VENOM & GLORY

S. WILLIAMS

Copyright © 2017 Shanora Williams

All rights reserved. This eBook is licensed for your personal enjoyment only. This eBook is copyright material and must not be copied, reproduced, transferred, distributed, leased, licensed or publicly performed or used in any form without prior written permission of the publisher, as allowed under the terms and conditions under which it was purchased or as strictly permitted by applicable copyright law. Any unauthorized distribution, circulation or use of this text may be a direct infringement of the author's rights, and those responsible may be liable in law accordingly.

Thank you for respecting the work of this author.

Published September 2017

Cover Art and Design by By Hang Le

Editing by Librum Artis Editorial Services

Trademarks: This book identifies product names and services known to be trademarks, registered trademarks, or service marks of their respective holders. The author acknowledges the trademarked status in this work of fiction. The publication and use of these trademarks is not authorized, associated with, or sponsored by the trademark owners.

BEFORE YOU READ

Venom & Glory is the third and final book of the Venom Trilogy and cannot be read as a standalone.

Visit www.shanorawilliams.com to find Passion & Venom and Venom & Ecstasy, the first two books of the trilogy.

ALSO BY SHANORA WILLIAMS

SERIES

FIRENINE SERIES
THE BEWARE DUET
VENOM TRILOGY
SWEET PROMISE SERIES

STANDALONES

DIRTY LITTLE SECRET
100 PROOF
DOOMSDAY LOVE
TAINTED BLACK
UNTAINTED
INFINITY

To my beautiful mother.
I love you.

PROLOGUE

This was never supposed to happen.

I betrayed his trust, shattered his loyalty, and broke his already broken heart.

What the hell was I thinking—no, what the hell was *he* thinking?

He never should have trusted me. He never should have taken me. He should have just killed me, the same way he did Toni, because being dead would be a hell of a lot easier than what I now realize is being brokenhearted.

He was once the monster in the dark—the man who haunted my dreams and stole my happiness. He was once a man I loathed—someone I would never be able to forgive.

That's what I thought.

But the man who was once a monster in the dark has become everything I've ever wanted. He has become the only ray of sunshine I have—my only hope. He is the one who restored me—the one who showed me what I am capable of, and who I really am.

He is the only reason I still wish to live.

Without him, I may as well be back in that shed again—chained. Broken. Beaten. Starved.

Without him, I may as well be dead.

2

DRACO

I have been disappointed by a lot of people.

I have been fucked over and cheated. Beaten and disrespected. I have seen things—things that have haunted me, turning my dreams into vicious nightmares.

I have seen blood and gore. I have seen my own father cut off a man's arm with a chainsaw in our cellar, and despite all the brutality I have witnessed, I have never wavered. Never flinched. Never cared about those people.

But this...*this* is something that I will not be able to accept.

I feel her looking at me.

I hear her sniffling.

I can't even fucking look at her.

The van runs over a pothole, shifting me over, closer to her. She grabs my hand. I pull away.

"Draco," she pleads.

"Shut up. No talking," one of the *putos* in the front seat commands. I want to break his fucking neck for speaking that way to her—to *me*. He has a black handgun pointed at my face. If my head weren't spinning so much, my fingers so numb, I would snatch it away and shove it down his goddamn throat.

"Draco," she whispers.

I keep my eyes ahead, jaw flexing.

The van finally begins to slow down, and I look out the window. The church is a few yards away, my men already lined up, armed, and waiting. They lift their guns as soon as they see the van coming their direction, ready to fire if necessary.

The driver parks and the man in the passenger seat pushes his door open and steps out. With a smirk on his lips, he walks to the side of the van, pulling the back door open.

"Take your feisty little bitch, and get the fuck out of here," he snarls at me when I step out.

I glare at him. Cold. Hard. His neck is right there. His throat. One grip and squeeze and I could end his fucking life.

His throat bobs when he notices I'm staring at it, a clear sign of fear, *weakness*. I hate weak motherfuckers that can't back themselves up.

"Watch your fucking mouth before I punch you in it," Patanza speaks from behind him, pointing a gun at the back of his head.

Several men in the trucks behind the van step closer, holding their guns high, aiming at us. I keep my eyes on the guard, *el hijo de puta* in front of me, and then I finally blink, lifting a hand in the air, a silent command for Patanza to stand down.

"Help her to the car," I order. I don't even recognize my own voice. The icy chill to it, the dry, gruff timbre.

Patanza hurries for Gianna, grabbing her elbow, nearly dragging her to the truck. When she's secured, and the door is shut, I fix my eyes on the guard again, taking a step closer, eyeing him even harder now.

"You may feel proud now, about what you think you and your cunt boss have accomplished, but don't you *ever* forget who the fuck I am."

He steps away, trying to laugh it off, but I see the panic in his eyes. He watches his back as he climbs back into the van, ordering the driver to hurry up and go.

I watch every single vehicle leave. I know at least one of them will linger. One of them will pretend to go, but wait somewhere to try and follow me back to my mansion.

I'm not fucking having it, so I wait.

They continue down the road, a trail of dirt and dust curling behind them.

When I snap my fingers, boots instantly crunch on the ground. My gaze is still ahead, still watching the vans drive away.

Four loud whistles zip past my ears, shooting through the air like cannons.

Then there's fire.

So much fire.

It billows, the way my trucks did when they attacked me by the Blue Betrayals. It's fierce and strong, like my anger in this very moment. The explosion makes the church bell ring, a small chime resonating deep in my bones.

Four vans—all of her fucking vehicles—are exploded by missile launcher guns. This was my Plan B. If something were to happen to Gianna or anyone I cared about at all, I made it clear there was going to be hell to pay.

I told her this would mean war.

And so it begins.

"They've fucked with the wrong one," I growl in Spanish, turning for the truck. "We head to the house, you pack as much shit as you can, and we fly out within the hour."

"Si, Jefe," they all say in unison. I climb into the truck and slam the door closed, but I feel her eyes on me. I don't look. *Can't* fucking look.

"Drive. Now," I command, and the truck pulls off in an instant. We drive toward the exploded cars and as we get closer, I see a figure moving. "Stop the truck."

I demand one of my men to give me their gun. When he hands me a pistol, I hop out, taking slow, measured steps toward the *hijo de puta* who had so much shit to say on the ride here—the one who was so happy and willing to point that fucking gun in my face.

"You know what's so sad about Yessica and her men?" I cock my gun and aim it at his forehead. He reaches for me with bloody fingers, his face streaming red and lips split, mouth filled to the brim with blood. "You never learn to watch your fucking backs."

I shoot him through the forehead, the sound echoing to the church bell, loud enough to pierce my ears. All is quiet when his head hits the ground. There is only the crackle of the flames, the sizzle from the fire.

I assumed this would give me satisfaction, but it doesn't. It only pisses me off more. My jaw ticks when his hands fall. Rage ensues, sparking the darkest parts of me—the parts of me I never wanted to feel again—and I *kick* him. I kick his head repeatedly, foaming at the fucking mouth, the longer strands of my hair slapping me in the face.

"MOTHERFUCKER!"

I hear screaming. Wailing. I don't give a fuck. I keep kicking.

"Draco!" Gianna screams, her hand wrapping around my wrist. I spin around quickly, pointing the gun at the center of her forehead.

"Don't fucking touch me!" I press the gun to her head, listening to someone stepping closer.

"Jefe." I look over and Patanza is staring at me, head shaking. "We have to go. *La policía ya viene en camino.*" *The police are on their way.* "Cameras will only be cut off for ten more minutes in this area." Her eyes shift over to Gianna, who is facing the gun, like she'll take the bullet if she has to.

"Get in the fucking car, and don't say a word," I growl at Gianna.

She stares at me with those bright green eyes, challenging me. She's trying to read me, but I know she can't. She can't because I don't fucking want her to.

When she realizes it, she turns and woefully climbs into the SUV. I follow her inside, and the driver pulls away.

Heart still pounding.

Body numb.

Mouth dry.

Bones aching.

I tell them, "I will kill every single fucking one of them. Anyone associated with that traitorous bitch will fucking die, and that's my fucking word! *Esa puta me la va a pagar!*" *That bitch is going to pay.*

3

GIANNA

We pull up to Draco's mansion, and he jumps out of the SUV before it can even stop, pointing and giving orders in Spanish as he storms into the house.

Patanza appears at my door and snatches it open, cocking her head, silently ordering me to get out. I step out and walk toward the mansion, the pebbles crunching beneath my feet.

Inside the mansion, I hear doors being opened and some being slammed closed. I hear things being tossed around, men yelling in Spanish, and even see some of the maids rushing out the other doors with suitcases.

I hurry through the foyer.

There are several men marching the hallways with black cases—cases I assume have guns and other weapons stored in them. More men come through the dining room and down the corridor, some with portraits and other valuables.

"Upstairs, to Jefe's room," Patanza snaps at me, nudging me on the shoulder.

I glance over my shoulder, but she's already watching. She stares with so much vile and disgust, my chest caves in on itself. As I walk up, I try to look for Draco over the guardrail, but I don't see him anywhere. I don't even hear him.

I step around the corner and as soon as I meet up to Draco's bedroom door, Patanza says, "Hurry and change. Better wear something comfortable."

"We're leaving?" I ask when she walks past me. Her nostrils flare, and as if she has no time whatsoever for my questions, she charges past me, entering the closet and pulling down a cotton dress without even really looking at it. When she comes toward me again, she practically shoves it into my chest, causing me to frown.

"Get. Dressed. We're flying out in twenty minutes." She stalks to the door and slams it shut behind her. My fingers tremble as I hold the dress up. I walk to the closet, noticing some of the other dresses are missing. They've most likely been packed up.

Fortunately, this dress is knee length and made of cotton. It's comfortable and black, matching my mood.

I dress quickly and walk to the bathroom, taking note of the missing makeup case. I look into the mirror, my face still pale from the horror, my eyes still wide with shock.

It takes me a moment to let it all sink in.

Is this what they're seeing? A weak Gia? A *scared* one?

There is a pounding on the door, and Patanza barges back in, waving a hand. "Let's go! You don't have all day! Jefe is waiting!"

She walks up to me, gripping my elbow, nearly dragging me out the door.

"Wait—Patanza! What the fuck!" I snatch my arm away from her, frowning when I meet her eyes. "Why are you being such a bitch to me? I'm not your fucking prisoner anymore!"

Her upper lip twitches and she takes a large step forward, getting in my face now. I don't back down, not even when she says, "You may as well be a fucking prisoner, Gia. You aren't my Patrona anymore. You're just a stupid *bitch* who doesn't know how to stay in her fucking place." She turns her nose up at me. "He told me what happened with Thiago." She swallows hard. "I thought you would be different. Turns out you're no better than the rest."

My mouth gapes, and her frown gets deeper. "Patanza, I—I thought we were—"

"Thought we were what?" she snaps, brows stitched. *"Amigas?"* Her laugh is bitter as she looks away. "Yeah," she mutters, turning her back to me. "I thought we were friends too, and I'm sure Jefe thought the same." She peers over her shoulder with a grimace. "But friends don't stab friends in the fucking back." Her back is fully turned to me. Before she's out the door, she shouts, "Let's fucking go!"

My feet move to her command before I can even process my thoughts.

4

GIANNA

Everything happens so quickly once I'm out the door of the mansion.

I'm literally tossed into the back of the SUV by Patanza, the driver pulling away without a moment's hesitation as soon as her door slams shut.

It's only the driver, plus Patanza, who is sitting in the passenger seat, and me in the vehicle. I twist around, looking back at the mansion as his men and even some of the maids rush in and out, stuffing suitcases and bags into the other cars and SUVs.

"Where's Draco?" I ask, turning back around, focusing on Patanza.

But she acts like she doesn't even hear me, looking out of her window instead.

"Patanza, where are we going?" I ask, making sure my voice sounds more demanding than terrified.

"Just shut up and ride." Her voice is calm. Too calm. She doesn't seem the least bit worried, and since she isn't, I assume I shouldn't be either.

We ride for a long time—I want to say for over an hour.

By the time we stop, the sun is blazing in the sky. The tires of the SUV slow to a creep and then the driver parks. Both the driver and

Patanza jump out, Patanza coming for my door while the guard hustles for the trunk.

I slide out of the truck and she turns, walking to a warehouse not too far away. I follow her, the driver behind me, suitcases in hand. She enters the building, and there are people inside. I pause a moment, stunned.

I wouldn't be so surprised at the sight of them if they weren't all completely naked beneath black aprons, standing in front of mountains of pure-white cocaine, measuring and bagging it all carefully.

There are three guards posted at the doors, keeping their eyes on the people.

What shocks me most is that none—and I mean *none*—of them look at us when we come in. They remained focused on their work, not even batting an eyelash. This must be one of Draco's many production centers.

I follow Patanza through a gray door with a *SALIDA* sign above it. *EXIT*. As soon as we're out, a jet comes into view. I slow my pace, but Patanza keeps marching, as well as the driver, who hurries past me without even looking my way.

The jet is sleek and white, the engine already humming loudly as I make my way there, slowly but surely.

There is a tall, gangly man wearing a black baseball cap standing beside the staircase. His skin is heavily tanned, his eyes an electric green when they flash up to meet mine. He asks Patanza something, and when she responds and they both look my way, I know they're talking about me.

I finally meet up to them, and she orders me to get on the jet.

"Is Draco coming?" I ask, my eyes locking with hers.

She narrows her gaze. "Does it matter?"

"Yes, it matters. I have no idea where I'm going, and I don't know where he is."

Patanza steps to the left, holding a hand out and raising a stern brow, gesturing for me to get on board. I challenge her stare, narrowing my eyes.

Her hand drops, her agitation on full display now. "Get on the fucking jet, Gia," she snaps at me.

"It's Patrona to you," I bite out.

Patanza bares her teeth and starts to charge me, but the man beside her presses a heavy hand to her chest, simply shaking his head.

"Calm down. She is still The Patrona," the man says in his native tongue. He steps around her, extending an arm, gesturing to the steps of the jet. "This jet will lead you to a safe house, Patrona. This was Jefe's order. I'm sure he will contact you soon about it."

"Why isn't he with me now?" I ask in Spanish.

"He has a few more things to handle here before he can be with you."

I swallow hard, looking from him to glare at Patanza. Without another word, I board the jet, stepping into the first cabin. I notice there are two, both complete with ivory leather recliners.

The cabin I'm standing in has a table set up in front of two recliners, and a three-seated sofa in front of the windows. Across from the sofa is a flat screen TV on top of a wooden stand. It's all bolted and secured.

It's luxurious, and screams *Draco* for sure.

With a sigh, I walk to the sofa and sit, staring out the window at the empty desert. The jet shakes as someone boards, and Patanza appears. She glances at me briefly, but turns to go to the other cabin. A door slides closed from her side, and I'm fucking glad. I don't want to deal with her right now.

The driver comes on next, reaching above one of the leather recliners to the right to tuck the suitcases into the bin. He doesn't even look at me. He shuts the compartment and is gone in a matter of seconds.

The man, who apparently is the only one with some respect around here, comes on next, smelling of tobacco. The door shuts when he's on board, sealing us in. He's taken his baseball cap off, revealing shiny raven hair, which makes his green eyes stand out even more.

I've never seen him before. Never met him.

"You should sit in one of the chairs for now, Patrona," he suggests, pointing at one of the recliners. I realize he must only speak Spanish. "We'll be taking off in less than a minute and these are the only chairs with seatbelts. You will have to buckle in until we're clear to roam around."

I don't argue. I just do it.

As soon as I'm buckled in, I plant a fist beneath my chin and look out of the window.

"A drink before we leave?" He points back to the kitchenette across from the lavatory.

I peer up at him.

"Rum, please," I murmur. Rum was my mother's go-to drink whenever she was stressed.

He bobs his head, taking off. I hear glasses clank and ice rattle, and then he's back in no time with a short tumbler in hand, filled halfway with brown liquid and ice. He hands the cold glass to me and I take a sip, loving the crisp taste.

The man sits in the recliner across from me and buckles in. He pulls out his cellphone to text someone, and then he places it in his cup holder, looking right into my eyes.

His smile is soft, eyes gentle. He seems nice, but I can tell he wouldn't have a problem killing someone if it came down to it, just like everyone else.

"Why have I never met you before?" I ask when the wheels of the jet start rolling. He cocks a brow, his head going into a slight tilt like he doesn't understand what I'm saying. *Yeah, he definitely only speaks Spanish.*

I ask the question again, in Spanish this time.

"Ahh." He presses his lips. "I work the cities, the jets, the factories and warehouses."

"So you're not one of his guards?"

"I'm more of a…manager, I suppose. I handle some of the shipments, set up the schedule for his flights whenever he needs one, and handle the employees' paychecks."

"The employees? Being those people in the factory?"

"Yes. As well as his guards."

"What's your name?"

"Emilio."

I nod, giving him one more sweep over with my eyes before returning my focus to whatever is outside the window. "I'm sure you know what's going on. You're probably pissed at me too."

He gives a throaty chuckle. "How can I be pissed when I wasn't very close to Mr. Thiago? Not to sound cruel, but in this business it happens. Constantly."

I glance over at him. "He...didn't deserve what happened to him. I'm sure everyone thinks it's my fault. I know Patanza does. And it is. It's all my fault."

"I would not worry, Patrona. Shit happens." He shrugs, as if it's that simple.

"Draco blames me too. He hasn't said it, but I know it's in the back of his mind. He hasn't spoken to me since they . . ." I swallow hard, and it hurts like hell to get it down. I take a sip of my rum to ease the gulp. "Since they shot him right in front of us."

Emilio's lips press thin, those bold green eyes hard on mine. With a heavy sigh, he says, "Relax, Patrona. Sleep. You need it. We won't be on here for too long. Don't worry about that right now. You're safe."

I pull my eyes away, sinking into the cushion of my chair. The jet is in the air now, the turbulence a bit rocky. Once it settles and the jet is flying smoothly, I finish off my drink and tuck my feet under my bottom. I try to sleep, but it's fucking impossible. I shift and twist, squeezing my eyes shut, all of it to no avail.

When we're in the clear to roam, Emilio stands and gives me privacy, but even with him gone, I can't sleep.

About an hour into the flight, I hear the door Patanza closed slide open. I watch her turn the corner where the kitchenette is and pour something.

She steps around the corner with a cup of clear liquid on ice inside it. She takes the seat right across from me and I sit up, brows creasing, ready for her to blast me again.

"Relax," she mutters. "I'm not allowed to hurt you...even though I really want to." She sips her drink—vodka or tequila I assume—and then releases a sharp breath.

She slouches back in her seat, eyes closed. It's the first time I've seen her drink alcohol, let alone let her guard down like this.

"I've had time to cool off," she states.

I don't speak. I don't know what to say.

She finishes off her drink in a matter of seconds, and the ice clinks against the glass when she places it in her cup holder.

She lets out a long sigh. "Do you know how long you've been here? Around Jefe?"

My eyebrows dip. "I haven't given it much thought."

"Two months. We took you in June. It's August 10th now."

"Oh."

"Jefe has never trusted anyone that fast—not within a two-month time frame."

I blink quickly, putting my line of sight on something else. My chest feels tight and raw again.

"How do you know he trusts me?"

"Because he told me, *idiota*."

My lips push together, and despite where we are and what we're going through right now, my heart flutters.

"He said we were supposed to do whatever you needed—before all of this shit happened. He didn't care that you walked the beach alone, or swam alone, or even if you wanted to go to town again. He would have let you because he knew then that you were smart and would return. He knew you weren't going anywhere. He knew you weren't *stupid*."

I lower my gaze, focusing on my red fingernails. "He never should have trusted me."

"No," she scoffs in agreement. "He shouldn't have." I tilt my head, locking my eyes on hers. She picks up her glass, swirling the ice around. "You know, Thiago promised me something the day before he got caught."

"He did?"

"Yes." Her head drops, her black hair curtaining her face. "He promised he would take me away from here. He promised me I wouldn't need to be a guard anymore. That we would run away together."

Oh my God. I squeeze my seat belt, blinking rapidly. "Wait...I thought you guys hated each other."

She looks beneath her eyelashes, shrugging a bit. "It's...well, it *was* complicated."

"How?" I ask, and when she drops her head and looks out the window, I see a side of Patanza I've never seen before.

Vulnerable.

Weak.

Lonely. I see now that she needs a friend. She wants to talk about it.

I unclip my seatbelt, sliding to the edge of my seat. "Patanza, tell me how."

Her eyes slide over to mine. I can tell she doesn't want to tell me, but that she would never confess this to any of the other guards. No, she wouldn't confess this to any man—just another woman like me, who will understand all too well. I know how it is to suppress feelings for someone I shouldn't care about.

"Thiago wasn't the type to settle down," she admits. "He only came around every few months, and whenever he did, we would hook up in private. We'd meet somewhere after hours and sort of hate-fuck." She huffs a small laugh, like she remembers something funny. In a matter of seconds, her face is serious again. "But during his recent visit, I was trying to stay away from him. I didn't want to hook up again because every single time he had to go, we would leave on a bad note. He would tell me all these things beforehand, about how he loved me, how he needed me, how I was unlike any woman he'd ever met, but after saying all that, he would be gone the next day, with no sort of goodbye. He would just *leave*, and wouldn't get in touch with me while he was away. He knew I had my own phone. Draco gave him my number every time I had to swap my phone out, just in case he needed to reach out to one of us, but he never called it. Ever."

"Maybe he was busy," I offer to hopefully make her feel better.

"We're all busy," she grumbles. She sits up in her chair, exhaling. "There was something about him returning this time, though. He wanted to meet in private a lot more. Even during the day, when he knew the other guards were watching. A few times we did things, yes, but he talked a lot more about how he wanted to get away. He talked about how he was going to complete one last shipment for Draco and then he was going to drop out and do his own thing—run his own empire. Not with drugs but, believe it or not, he wanted to open a T-shirt printing company."

"Oh," I breathe, smiling a little. "Wow."

"Yeah. It's sounds cheesy and stupid, but he was good at it. He'd made a few shirts for fundraisers in the city. For kids who were homeless. He and Jefe always gave more than they received..." She exhales. "The night before his shipment, he told me, 'Patanza, I want you to come to America with me. We'll live in a house on the beach in Miami. We'll make love and fuck like we always do. We'll get away from all of this.'" She laughs a little. "I told him he was an idiot. Jefe wasn't just going to let me go that easily. I'm his best guard. He trusts me the most. He wouldn't just let me run away with Thiago, plus I'd made an agreement to Draco that I would work for him and give my life for his, no matter what."

"You deserve to be happy too, Patanza," I say. "You work the hardest. You're always there for Jefe. I'm sure he would have understood."

"I obviously don't deserve happiness." She glares at me. "Thiago is *dead* now. Whatever freedom I thought I was going to get is gone. I...I wanted to run with him. I wanted to get away from all of this —*killing* people. Always on the run, like now. Having to watch my back because everyone knows I work for The Jefe." Her breathing is ragged. "I just wanted a normal life for once, so I told him I would go if he told Jefe that he was taking me with him. Jefe would have been upset, but he would have let me go in the end. He's protective, but also more lenient with me. He knows what I've been through in my childhood and teen years. But working for Jefe is pretty much all I've ever known. Truthfully, I was afraid of normal. But Thiago promised me it would be okay. He promised we would go and be happy, drink margaritas and wake up to silky sunrises." She releases a ragged sigh.

"I'm so, so sorry, Patanza," I whisper. "Thiago didn't deserve it, and I feel awful about it. I know you blame me for stealing your freedom, and I'm so, so sorry, but I promise you can still get out. If you really want to get away, just tell Jefe. Tell him you want to go. He trusts you. He knows you would never give him away or rat him out."

"No." She sits up, shaking her head hard as she looks me deep in the eyes. "After what happened, I'm not going anywhere. I *have* to be here for Jefe."

"Draco can take care of himself."

"I have nowhere else to fucking go," she snarls at me, picking her head up. "Plus, I have to watch his back for sneaky bitches like you."

I sit back again, plucking lint off my dress. "I feel bad about it, Patanza. That girl was just so…cold. And then Henry." I squeeze my eyes shut tight. "I just thought he was telling the truth—I thought he was an honest person. I never got the impression that he was lying, and I didn't think he was in that deep with Yessica."

"Yessica," she spits. "Yessica is just a stupid fucking bitch who's pissed at Draco because he told her he would never love her. She most likely got pissed when she heard there was a woman in Draco's life that was being called Patrona, and she came for you. She doesn't give a damn about No Arms. She would have left him in that cell to rot forever, but without him escaping, she never would have gotten to you. Too bad we just didn't fucking know it."

"I know that now. But Draco was willing to let him go too…he believed me until she—"

"*Dios mío!* He fucking loves you, Gia!" she barks at me, looking me hard in the eyes, and my heart pounds down in my chest. "He's so fucking in love with you—I've never seen it before. But after that happened, I don't know how he can. I mean…*Thiago.*" She says his name like it hurts. "Thiago was his closest relative besides his mother, and he watched him *die*, just like that." She snaps her fingers. "Within the blink of an eye he was gone, and it's all because of a mistake you made."

We both sit in a thick, uncomfortable silence, her staring at me, me staring at her.

"He can't love me," I tell her. "He *shouldn't* love me."

"Well you know what?" Her tone is rhetoric as she stands up. "He does. I'm sure he wishes he didn't, but he does. If there is one thing I know, it's that you can't fight love. You can't ignore it. You can try, but it won't work. It will only make you think about the person even more." She walks past the second recliner, into the aisle. Her eyes don't meet mine when she says, "We'll be landing soon."

She says that, and not even thirty minutes later I spot palm trees and, beyond them, a crystal clear blue ocean. Emilio returns and tells me to buckle back in. I do so, and the jet lands in a matter of minutes.

Emilio stands, reaching up to the bin across the aisle and taking down the black suitcases. When he has the handles clutched in hand, he asks me to follow him out. I follow behind him just as Patanza appears.

I notice, before I get off, that her eyes are red around the rims and puffy. She has a hat on now to shield her eyes, and immediately puts on a pair of sunglasses before getting off the jet, but I notice.

I don't bother trying to comfort her. Instead, I follow Emilio down the stairs to the sleek, white Mercedes parked ahead. There is a driver standing beside the car. When he spots us, he opens the back door right away.

"Go ahead and get in the car, Patrona," Emilio says over his shoulder, heading for the trunk. I climb into the backseat, and Patanza gets in behind me, avoiding my eyes.

Emilio is in the passenger seat, and the driver climbs in, smelling of way too much cologne. He pulls off when Emilio's door is closed, driving down a long, winding road.

I have no idea where we are until we reach the end of a road and a street sign appears.

Los Cabos.

We're in Cabos?

I look over at Patanza. She finally looks at me, pressing her lips thin. The drive continues for nearly fifteen minutes before we're pulling into a residential area.

There is a home here, much smaller than Draco's mansion, but still beautiful nonetheless.

It's a wide, two-story home, made of white stucco, the shingles on the roof a bold, muddy orange. We park and step out, Emilio leading the way to the door with a set of keys. He unlocks it and lets me right in.

I step onto waxed white marble, and the scent of cinnamon and sea-salt hits me. I hear gulls calling and walk past the den and through the living room set up with plush, clean furniture. Every surface is clear of dust and lint.

Ahead of me are two open glass doors, with a deck overlooking the sea. I meet at the doors and the wind pushes my hair back, soothing my sweat-dampened skin. Down the steps is an infinity pool with not a trace or speck of dirt inside it. It's sapphire blue, clear, rippling, just like the ocean that's not too far beyond it. There is even a bar set up inside the pool.

It's marvelous, and for a second I have to admit that this home is much more beautiful than his mansion. Unlike the mansion, this home has many windows, allowing the sun to stream through, highlighting the tables and white, L-shaped sofa. Unlike the mansion, this place is homey and somehow it feels secure.

Quaint.

Simple.

Comfortable.

"If you like it out here, you should see the master bedroom," Emilio says, popping up beside me. I put on a light smile for him, turning and following him to the bedroom. Patanza is nowhere in sight now.

Emilio walks down a long hallway and then turns for the second to last door on the right. I'm in awe of the bedroom as soon as the door swings open and he places the suitcases down on the floor.

It's massive, with a private terrace over looking the ocean too.

I take a step closer, spotting a hot tub outside the terrace, a tray set up there with bread, fruits, and even a bottle of merlot. The bed is a

California king, swathed in puffy white bedding and brown pillows, a thick white headboard matching the sheets.

"I know it's only two in the afternoon, but the fruit and merlot is for you. Please let me know if there is anything else I can get you, Patrona. The kitchen is fully stocked and there is even a bar in this home and by the pool. You can call me, or you can go out and help yourself to anything." Emilio takes a step back. "You probably want to be left alone, so I will go to my room and let you settle in." He picks up a black device on the TV stand. "Press the green button on here when you need me."

"Okay." I nod. "Gracias, Emilio."

"Por supuesto, Patrona." Of course, Patrona.

He starts to turn, but I call for him quickly before he can get out the door.

"Si, Patrona?"

"Will…Jefe be here anytime soon?"

Emilio studies my eyes, but then pulls his gaze away. "I'm not sure when Jefe will be arriving, Patrona, but you are safer here."

"Do you mean I'm safer away from him than *with* him?"

His green eyes sparkle from the sun. All he gives is a curt nod, and then he's gone, shutting the tall brown door behind him.

I turn back around, walking to the hot tub, focused on the fruit and bread, but I don't have the stomach to eat.

Instead, I pick up the bottle of merlot and then grab the bottle opener, popping it and pouring it into the empty glass on the tray.

There is only one glass, meaning I will probably be alone for quite sometime. I take a full sip of the merlot, and then place it down. Pulling my dress off, I toss it aside and then step into the hot tub, sinking into its warm oasis with just my panties and bra on.

I press my back against the edge of the tub, pick up my half-empty glass, and I just…*breathe*.

For the first time since this all began, I breathe, and then I let it all sink in.

Draco won't be here for a while. He sent me away, probably because he couldn't stand the sight of me anymore. I know he won't show up anytime soon—or probably at all. I'm safe here, yes, but I don't know what the hell I'm supposed to do here by myself.

This home is beautiful—gorgeous really. It's everything and more, but without him around, I may as well be back in that cell, rotting away. Alone and afraid. Worried about what's to come, and how to handle it.

Tears sting my eyes, but I take a sip of wine to ignore the burn, looking at the ocean.

I know Patanza said he loves me, but by now he has to hate me.

I hate myself.

I stole the happiness from Patanza—a happiness that seemed so bright and freeing. I snatched it away from her, and she'll never forgive me for it.

Because of me, Draco's cousin and closest confidant is gone.

Because of my stupidity and self-righteousness, everything is *ruined*.

5

GIANNA

The hours spent here are long and exhausting.

I'm waking up to an empty side of the bed.

Cold. Vacant. I'm not used to it. Being without him terrifies me now.

Breakfast isn't served at a table, it's brought to me by Emilio, who hardly says anything, only asks me if I need something or to call for him if I do. Patanza has been around, using most of her time sitting in the one spot that gives view of the city.

On my second night here, I walk past and see her sitting in a lounge chair with her head hung low. At first, I can barely recognize her. She's wearing black lounge clothes, her hair long, shiny and damp. It's dark, and other than the lights sparkling from the pool, you can't make out much but the city lights beyond the patio where she sits.

I see her sitting there with her back facing the closed door, her hair like a curtain around her face, and I swear I see her shoulders shaking. If I'm not mistaken, she's *crying*. My feet move, the urge to go out and talk to her high and demanding.

But when she reaches up and swipes hard at her face, then stands and stalks away into the darkness, I stop before I can reach the door, realizing she only wants to be left alone.

By the third day, I am a mess. I can hardly eat. Hardly sleep. I can't get that image of Thiago out of my head to save my life. The way he had my back and protected me when we were in that tunnel—how he would have done anything to protect me because he knew how much I meant to Draco...it was too much. Too real.

He gave his own life for me. For *his cousin*.

"You need her more than me anyway." His words haunt me, the tears lining my eyes, hot like fire. I roll over and somehow, after letting go of a river's worth of tears, I fall asleep.

The next morning, I walk out of the bedroom after taking a quick shower, and Emilio is in the living room, his back to me, talking quietly on his phone.

"Si, Jefe. Ella esta bien." *She is okay.*

"Is that Draco?" I ask in Spanish, rushing in his direction.

Emilio spins around, eyes stretched wide as he stares at me. I don't even bother asking for the phone. Instead, I take it away, pressing the receiver to my ear.

"Draco?" I call. "Draco!" There is no response.

I lower the phone and look at the screen. The call has ended. He hung up.

I glare up at Emilio. "Where is he? Is he on the way?"

Emilio presses his lips with a slight shrug.

"What did he want?"

"He was just checking on you, Patrona."

"Why doesn't he just come and check on me himself?" I snap, and I know I shouldn't be angry with Emilio, the only man showing me respect right now, but I can't help it. I feel like I'm on the brink of a mental breakdown.

"He will talk to you when he feels like it," Patanza says from behind me in her native language. I turn and look at her. Her face is pale, eyes dark and empty. She seems almost . . . *lifeless*. "Stop pressuring Emilio, when you know he can't give you solid answers. Haven't you caused enough fucking trouble?"

"Patanza," Emilio warns.

But I don't stick around long enough to hear what else she has to say. I return the phone to Emilio and walk back to my bedroom.

I'm on edge for the rest of that day. By nightfall, I'm calling Emilio for a bottle of wine to help take the edge off. I down three glasses of red wine, eyes wet, heart pounding.

I don't know when I finally fall sleep, but when I wake up, it's still dark, and the heavy smell of marijuana rolls past my nose. The door to the terrace is cracked open. I gasp, shooting up straight, staring through the glass.

Dropping one foot on the marble floor, I tiptoe to the door, cautious, heart racing. I pause for a second when I hear a throat clear, deep and heavy. I look around for something to defend myself with, but there isn't much here. Just the half empty bottle of wine and the silver tray. On top of the tray is a knife I used to cut my apples earlier.

I grab it, pulling the door open and peeking around the corner.

When I see the broad shoulders and chiseled jaw, my racing hearts works overtime. I immediately lower my guard, something I normally wouldn't do around him, placing the knife down on the chair behind me.

I can't help but lower what's left of my defensive walls.

Draco is standing on the terrace with a joint pinched between his lips, overlooking the city of Cabos. The moonlight makes his skin look clear and smooth, highlighting the dark stubble on his jawline and around his mouth. He's wearing an unbuttoned dress shirt, his hair a disheveled mess.

I almost don't go out. He looks calm, if only for now. Maybe I shouldn't bother him. Give him his space until morning.

I start to step away, but I bump into the side of the house, causing a thump.

He looks over when he hears it and immediately reaches for his gun, drawing and pointing it at me. I hold my hands in the air, and when he realizes it's only me, he lowers it right away, sighing heavily as he tucks it back into the holster.

"Sorry to scare you," I whisper.

"Nothing scares me," he grumbles, pulling the joint from his lips. "It's called watching your back."

I look him over. His eyes are hard, but deep in them I can see the pain. I see his agony, and I want to cry for him. I know he hasn't dared shed a tear. He's kept himself busy and distant for a reason.

"Draco," I call, stepping closer to him, cutting right to the chase. "I am so, so sorry. I swear, I didn't—"

"Just shut up, Gia," he mutters, looking away. "There is nothing you can say that will help the situation we're in. It happened, and it's done. Time to move forward now."

"I just want to apologize," I tell him, still cautious, but still moving closer to him.

"Apologies are worthless. They don't help or motivate me. They only piss me the fuck off."

My mouth clamps shut. I stop only a footstep away from him. He puts out the joint and bends over, placing it on the ground.

"What took you so long to get here?" I ask.

"Had work to do. Shit to handle."

"You killed someone?"

"I've killed a lot of people."

I look down. He's so cold, intentionally driving a wedge between us. It hurts knowing he doesn't want to speak to me; that he probably doesn't even want to be around me.

"You told them I was safe here. How am I safer here?"

"Because *she* doesn't know where you are. It allows me to do what I need to do until I can get to her again."

"You haven't seen her since—" My sentence cuts short. I'm afraid to say it around him. Saying it will make it real.

He takes note of my hesitance, cocking a brow, fixing his gaze on me. "Since what? Since she killed my *cousin?*" His tone is harsh and unforgiving.

I nod pathetically.

"No, and she better be fucking glad I haven't seen her, otherwise I'd gouge her fucking eyes out and then bury her alive."

The menacing chill in his voice makes the hairs on the back of my neck prickle. "What will you do to get to her?" I ask, voice low. "I want to help, Draco. This is my fault. I need to do something too, not just hide out here."

His head shakes from side to side, his face seeming much paler now. "I blame myself for ever sending him out there. I knew something was wrong—I could feel it deep in my gut when he didn't answer the damn phone. He always answers for big deals. Always, but I ignored that churn in my gut and automatically assumed he was going against me." His eyes flash up to meet mine. "But I bet that's what you want, right? For me to blame myself. For me to put everything on my shoulders? Well, *fuck that.*" He points a stern finger at me. "You are to blame too, Gianna. *You.* If that no-armed fucker hadn't been set free, they never would have found Thiago in the first place! He knew *everything*! He listened and watched for months, and you just let him go, like he was a fucking saint!" Nostrils flared, he takes a step back, going to the door. "I'm really starting to think I should have just killed you the same day I killed Trigger Toni. If I had, none of this shit would have ever happened."

His words are a solid punch in the gut—or maybe to the face. Either way, it knocks the breath right out of my lungs.

He walks right past me before I can even stop him.

6

GIANNA

He doesn't sleep in the room with me.

After last night—after what he said—how could he?

It's well past 8:00 a.m., and since he walked off last night, there has been nothing but silence.

I push out of bed and walk to the door, hoping he's still around. Stepping around the corner that leads to the dining room, I hear glasses clanking and forks scraping china. I enter the dining room, and am utterly surprised to see Mrs. Molina sitting there with a newspaper on the table.

She's reading the newspaper, a bowl of hot cereal and fruit in front her. It's a much smaller table, only able to seat six. She hears me coming in and lowers her paper, smiling wide at me. From that smile alone, I'm assuming she doesn't know what I've done…at least not yet. Draco is nowhere in sight.

"*Buenos días, cariño!*" she sings, dropping and folding her paper. She sits up in her chair, smiling up at me. I take the seat across from her, warmth coursing through my bloodstream. She doesn't know. She can't know, otherwise she wouldn't be smiling right now. "How are you?" she asks.

"I'm great!" I try and sound positive and uplifted. I'm far from it.

"Are you loving it here? You've been here longer than I have, right? I arrived around midnight last night."

"It's beautiful," I tell her.

She smiles, and Emilio steps around the corner, coming from the kitchen. "What would you like this morning, Patrona?" he asks.

"I'll take what Mrs. Molina has," I say, and he bobs his head. "Thanks, Emilio." Mrs. Molina takes a sip of her apple juice. "Will Draco be eating with us too?"

She shrugs. "I have no idea. It is not like him to miss breakfast, but he's told me he has a lot of things to handle this morning, so he'll probably be a little late. He told me you would be joining me though. If you couldn't tell, I was waiting." She winks.

I smile a little and then twist my lips. We're quiet for a moment. She takes a bite of her green apple. I grab a red Honey crisp from the bowl. "It's not weird to be taken away from one home and put into another so quickly?"

She waves a highly dismissive hand. "Oh, please. I am used to it. His father did it all the time. No one place is ever safe for long when you are a Molina. That mansion we were in was just our favorite one." She looks around. "But this one is starting to grow on me, too. It's... simple. And we don't get much simplicity in our lives."

My upper lip twitches to form a small smile. Emilio returns with a hot bowl of cereal and places it in front of me. It smells delicious, like cinnamon and honey. "Enjoy, Patrona."

He takes off, eyeing Mrs. Molina briefly before stepping around the corner. Though I have no appetite, I dig into my food anyway, eating without really tasting it, while she reads more of her newspaper.

A door shuts from a distance, and I hear slow and measured footsteps. When Draco steps around the corner, my heart goes mad, banging like drums, my pulse loud in my ears.

He doesn't even look at me as he walks around the table, gives his mother a kiss on the top of her head, and then takes the seat to the left of her, at the head of the table, of course.

"Buenos días, Mamá," he sighs.

"Good morning, *hijo*." She drops her spoon.

Draco looks over at me. "Gianna."

"Morning," I murmur.

He looks away, at the entrance of the kitchen. Emilio appears with a bowl of cereal for him, too. This isn't like the meals we had at the mansion—the multi-option, wholesome meals that I used to die for.

This hot cereal is basic, simple. Just enough to get you through the morning. Now that I think about it, most of the meals I've had here are very simple—chicken with rice or potatoes. Breakfast would be waffles with fruit, or toast with eggs.

"I think I will read by the pool today," Mrs. Molina says after finishing up her food.

"Go and enjoy yourself," Draco mumbles before taking a bite of his meal.

She nods, and Emilio steps up and grabs her bowl. "Would you like me to get anything for you while you're by the pool, Mrs. Molina?" he asks in Spanish.

"No, honey. I will be fine, but thank you." She smiles at him, and then me, and then takes off, humming.

When I can no longer hear her happy tune, Emilio leaves, and I look over at Draco. "You haven't told her."

"Told her what?"

"About Thiago."

He looks at me with cold, dead eyes. No response.

I sigh, my appetite completely gone now. "Maybe I should tell her."

"You won't speak a fucking word of it," he snarls at me, brows stitched.

"She deserves to know. She loved Thiago."

"I know she did, and if she finds out why he died and what you did, she will fucking *despise* you. She is the only one who thinks you are an angel, and I want it to stay that way—not for my sake or yours—but for Lion's. You need her to have your back, because if she doesn't, you may just end up dead around here." He shoves back in his chair, causing a screech on the hardwood floorboards. He stands up tall, glaring down at me, pointing a stern finger in my face. "You will not say a fucking word. She doesn't need to know another family member of hers is dead. She doesn't know we are under threat—not this severely—so keep your fucking mouth shut and stay out of her goddamn way."

He stalks away, and before I know it, a door slams, making the walls shake. I flinch when I hear it, eyes wet, throat thick with emotions I can't stand feeling. I stare down at my uneaten food.

My hands are fucking shaking, my heart still racing. My gut feels twisted into a thousand knots.

No one here is on my side. No one but Mrs. Molina, and even I know that won't last for long—not when she finds out what really went down.

For the rest of the day and the next, Draco doesn't say a word to me. Breakfast, lunch, and dinner are set up, but only his mother is at the table. He doesn't show, though I know he is around.

Mrs. Molina makes excuses for him, saying he's been very busy lately, but she has no fucking idea what is even going on.

Mrs. Molina and I spend time together at the pool after several meals, but I don't dare bring up Thiago or even Draco. Instead, I encourage her to talk about Los Cabos, this home, and even about what book she's currently reading. Though she is engaging and lively, I find it hard to concentrate on what she's saying. Every time she speaks, her voice becomes a hum, distant in the background.

Instead, I hear the ocean roaring from far away, the crunching of cars running over asphalt and gravel. I hear my slow, thudding heart, and the raging, screaming thoughts in my head. I am aware of every single thing, including how close I am to losing my sanity.

Mrs. Molina is still out by the pool when I decide to grab some bottled water. As I enter the kitchen, I see Draco outside on the terrace. He has a phone glued to his ear, his back facing me. His shoulders are hunched, and his hair is a disheveled mess being tousled by the wind.

He turns a fraction, the first few buttons of his shirt undone. There are bags beneath his eyes, and his eyebrows are dipped and glued together.

He is furious.

He orders something into the receiver of the flip phone, and then he slams it closed right before slamming it down on the ground and breaking it in half. He grips the guardrail in front him, shoulders still hiked up and tense, breathing heavily like a savage beast.

He finally turns, peering over his shoulder, and his eyes find mine.

I don't speak. Really, what can I say? I expect him to come in and talk to me—to say something, even if it's rude or mean or whatever. But he doesn't. He comes inside, but his eyes are no longer on mine.

"Everything okay?" I ask, but he completely ignores me, marching right past with his chin up and his jaw flexed.

The next morning I hear doors slamming. Something falls to the floor and then another door slams shut. Gasping, I sit straight up, hurrying for my robe and sliding my arms into it, wrapping it around me and covering my gown.

I rush out of the bedroom, but the living room is completely empty. The pool water is still. There is utter silence.

I walk to the empty kitchen, checking the patio. I start to think it was all in my head—that I was hearing things—until I hear stomping and Mrs. Molina asking, "WHERE IS SHE?" in Spanish.

She storms into the kitchen, her eyes puffy, gray hair a frizzy mess. I've never seen her so distraught. So...unhinged.

She charges for me, pointing a fierce finger in my face.

"You! What have you done?" she roars in Spanish. "What have you done, Gianna!"

I blink rapidly. Guilt courses through me, taking over every single fiber of my being. "W-what are you—"

"No!" she snarls. "Do not play dumb with me!" She's still speaking Spanish, the words flying at me like sharp spears. "He is dead because of you! My only nephew is dead! Why didn't you listen to Draco? Why? He trusted you!"

I feel my bottom lip quivering, my eyes bulging out of my head. Emilio and Patanza appear behind her. Emilio grabs Mrs. Molina by the shoulders but she shrugs him off.

"Señora, please," he pleads, grabbing for her again.

This time she doesn't shrug him off, but she does glare at me. Hard. Cold. In this moment she looks exactly like her son—ready to defend and kill if she must.

"He trusted you. *I* trusted you." She points at herself, stabbing a hard finger into her own chest. "I thought you would be good for him. I thought you would give him some hope, but all you did was snatch that hope and light away from him. You've *ruined* him!" Her voice breaks.

"I'm so sorry," I whisper, holding my hands out, but she shakes her head, standing up tall.

"You are not sorry! You are *weak* and just like the others! You had a chance, and you blew it. Thiago was all we had, Gianna. All we had." Her tears are continuous, like waterfalls, overflowing. "Because of you…he is gone. They took him, because you didn't trust my son enough—because you wanted to be *better* than him. You did the wrong thing." She sniffles hard, and my throat thickens with unwanted emotion. "I will not be surprised if he never forgives you, Gia." Her head shakes swiftly as she swipes a tear away. "Your father would be so disappointed in you."

When she airs her last sentence, I feel a crack form in my chest. My heart, which was pounding in my chest, stops. My hands, which were shaking with adrenaline, are cold and still.

I didn't know my heart could be any more broken than it already is, but she just did me in.

The pieces are crumbling and wilting away, but only because I know what she says is true.

Daddy would be angry.

He wouldn't have forgiven me, if I'd done this to him.

And because I know this godawful truth, I am devastated. What the hell have I done?

Emilio finally gets her out of the kitchen, looking back at me once with sympathetic eyes. Patanza still stands there, her lips pressed. With one shake of the head, she turns her back to me and walks away.

When they are gone, I sink onto a barstool, dropping my face into the palms of my hands. I don't cry. I can't cry. Instead, I fight the tears, though it's hard as hell to do.

I hear footsteps, but I don't look to find where they're coming from.

I don't care who it is—that is until the familiar voice says, "If you want to cry and be useless, go to your fucking room and do it. I don't want your tears on my countertops."

I pick my head up, frowning at Draco, who is standing at the door of the kitchen. His first words to me in nearly forty-eight hours, and that's what he has to say?

I push off the stool, walking up to him, getting in his face. "You think I don't feel bad about this?" He doesn't answer me. He matches my stare, challenging me in all the wrong ways. "If you are so angry, why haven't you punished me for it yet? If I'm just like the others, why am I still here? Why?" I demand.

Still, nothing.

His jaw ticks as he pushes me aside and walks toward a liquor cabinet, taking down a box of cigars. I watch him as he sniffs one and then locks it between his teeth.

After putting the box back where it belongs, he's walking in my direction again, but he goes right past me, his eyes far away from mine.

Just like that, he's walking away too.

7

GIANNA

The next day, I am completely fed up.

I eat breakfast alone. Lunch alone. Dinner alone. All meals have been delivered to my bedroom. I haven't seen Patanza in two days, and I haven't seen Mrs. Molina since she confronted me.

The guilt is eating me alive. All I want is to feel human—to speak to someone and voice my opinions, but no one wants to listen.

I can understand why. I've destroyed the relationships I had, demolished by my own bad decisions. The people that trusted me, no longer can. The people who gave me a chance now regret that decision.

Though the view is gorgeous, all I see is black and white. There are people who would kill for this kind of room, this paradise, yet here I am, with the right side of my face on the comforter, drowning my sorrows with bottle after bottle of wine.

The sun is setting now—I can see it from here.

The house is quiet. I haven't seen anyone but Emilio all day.

I continue asking for bottles of wine, but sooner or later I'm going to need something much stronger than this.

I have to do something to win back their trust.

I have to fix the damage I caused. But how? How, when no one is wiling to give me a chance—when no one will even look me in the eye?

Nightfall arrives, and I roll over, staring up at the twirling ceiling fan. It's still quiet, the ocean roar peaceful, the city lights bright and flashy.

I step out of bed and walk to the door, on the search for something stronger now. Tequila, or even rum will do.

I walk to the empty kitchen. The countertops are spotless, and of course the wine fridge is out of my favorite wine. The bar inside doesn't have a very good selection, which only leaves the pool's bar.

With a sigh, I turn around and walk out, going into the living room, past the clean, untouched furniture. I look out at the pool bar, but then I see a shadowy figure sitting close to the rails. Chains of smoke surround him, and I notice a short tumbler in his left hand.

I quietly open the door, walking barefoot past the pool. The scent of his cigar is strong and powerful, but I suck it up and keep it moving. I know I shouldn't. I should just grab my bottle and go about my way, but I can't help myself.

I step up behind him, and he peers over his shoulder with a solid frown. The city lights highlight one half of his face, the other half shadowy in the moonlight.

"What are you doing out here?" I ask.

He looks away, taking a slow pull from his cigar.

"Can't sleep?" What a stupid question. He never fucking sleeps. I sigh. "Draco, can we please just talk? I need to tell you how I feel." I pause. "I want to help you."

He clears his throat, shifting in his chair.

"What happened is my fault, okay? I know now, and I know you're pissed. I blame myself for it, and I always will. I regret what I did. I was selfish and I wasn't thinking. I was stupid, thinking I could— could *own* you in some fucked up kind of way. Testing your limits. I thought I had you wrapped around my finger. I thought I . . . I don't know. I just thought I didn't need you. But I do. More than you think. So please, just say something."

He picks up his glass and downs whatever liquor he is drinking. When he's done, he sets it down on the ground and then stabs the butt of his cigar on the concrete. He starts to push out of his chair, but I walk forward and stop him from getting up, pressing him down by the shoulders.

A million thoughts take over my mind, but I don't let them consume me. He's only wearing sweatpants, and I immediately go for what I want.

I lower to my knees to get between his legs, yanking his pants down as he tries to push me away. "Get off of me," he growls.

But I don't. I keep going, wrapping my fingers around the hem of his pants and tugging, tugging, until I see nothing but his briefs. He barely lifts his hips, making me work for it, eyes hard on me. I continue, focusing on the edge of his briefs, my heart beating faster.

When his thick, soft cock is free, I push up and wrap my hand around the base of it, bringing his tip to my lips and swirling my tongue around it. He sighs heavily, and when I look up, his eyes still hard and intense on mine.

I close my lips around him, my hand still wrapped and stroking. He's getting harder by the second. When he's as hard as a rock, I have to work harder to fit him in my mouth, but I don't stop. I keep sucking and licking, dying for a taste of him. Needing him to want me again.

I gag around him when I take him too far and hear him curse beneath his breath. But still, I don't think or stop. I just do.

I finally let him go when he's fully erect, climbing on top of his lap. I'm not wearing any panties or shorts beneath this gown, so sliding down on his thick length, inch by slow inch, is easy to do. My lips part, a gasp spilling out when I feel him completely inside of me.

His nostrils flare, his fingers digging into the arms of his chair.

He doesn't want me.

He *does* want me.

I can't tell.

I don't stop.

I ride his cock, lifting my hips up and down, circling and dipping, my fingernails sinking into his shoulders. During all of it, he's staring right into my eyes, breathing harder, pretending he isn't enjoying it. But by his small grunts of resistance and how he clenches his jaw, I can tell he does.

Then he's gripping my ass in his hands and slamming into me from below, and I know for a fact he's enjoying it. A clapping noise fills the air, the sound of his body slapping against mine, and I gasp out loud, holding onto him tighter, my arms wrapping around him.

He squeezes my plump ass in his hands, and I work my hips in sync with each thrust he provides. He's filling me up more and more, making me wetter. Making me hungrier for him.

Not a word uttered.

Only breaths mingling, and grunts and moans flowing with the warm breeze.

I can see he wants to hold off and pull away when our eyes connect. His mouth lands on mine, and he sinks his teeth into my bottom lip, biting hard, so hard that I taste blood, but the pain is overpowered by the pleasure.

I force him back and ride him faster, feeling his cock hit the most tender of spots inside me.

His head falls backward as he gives himself to me, just what I wanted, and he curses beneath his breath in Spanish.

"Forgive me," I breathe in his ear, kissing my way down to his neck. A groan bubbles deep in his throat. He opens his eyes, looking right at me. I feel myself on the brink, so close to tipping over. "Please," I beg, kissing his lips while my pussy clenches his cock. "I'm so sorry."

His large hands are still holding me tight, delivering full, hard strokes. His strokes are quick and hungry, like he can't get enough, and I squeeze my arms around his neck, climaxing like never before from the power alone.

I come so hard around him, never wanting to let go—loving how full and swollen he feels inside me.

"Shit," he groans, his body now stiff and tense. I feel him coming inside me, the warmth he provides, twitching every time I squeeze my walls around his sated cock.

I'm breathing hard, but when I pick my head up to look at him, he's no longer looking at me. He's slouched in the chair, staring ahead at the city. I wait for him to say something—wait for him to kiss or caress me.

He doesn't. Instead he says, "Get off and go back to your room."

I frown, slowly climbing off his lap and standing in front of him. "We should talk," I breathe.

Avoiding my eyes, he stands up tall and pulls his briefs and pants up to his waist. He starts to walk past me, and I panic, shooting my arm out before he can get away.

"No!" I grip his wrist and yank him back around to face me. He glares down at the hand I have wrapped around him, like he wants to cut it off.

He grimaces. "Let go of me."

"No." I step toward him, my bottom lip trembling now. "Stop walking away from me! Face me like a fucking man, you coward!"

"Fuck you, Gianna!" He snatches his arm away, taking a small step closer to me.

"You did just fuck me, and I *fucked* you, and you *loved* it."

He doesn't blink. "You stay out of my way, and I'll stay out of yours. It's that simple."

"Draco, please," I beg, staring up into his eyes. The tremble in my lips is worse now. I'm on the verge of tears. I hate this. "Just fucking talk to me. I can't live like this! Your mom fucking hates me now! Everyone around here hates me!"

His glower is terrifying. I can tell he's angry, but that he's also disappointed. I can tell he wants to talk, but it's not in his nature to talk about how he's feeling.

This is El Jefe, the broody, dangerous man who has wanted to kill me on more than one occasion, and somehow I keep forgetting that.

This is the man who was ready to kill me when he first heard about me. This is a man who never shows mercy or pity, yet he has for me—*repeatedly*. He doesn't know what the hell to do with me, and I don't know if I should be upset or glad about it.

His jaw ticks, and his throat bobs as he finally pulls his gaze away, like he can't even stand to look at me. "I have nothing to say to you, Gianna."

"Yes, you do. I'm sure you want to yell at me—or beat me. You can do whatever you want to me—punish me for days if you have to—do anything you want, as long as you *talk to me*! As long as I know there's a way through this! As long as you're not still angry with me!"

He frowns when my last sentence hits him. "Why *wouldn't* I be angry with you?" he barks, voice harder, colder. "You disobeyed me! You didn't fucking listen! I told you that motherfucker was no good, but you went behind my back and set him free anyway! And look what happened. My cousin—my only cousin and the only real family I had left other than my mother—*died* because of *you*. Because that no-armed fucker heard all about our plans, knew every fucking thing we were doing, and you set him free like a *perra estupida!*" *Stupid bitch.*

He gets closer to my face, baring his teeth now. I hold his gaze, barely breathing. I don't even blink. I can't. I'm stuck…shocked.

"You want me to talk to you—tell you how I feel? Fine. I'll tell you what I feel," he seethes, holding my eyes, his fierce and dark. "I never should have trusted you. I should have left your spoiled ass in that cell to fucking *rot*. It would have spared me all of the trouble and would have prevented all of the mess that I now have to clean up because of you. I *never* should have tried to love you."

My heart nearly fails me.

He stands up straight again and walks by without another word. I stand there like the pathetic, useless girl I am. Draco isn't known for walking away from his problems. He handles them and even owns them, but this time he refuses.

I can't even turn to see him go. Though it's nearly eighty degrees outside, I'm frozen all over.

My eyes sting, and I feel the unsteady emotions thickening in my throat, my breaths becoming labored. There's a squeeze in my chest, a tug around my heart, like someone has lassoed it, pulling with all their might.

It doesn't take long for me to realize where the pull is coming from. With each step he takes away from me, the pull is getting stronger and stronger.

With those words, he's ripped my heart right out of my chest and, because he's so hurt and misguided, he doesn't even know it.

8

GIANNA

I decide not to go back to my room afterward.

I sit in the living room instead, staring through the spotless glass in front of me.

The sun is just rising now. Dusk is calling.

Someone shuffles by and I look up, spotting Patanza who is fully clothed. She's tugging a pair of fingerless black gloves over her hands. Her face has a little more color to it now, but when she looks up, her eyes are still just as dark and dangerous.

She gives me a brief look with a slight frown before walking to the door and leaving the house, the door clicking shut behind her.

Sighing, I push out of the leather recliner and start to make my way to the room. I should try and sleep. I have no energy and I need to refuel, but my mind is thrashing with unwanted thoughts.

My body is yearning for him.

I can't stand it.

I start to walk to my room, but stop at the door when I hear something crash. Brows narrowing, I pull my hand away from the doorknob to the bedroom, and walk toward the sound.

The crashing continues, getting louder with each step. I'm holding my breath when I see light seeping through the cracks of a door.

"Fuck!" Draco curses loudly, and I gasp, hurrying for the door. I grab the handle and push in, but there is another door ahead. It's parted, so I can only see a sliver of what's inside the room.

There is furniture made of black leather, mirrors on many of the walls, and glass tables. There are guns on a wall that I can see from this angle, and then Draco appears, walking by the door swiftly.

I hold back on a gasp, spotting his tall, broad figure. He's shirtless, his skin and hair slightly damp, like he's just finished taking a shower or a swim. A gun is in his hand, directly at his side, his finger wrapped around the trigger like he's ready to fire it at any given moment.

My breathing becomes shallow as I watch him. I watch him curse. Watch him holler. I watch him unload the gun and dump all of the bullets on the floor, and then he flings the weapon, sending it crashing into one of the mirrors in front of him.

"La mataré!" he barks. *I will kill her.* "I will squeeze the breath out of her body! I will fucking end her!" He is in a blinding rage, and for a moment I panic, assuming he's talking about me.

He grabs his cellphone, asking about the whereabouts of Hernandez, and relief strikes me. I realize he must have been talking about her. I close my eyes, still holding my breath for fear that he may hear me, backing away slowly.

When I'm out in the hallway and the door is shut behind me, I start to turn but bump into someone.

The person's hands lock around my upper arms, and I let out an even louder gasp, my heart racing as I meet his bright green eyes. Emilio pulls his hands away, lifting one finger up and pressing it to his lips, shaking his head.

"Leave him, Patrona. Let him grieve," he whispers. With a sigh, he looks at the door Draco is behind. Without another word, he steps away from me and turns around, walking back down the hallway, stepping around a corner, and disappearing.

I draw in a deep breath and hurry for my room.

He is losing it.

Unhinged.

Damaged.

Broken.

And we all know it.

And since he won't let me help him, the only thing I can do is stand by and watch—watch as he self-destructs.

9

DRACO

I can't do this anymore. She is driving me out of my motherfucking mind.

I see her walking around, looking for me, and I hide—I fucking *hide,* because I can't face her. I can't look into her eyes and know for a fact she feels just as awful as I do.

I have to hate her.

I have to forget her.

I have to hold onto that urge of wanting to choke the shit out of her just enough—just enough until she thinks she's on the brink of dying.

If only I could. If only I had it in me. But I don't. So instead I pretend to be a ghost to her.

I thought I could handle it—having her around. I thought I could ignore her—pretend she doesn't exist—but that is fucking impossible to do. She's around. I know it. I *feel* her. I hear her when she cries—which she does, every single night—when I stop by her door, just to listen.

She's drowning her sorrows, bottle after bottle, and I am not doing a damn thing to stop it.

It's not like me to reward or give solace for the fucked-up shit she's done.

It's not like me to forgive and forget. It's not in my DNA.

She almost had me out by the pool—she was so fucking close to getting me to crack. Her sweet, wet pussy wrapped around me was enough to make me weak and almost enough to make me say the words: Okay, I forgive you.

But I didn't.

I couldn't.

I can't.

I can't fucking forgive her, because if I do, she'll want to stay.

She needs to be pushed away. She needs to think I don't want her. She needs to know that there are things far more important to me than whatever it is I feel for her.

I know what I am about to do is wrong. What I am about to do may cause her to hate me forever. What I am about to do is shattering me, inside and out. It's ruining me—making my fucking chest hurts. She's given me an ache I've never felt before.

Emilio appears at the door after making the first delivery, lips pressed thin as he pulls his gloves off. I'm certain there are a million questions racing through his mind, but he knows better than to ask them.

I set a clean glass on the silver tray with the champagne I told him to bring. "Take it to her," I order, looking away. He picks it up right away, hurrying out of the room.

Never in my entire fucking life have I felt a burn this fierce in my chest—a fire this strong swarming in my veins. I down my tequila, hoping—no, *praying*—that it will make me go numb.

It does nothing but fuel my emotions, drawing out the darker parts of me again.

"Shit," I curse, slouching down in my chair, shoving rough, thick fingers through my hair. I hear the voices in my head—the voices that constantly drive me to do the mad shit I do.

Don't.

Stop.

Do not become weak for her.
Fuck her!
And then there is the other voice.
Go.
Run to her.
You fucking need her!
Go!

It's overwhelming as fuck. Every battling chant, every consuming thought of her.

Mi reina. Mi patrona. *Gianna*.

I shoot out of my chair, glass still in hand, and throw it at the wall across from me. The glass splinters into pieces, sharp shards scattering all over the room. But I don't care for the glass, because on that same wall, right across from me, is a mirror.

I see myself.

Face pale.

Dark, empty eyes.

Being away from her is destroying me. Being away from her makes me hostile. It makes me want to fight and ruin. Despite how angry I am, how I want to blame her, I can't, because I want her so fucking much.

And that's exactly why she has to go. All I can think about is having my cock inside her, my lips on every inch of her skin. All I can think about is how I want her to sigh my real name—the name only she can call me and get away with it. Her laughter, her cries, the way she calls for me in her sleep and doesn't even know it…

Fuck.

She has to go.

10

GIANNA

As soon I walk out of the bathroom after my swim, my eyes shoot over to the flowers that appeared less than an hour ago. They are stored in a glass case, with a big, bold note taped to the vase that says: DO NOT TOUCH THEM.

They are a beautiful, bold indigo. No thorns like the Blue Betrayals. No darkness like the Chocolate Cosmos. These are vibrant and full of life. Too pretty not to touch. In front of the flowers is a folded card and a pair of gloves. I pick up the black leather gloves again, turning the note over to read it once more.

Death by Indigo. That's what they are called.
They are beautiful, alluring. All you want to do is touch them—feel them. See how they smell. You can smell. You can look. But you cannot touch. One fistful without gloves can ruin your life. They are the deadliest flowers on earth. They are banned because one touch on one tiny finger could paralyze a whole hand.
They are poisonous and toxic. They are exactly what you have become to me.

I know the handwriting all too well.

This note hits something inside me. I feel another ache, deep, deep down every time I read it. I feel a hand crushing what's left of my heart.

My heart in his hand.

Crushing until nothing is left.

I get the urge to open the case—to touch them, to put an end to all of this.

But I am not weak. I won't cave. He is angry now, but he has to forgive me. I am not his enemy. Not anymore.

There is a knock on my door several minutes later. I pull my gaze away from the sunset, telling the person to come in.

Emilio steps into the room with a silver tray in hand and a wary smile. "Would you like some champagne, Patrona?"

"Champagne? What are we celebrating? How I'm so great at fucking things up?" I ask, sarcasm laced in my voice. His mouth twitches. He just stands there, unsure how to respond. I sigh and answer, "Why not?"

Nodding, he steps up to a table in the corner and sets the tray down. He pours the champagne and then walks to me, holding the glass out.

When I accept, he says, "We all do foolish things, Patrona. Even the best of us—the strongest and most powerful—do things that don't make sense sometimes. We are humans. We can only live and learn from our mistakes." He forces a tight smile at me, and then he turns quickly.

He's out of the door before I know it.

I sip my champagne, needing anything to pull me out of my gloomy mood. I walk to the closet and change into a silky pink gown, then shut off the lights, tucking myself beneath the sheets with my glass in hand. The pillows are plush and comfortable behind me.

From this spot, I can still see the ocean. If I listen hard enough, I can even hear it.

The soothing waves crashing to shore.

The soft swish.

I sip.

Sip.

Sip.

Until everything becomes dark and my body feels weightless.

I don't feel anything, but I can still hear.

I hear a deep, heavy sigh.

Mumbling.

Whispering.

Arms wrap around me.

Lips are on my cheek.

Warmth is on my back, like someone is holding me.

I hear myself whisper his name, "Draco." His name is a sweet, soft tingle on my lips.

"Damn it, Gianna," I hear him murmur. And then it's cold again.

Quiet.

He's gone.

11

GIANNA

A hard gasp shoots out of me.

My eyes pop open, and I pant heavily, looking all around me. The space I'm in is familiar. Ivory leather. A sweet, cinnamon scent. I'm strapped into my seat. I'm on the jet again?

I'm still wearing the pink gown, but with a trench coat covering it. My lips feel numb. My body is tingling. I can't get a good grasp on my breathing.

My eyes sting, tears blurring my vision, but then something catches my eye from the left.

No, *someone*.

Emilio is standing there. He's been standing there this entire time.

"Emilio," I breathe. "W-what the hell is going on? Why am I on the jet again?"

His face is sullen, and I see the guilt in his eyes. Though I ask in English, its like he can still understand my question.

"You put something in my drink, didn't you!" I shout in the language he can understand.

"I didn't put a thing in there, Patrona."

"Then who did?" I demand, eyes still burning

He sighs. "I think you already know who did."

"Draco?" I whisper, and he immediately pulls his gaze away. He turns his back to me and walks to the recliners behind him. With wide eyes, I slouch back in my chair, staring down at my lap. My heart is galloping in my chest, my palms sweaty. Sweat has even beaded up on my forehead and above my upper lip.

Despite it all, I stand up, focusing on Emilio. "Take me back to him. Now!"

His lips smash together. "You know I can't do that." He looks me over. "Please sit, Patrona. There is something he wants me to give to you."

I look at him sideways, eyes shifting over to the windows. Surrounded by clouds. Up in the sky. Something tells me it's too late to do anything.

With a hard sigh, I finally sit, and Emilio takes the seat across from me and leans forward. He extends his arm, holding out something in his hand. A cellphone. I glare down at it warily, taking notice of the folder in his other hand.

"Jefe wants me to make sure you listen to this before you land," he says softly.

"What is it?" I ask, voice dry, thick.

He sighs, making the screen light up and unlocking it. He scrolls through and then stops, handing it to me with the screen up.

It's showing the voice recordings. With a tilted brow, I take it, eyeing him briefly before looking down at it.

There are four recordings on here.

Emilio stands, handing me the manila folder. I blink up at him, taking it and placing it on my lap. "I'll let you have your privacy," he says softly.

I swallow hard, but my throat is still dry, desperate for moisture. I'm too anxious to hold off on listening to these. I press play on the first recording, and Draco's voice fills the small space around me.

"Gianna Natalia Nicotera." He sighs, long and hard. *"You are confused. Angry. Probably downright pissed. I don't expect you not to be. You're wondering what happened, and why I did it. Well, I'll tell you what I did. I dropped a small dosage of rohypnol in the champagne, enough to keep you barely conscious. You probably don't remember what happened after you drank it. I really wish you wouldn't remember any of the events that happened before this."* His voice breaks a little, just barely. But I can hear it. I can hear the agony in his voice, how much this is hurting him, and my throat thickens, chest heavier now.

"I am not a good man, Gianna. I am a fucked-up man. I sell drugs and kill for a living, and I consider that the norm. I've punished women and never gave it a second thought—not until you." When he says that, my heart beats faster. The recording ends so I go to the next.

"There is one thing I wish, and that is me wishing I had never ordered my men to take you that day. I think having you killed would have been better, because even as I record this message, I am fucking torn. I am torn between doing the right thing—which is sending you away from danger—and keeping you here with me and risking everything I have worked so hard for. If I had kept you around, it would have cost me. They know who my heart beats for now. She knows the great lengths to which I will go to keep you safe...and because of that, I couldn't let you stay. You are a liability to me, Gianna. Yes, you broke my heart, and yes, I trusted you, and you betrayed me, but despite all of it, I love you so much, and I don't think that will ever change."

A tear escapes me, but I swipe at it quickly, holding the phone tighter, clicking the next recording.

"You're wondering where you will go. Don't worry. You'll be with family—family that I know you trust, not the motherfuckers that will try to marry you off to a worthless family to rebuild the Nicotera name." He pauses. *"Open the folder Emilio gave to you."* I place the phone on the arm of the recliner, opening the folder.

I frown a little as I flip through them realizing all of the images are of me. They each have time stamps on them, some going way back to when I was first taken. Some are in color and some are in black and white. There is one with me on the beach. One of me at the pool. One of me eating breakfast with Mrs. Molina and laughing.

There is even one of me sleeping in Draco's bed in only my panties, no bra, the sheets halfway across the backs of my thighs. I question if he took these images or if someone else did. But he would never let anyone get that close while I was naked and vulnerable this way. It had to be him.

"I sent these images and more to your family to let them know you're safe. All but that last image anyway. I sent a new image to them every single week to let them know you were still alive and well. That you would stay well, as long as they didn't come looking for you. I threatened that if they did come looking, or if I found out they hired someone to come for you, I would kill you." He blows a heavy breath. *"I wouldn't have killed you,"* he murmurs, and I sigh in relief. He knows me too well.

"You may not understand at first, but I'm not doing this for myself, Gianna. I'm doing this for you. I don't give a fuck about this life anymore. I don't give a damn about running this empire, but my pride will not allow it to fall that easily. I refuse to let that bitch win. The truth is, I wanted to run away with you—to a private island I bought—and fucking marry you. I wanted to have a child with you. I wanted to create an entire fucking life with you. These thoughts alone make me feel pathetic, but I don't fucking care because it's what I want, and it is the truth. I wanted to make you my fucking world. But at the end of the day, my reality is this: being El Jefe. All of the world should know that I am not to be fucked with. And that's why Hernandez has to die. But I cannot go after her with you around. Your family will protect you. You're probably out of the country by now. Your familia will be waiting on a private runway. They will pick you up, and they will most likely try to ensure that you never see or hear from me again."

My heart breaks when those words run through my ears. Never see him again?

I play the final message.

"Even if I die—even if I lose everything in the process—it will not matter. You will be safe. I will make sure all of your threats have vanished. You will no longer have to worry about watching your back in this world. You will finally be free. You're probably wondering why I couldn't tell you this face-to-face. I just...couldn't. I am no coward. I am known for facing my issues and handling them like a man. But you are an issue I can no longer face. You are my heart. And I cannot say goodbye to you."

I break down without even letting all of his words sink in. The tears have completely blinded me, but his voice continues, making me weak, each word crippling my heart.

"Yo no soy un buen hombre," he whispers, voice cracking, breaking. I am not a good man. *"I wish I was, for you, but I will never be good. I sometimes wish I was still the little boy who saw you and fell hard for your big, green eyes. I wish I was still that innocent kid who had a raging crush on you—the kid who didn't give a damn about the guns, the drugs, the cartel, or any of this cruel, vile shit. The kid who made a simple promise to marry you. Cherish you. Protect you. Be good to you. But I cannot be that man. I am broken and cruel. I am corrupt and I enjoy all of this more than I care to admit. I thought I was heartless, but having you around proved me wrong."* He pauses. *"I see now that in order to live this life, sacrifices must be made. So this is my sacrifice. I am letting you go. Not for my sake, but for yours. I have only caused you misery and pain, but you, mi reina, deserve to be happy...even if some of the things you have done may have just cost me my life."*

Those are his final words.

This is his goodbye?

I can't accept it.

I feel the same way. I have only caused him misery and suffering. I am the reason he will lose everything.

I have been a burden all along, and he knew that, yet he still dared to love me.

He risked his life the moment he decided to give his heart to me.

12

GIANNA

This flight is longer than expected.

I'm still thirsty; I have to use the bathroom, but I can't pull myself together enough to stop the tears. I hate crying, especially now, after feeling like I was on top of the world—like nothing could stop me.

This was never supposed to happen.

I betrayed his trust, shattered his loyalty, and broke his already broken heart.

What the hell was I thinking—no, what the hell was *he* thinking?

He never should have trusted me. He never should have taken me. He should have just killed me, the same way he did Toni. Being dead would be a hell of a lot easier than being brokenhearted.

He was once the monster in the dark—the man who haunted my dreams and stole my happiness. He was once a man I loathed—someone I would never be able to forgive.

That's what I thought.

But the man who was once a monster in the dark has become everything I've ever wanted. He became the only ray of sunshine I had—my only hope. He was the one who restored me—the one who showed me what I was capable of and who I really am.

He is the only reason I still wish to live.

Without him, I may as well be back in that shed again—chained. Broken. Beaten. Starved.

Without him, I may as well be dead.

Someone taps my shoulder, and I pick my head up, focusing on the box of tissues. My eyes drift up to Emilio's, whose face is calm and complacent. I take the box, but I don't use the tissues. Instead, I look out of the window, tears staining my face, as he sits in the seat across from me.

He's quiet for several minutes. It's not awkward, either. He probably doesn't want to say the wrong thing, and honestly, I couldn't care less about what he has to say, unless he decides to turn this jet around—which I know he won't do.

Forget what I said earlier. I need to get back to Draco.

"I grew up with Draco," he says, voice low.

I continue staring out the window.

"He is not a bad man—well, not so much."

I side-eye him.

"You want to hate him. I get it. But he was right, Patrona. He is doing this for you. He can't see anyone else that is close to his heart die. His mother isn't even in Cabos anymore."

That gets my attention. "Where is she?"

"Somewhere Hernandez will never find her," he says. "Just like she won't find you. Draco wants to make sure of it, which is why you shouldn't come back. Your family knows you are on the way."

I swallow hard. "Great." Sighing, I slouch back in the chair, swiping a finger beneath my eyes. "Can I get a bottle of water, please?"

He nods, pushing out of his seat and going for the galley. He returns with two bottles of water, one for himself and another for me. I crack it open and chug most of it down as he sips his.

"She is a crazy woman," he says, agitation on his breath.

I frown. "Who?"

"Yessica."

Brows stitched, I sit up in my seat, in need of more details. "You've been around her before?"

"Plenty of times."

"Why is she out for him?"

Emilio cracks his fingers, sitting higher up in his chair. "Because he broke her heart. And from what my mother has always told me, *hell hath no fury like a woman scorned.*"

I blink slowly. "How did he meet her?"

"A territorial deal."

"When?"

"When he was twenty-two." He holds my gaze, and I stare back. He knows I need more.

"Tell me the whole story, Emilio."

"It is not my story to tell."

"I don't care. I'll never see him again anyway. I want to know how much of a threat she really is to him—why he never goes into detail about her with me."

Sighing heavily, he swipes a hand over his brow, lowering his gaze. "They met when they were twenty-two. Draco had started a new trade with a highly respected mayor in Venezuela. Yessica was an assistant for the mayor. She was from Mexico, always looking for her next power role—or at least, riding the coattails of the most successful men, to try to claim hers." He swallows thickly. "Jefe stayed in the mayor's mansion for three nights. He needed to earn his trust, and of course the mayor's assistant stayed there as well." Emilio's eyes harden, focused intently on mine. "Do you want me to keep going, Patrona? I don't want to hurt you or your feelings with what I am about to tell you."

"Keep going," I command, my voice scratchy, foreign to me now.

He runs his tongue over his bottom lip. "Yessica stayed in the mansion, and I was there as well. My room was next to his, but I always kept my door open to keep an eye on my boss. I would see her come while everyone was sleeping, and go to his room. Sneak in there. I would hear her moans of pleasure. Hear him cursing at her to get out, but not really doing a thing to stop it. I think he was having fun. Enjoying it."

I cringe inside, shutting my eyes for a brief moment. "Keep going." My words come out quick, biting.

"They became closer, and by the time he had to go, she begged him to take her with him. At first he refused, but Yessica is good at seducing. I know because she tried to seduce me too." He grips his bottle of water, pulling his gaze away from mine. "So she told him that she would do whatever he wanted. That she'd work around the house for him, take care of him in ways only a woman can. She was all in for Jefe, and he liked that. He liked women who were willing to beg."

My chest tightens. I hate every single word coming out of his mouth, but he can't stop. I need to know everything.

"She lived with him for four years, but each year she became greedier. Jefe wasn't as lenient with her as he was with you. Whenever she did something he told her not to do, she was punished severely. Beaten and whipped with belts and paddles. Choked while she slept until she begged for mercy. She was even knocked unconscious once. You would think I felt bad for her. I didn't. I didn't, because she asked for this to happen to her. She would yell in his face, tell him to do something about it if she'd made him angry. She was addicted to it—his punishments. She was fucking insane."

"So she's the reason he likes to punish." It's more of a statement than a question.

He nods, just barely. "He got a thrill out of it, but he was the worst with her. She'd intentionally show up late for breakfast, even when he constantly reminded her. One day she pushed too far. She spit on his food, and he stabbed her in the thigh."

My eyes stretch wide.

"One of the maids stitched her up. One day, during her very last week there, she told him she'd put up with so much of his shit that he needed to marry her. She demanded that he make her his wife. Jefe refused. He didn't love her. Truthfully, I think he was beginning to despise everything about her. He was on the verge of killing her, which was his only other option, because he couldn't let her go. She knew too much, and he didn't trust her. He told her to her face that he didn't love her and that he would never marry a psychotic bitch like her. She begged him to. Groveled. He refused every single time. I remember the day he told her: 'Love is useless. *You* are useless.' She'd changed after that. She no longer begged. She didn't show up for breakfast and didn't spend her nights looking for him. She hid in her assigned bedroom...and then one day she was just gone.

"We searched for her for years and got nothing. She'd completely disappeared...until one day she appeared during one of Jefe's meetings as an associate for one of his well-trusted dealers. We knew then that she had her own agenda, but Jefe wasn't concerned. He knew her threats were empty. He knew she was still the psychotic bitch who craved him day and night. He was still on top, and she was many levels beneath him. But one day, she was no longer the associate with the big dealer. She *became* the big dealer. She'd bought them out. Took over. She created her own empire and ran many of the small dealers dry. Now, she only needs one more big cartel dealer to rule all of Mexico—and that's Jefe's, but he's not handing it over without a fight. And she knows that—she knew when she first took you that he was going to start a war. She wanted this—to lure him out. At first, though, she didn't care to take what was his. Toni was dead, and she wasn't about to take her business down with him. Henry Ricci was a lost cause to her, but when Yessica heard about you, I'm certain she dug deeper. She needed to know more, and she knew she was only going to get that from Henry. Henry made himself way too easy for us to find after escaping. That should have been a sign to Jefe then that something was going on—that something bad was about to happen. She took Thiago, thinking he'd cave and tell her about you and where Jefe was. It's a very good thing he didn't."

He sighs, and I sit back in my seat, my pulse thudding in my ears now.

"Before that," he continues, "she mostly stayed out of his way. But when she heard about you, oh, Patrona, her jealousy *ignited*. I know it did, because you are the woman she wishes to be. He loves you, not her. He will never love her. He treats you like a queen and gives you so much mercy, while he treated her like a pile of shit. This is why you have to go. Because if she catches you again, she will kill you this time, just to make The Jefe just as miserable as she is."

13

GIANNA

The flight becomes rocky minutes after Emilio announces we will be landing soon. Fortunately, the landing smooths out when the wheels of the jet touch the ground.

The jet drifts along for two more minutes while I stare out of the window, at the mountains and the silky, blue sky.

I don't know what the hell I'm going to do. I can't be with family again after being around Draco for so long. He should know this. It won't be the same as before. A normal life doesn't suit me anymore—not after everything I have gone through while in his hands.

The only family I had left that I know of—and that I trust enough not to try and marry me off—is my dad's brother, Uncle Jack, and his wife, Aunt Minnie. They have two kids, from what I can remember, Clark and Jennifer, but we were so young the last time we saw one another that they probably don't even remember me.

Uncle Jack and Aunt Minnie didn't attend my wedding. They'd made up an excuse about how they didn't like to travel that far, but something deep in my gut tells me now that they just didn't like Toni.

I remember Uncle Jack coming around, but never directly speaking to Toni. Uncle Jack had even dropped out of my dad's business when he saw Toni getting higher rank, but he still ran his own business, which still required security guards.

Daddy has another brother, and a sister.

My uncle Ken will try to marry me off.

My aunt Natasha will try to marry me off, too.

Even my grandmother Veronica, will try to marry me off—all for the money. All because they know how much I am worth, and that the vilest men in his world will pay a pretty penny, just to get me pregnant and weave our bloodlines.

Dad never trusted any of them but Uncle Jack. Yes, he had Ken working for him, but it was always at a distance. Ken never sat at my dad's table. He always kept me close and kept them at arms length. The only time we would all get together was for every other Thanksgiving or Christmas, and even then, Daddy always went with two guns, three knives and two of his best guards.

The jet finally comes to a stop, and as soon as it does, Emilio is standing and reaching into the bin above his head. He takes down two magenta suitcases and then looks at me.

"Are you ready, Patrona?"

Pressing my lips, I unclip my seatbelt and stand. No, I'm not ready. No, I don't want to go. But I know I have no choice. He won't let me stay. If I had a gun, I'd put it to his and the pilot's heads and demand they return me to him.

But I don't.

So I go.

Just as I start to follow after Emilio, I see a black SUV pull closer to the jet. A man in a navy blue suit steps out, sunglasses covering his eyes. He walks in front of the truck with his arms crossed in front of him.

I frown a bit. He's unfamiliar to me.

Emilio sees him too and places the suitcases down before he exits the jet. As he walks down the stairs, I see him draw a black handgun on the way. I rush to the window, watching as he holds it at his side. The man standing in front of the SUV immediately draws his when he spots it.

Emilio says something, and the man answers, and then the man steps around to the back door, pulling it open. A tall, familiar man with a thick, brown beard steps out. He looks much different than the last time I saw him—then again, the last time I saw him, I was fifteen years old.

He's wearing a black leather jacket, a collared gray shirt beneath it. He shuts the door behind him and walks toward Emilio, taking out his wallet and showing him his credentials.

Relief washes over me, only a small ounce. That's him. Uncle Jack. He looks different, like he's gained a few pounds, but in a healthy way. His brown hair is longer, curling behind his ears, and his smile is just as charming as he assures Emilio everything is alright.

Seeing it soothes the storm brewing inside me.

After Emilio reads over his information, he nods and hands it back, then turns for the jet again. He hustles back up the stairs and I ask, "Is everything okay?"

"Great, Patrona. Come with me." He grabs the suitcases and walks back down. I follow him out, surprised at how chilly it is. I'm only wearing a trench coat over a nightgown, and a pair of flip-flops. As I walk down, I see snow-capped mountains in the distance.

Where the hell are we?

I make it down the final step, and Uncle Jack steps forward, smiling broadly—until he notices what I'm wearing. His smile collapses, but he opens his arms, and I walk into them, wishing I was happier than I am in this moment.

Months ago I would have been eager and ready to walk into his arms—ready to be around anyone who wasn't Draco—but now…it's a hollow victory.

"He kept his word," he sighs.

"Who?" I ask, looking up at him.

"The man who held you captive. The Jefe." He frowns a bit. "Did he hurt you?"

"I'm fine," I tell him, shivering.

He notices and then looks me up and down. "Come on, let's get you to the truck where it's warm." He starts to escort me that way, but I pause, looking back at Emilio.

"It was a pleasure serving you, Patrona," he murmurs in Spanish, smiling softly. And I don't know what it is about his words, but it hurts my heart to hear them. Tears prick my eyes, but I nod quickly and pull away, walking to the truck with Uncle Jack.

I slide across the bench to the other side, not without noticing Emilio handing the suitcases to Uncle Jack's driver.

As soon as it's done, Emilio turns, pulls out his cellphone, and walks back on the jet.

It takes everything in me not to bawl where I sit. I can't cry. I'm assuming Draco wants them to still be intimidated—to still think he's dangerous and ruthless. He doesn't want his reputation ruined by me. He doesn't want them to know he is soft and that by sending me here, he was doing them and me a favor.

He never would have killed me...but they don't know that. To them, he showed mercy. They got lucky, and only because he respected my father.

"Did he not tell you where we live?" Uncle Jack asks me when his door is shut.

"No." My teeth are chattering. I rub my hands over the arms of my jacket to warm myself. Uncle Jack cranks up the heat using the knobs above. "Where are we?"

"Colorado. Estes Park, to be exact."

"You didn't live here before."

"No, I didn't. We moved here a while ago, right after Lion passed away. It's quieter here. Safer."

I drop my head. "Oh."

I can still feel him looking at me. I can't look him in the eyes right now. Not right now. I drop my arms and squeeze my fingers. "You weren't at the vigil I planned for him."

"I wanted to be."

"Why didn't you come?"

"Because I was out looking for the man who murdered him."

I look up into his eyes. They are so similar to Daddy's, bold and green. "Any luck?"

"Don't play dumb. I know who it was. The Jefe told me who when he sent me notification that you would be flying back."

My throat becomes dry and scratchy. "Oh. He told me, too."

"I'm glad he killed the son-of-a-bitch. If I'd known sooner, I would have strangled him at the funeral. A final favor for my brother."

The driver climbs into the car and puts it in reverse. As he rolls backwards, I stare ahead at the jet, hating each inch he's putting between it and us. He finally veers right, puts the car in gear, and drives away. I stop staring when I can no longer see it.

"I'm glad he killed him, too."

Uncle Jack grunts, shifting in his seat. He pulls out a cellphone but before he dials, he looks at me. "You sure he didn't hurt you?" He eyes my wrists, the scars from the ropes still visible. I rub them, remembering how raw they felt. How tender. How much I hated him then.

"He didn't hurt me much." *Not as much as I hurt him.*

"Well, I am glad we have you back, Gia. We tried to do everything we could to look for you, but after a while, he became hostile—made threats that he'd kill you and record, it just to prove to us that he didn't fuck around and didn't want you to be found. I think he realized how close we'd gotten to him at one point, and it made him angrier." He sighs, running a hand across his face. "I'm truly surprised you are still alive."

"He was close to Daddy. He had too much respect for him to kill me."

"I know he was, but he is still a cruel man. He is, and so was his father. The Molinas cannot be trusted. I don't know what your father saw in them." He brings the phone up to his ear. "Calling your Aunt Minnie. She's preparing a big, hot dinner for you. You'll love it."

I press my lips, forcing a smile at him. He returns a full, genuine one. I know I should be grateful for what he's doing—taking me in, possibly even risking his life without even knowing it—but how am I supposed to be grateful for something I don't even want?

I don't want to be here with him.

I want to be back with Draco.
I want to help.
I want to fight.
I want to be there for him, every step of the way.
But he needs space. He needs time away from me.
And I get it, because I really, really fucked up.

14

GIANNA

It's a twenty-five minute drive from the private runway to Uncle Jack's home. During the ride, I think of ways to get back. What do I tell them? Do I ask him to send me back to Mexico? Would he even do it?

Would he think I'm crazy?

I don't know, but I'm getting back somehow. I don't care if he thinks I'm crazy for wanting to. My place isn't here.

We pull up to a large, two-story log cabin made of smooth, golden brown wood. There are four long rectangular windows that make up the front top half of the home—windows that reveal some of the brown furniture inside. The gold chandelier is the most prominent object, giving the front of the home a warm glow.

Uncle Jack's driver—whose name I now know is Alvin—navigates around the circle driveway, parking the SUV in front of the house.

"Well," Uncle Jacks sighs beside me. "We're here, Gia. Home."

I don't look back at him. I can only look ahead. A new place. A new start.

I hear their seatbelts unbuckle, and Alvin is out first, opening Uncle Jack's door and then hustling around to open mine. I step out in

Uncle Jack's coat that he demanded I wear on the ride here, and the sole of my right flip flop rolls over a pebble.

"What do you think so far?" Uncle Jack asks, stepping up to my side.

"It's a nice home," I tell him.

"Come on. Minnie and the kids are waiting for you. I'll warn you now—that son of mine, Clark, is as hardcore and as blunt as they come. Don't let his remarks and crazy insults get to you. Don't know where he gets it from, 'cause it sure as shit isn't me. Might be his mother." He laughs, taking out his keys and sifting through them. "That woman is the feistiest little thing I know. Jen, she's everyone's friend. You don't have to worry too much about her."

My lips stretch into a small smile as he glances back.

He stuffs the key into the lock and unlocks the door, and as soon as he does, a waft of warm aromas hit me. A home-cooked meal. Fresh. Probably still being prepared.

Uncle Jack lets me walk in first, but I step aside to let him take the lead.

Their home is...beautiful.

To the left is a staircase, but not just any staircase. The railing is made of carved wood, dark and light grain. Between the railings are dark, intricate carvings, appearing smooth to the touch.

Ahead of me is a stone fireplace, flames already dancing, making the hard oak floors shine. Above are thick, mahogany beams keeping the beautiful cabin in place.

Clean, broken-in leather furniture is set up in front of the fireplace, with plaid red and black blankets, quilts, and tan throw pillows scattered over it.

I'm relieved when I don't see any animal hides or deer heads. I don't know why, but that has always creeped me out.

It's cozy here—a completely different setting than the homes Draco had me in. I like it.

I look up, at the guardrail to the left, and someone is already standing there. His short, cropped hair is black like the wings of a raven, his eyes a deep golden-brown. I can see the brightness of them from here. His skin is the color of mocha, tan and smooth.

He's wearing a black thermal shirt, dark blue jeans, and in the corner of his mouth is a toothpick. He chomps on it slowly, his nose in the air as he looks down at me and then at Uncle Jack.

"That her?" he asks, and I assume he's Clark. He's older now. More mature than what I remember. His jaw is square and cut, slight stubble surrounding his lips and the lower half of his face. I remember him being two years older than me.

"Who else would it be?" Uncle Jack says, moving aside and letting Alvin come in with my suitcases. Alvin places them down in the corner and then walks back outside, bobbing his head at Uncle Jack, who nods back.

"I'll see you tomorrow, Al," Uncle Jack tells him.

"Goodnight, sir."

"How long is she staying for?" Clark asks, now at the top of the staircase.

"For as long as she feels like it. Now stop asking questions and take her suitcases to her bedroom. She's been through enough."

Clark's face doesn't change. He watches me intently, but I watch just as carefully as he takes the steps down. When he's at the bottom of the staircase, he takes the four steps it takes until he's only a small step away from me.

He looks me over. Twice.

I do the same.

Then he shoots his hand out, revealing rough, calloused fingers. "I'm your cousin, Clark. My dad's told me all about you and about the man who had you." He looks down at his hand, waiting for me to take it.

I lift mine and grab it, shaking once before letting go. "Gianna."

"Obviously." He walks to the suitcases and picks them up. Before he can get to the staircase, he stops and looks my way. "My dad won't tell you what I said, so I'll let you know now. Don't fuck with me. Don't go in my room. Don't ask me any questions because I fucking hate questions. I like to be left alone. I don't like people who snoop or dig for shit they have no business digging for. You keep your distance, and I'll keep mine."

"Oh, shut up, Clark," Uncle Jack mutters. "Take the damn suitcases to her room."

"Trust me," I laugh softly, "you don't have to worry about that. I'm sure you aren't doing anything I haven't already seen happen."

Clark glares at me before turning and marching up the stairs.

When he disappears, Uncle Jack places a hand on my shoulder. "Ignore that idiot. Only reason he's living with me right now is because he doesn't know how to stay out of trouble. Come on. Let's go see your Aunt Minnie. She's in the kitchen."

I follow him down the hallway, hearing dishes moving and a sizzling noise, like something is being fried or sautéed. We step around the corner, into the kitchen, and there she is. Aunt Minnie. I remember her very well.

"Minnie," Uncle Jack calls, and she spins around quickly, her eyes wide and just as bright as Clark's.

"Oh! She's here!" Aunt Minnie drops her wooden spoon and turns around completely, wiping sauce-stained hands off on her apron.

She's still so beautiful. Brown skin, like the oatmeal muffins she used to make me for breakfast when I slept over, and bright golden-brown eyes. Her hair is still in those beautiful, wild corkscrew curls she always wore. She's a thick woman, with full hips and a full bosom. She's gorgeous.

The family was surprised Uncle Jack married her, but he loves her deeply. He refused to let her go and even put a ring on her finger as soon as he found out she was pregnant…or so I was told.

I wave and smile at her. "Hi, Aunt Minnie."

"Oh—don't you do that. Don't you get shy around me." She comes my way, opening her arms. "Come here." I step into her arms, and she squeezes me tight. She's so strong, but the hug is comforting. Welcoming, unlike her rude-as-hell son. She releases me, looking me in the face. "I swear you get more and more beautiful, the older you get."

I laugh a little. "Thank you."

S. WILLIAMS

She studies my eyes. "Are you okay? Were you hurt?"

"I'm fine, I promise. I'm alive, right? Still breathing. Daddy used to tell me that's all that matters."

"He sure did," Uncle Jack chuckles. "You take after him a lot. Even when you don't speak, you're just like him. He was always quiet, doing more observing than action. I still don't get how he could be so stupid around that man and let him take his life like—"

"Jack," Aunt Minnie scolds, staring at him. He clamps his mouth shut. "Please. Not now."

"It's okay." I wave a dismissive hand. "I'm just happy to be here. Thank you guys so much for taking me in."

"Of course, sweetie. We are glad to have you here, and you'll always be safe—"

"OH. MY. GOSH!" A high-pitched voice chimes from behind me, and I turn to look back, spotting a familiar girl.

Her green eyes are locked on me, her mouth parted, like she can't believe what she's seeing. Her hair is just as dark as Clark's, straight and pressed, touching the middle of her arm. She's wearing a coat, gloves, and boots, like she's just come from outside.

"Oh, Jen," Uncle Jack exclaims. "I was wondering where you were. Gia's arrived."

"I was chopping wood for the fire." She's still staring at me as she speaks, shrugging out of her coat and snatching off her gloves.

It's completely unexpected and catches me way off guard when she rushes my way after placing her coat on the back of a chair, throwing her arms around me and squeezing me tight.

For a moment I tense up, ready to shove her away, but I remember I'm safe.

They're family.

They won't hurt me...I don't think.

"You are still so pretty!" she says, and I'm assuming she's Jen, their daughter. "I still have a picture of us in my room. When we were like twelve, I think. When I had that sleepover. Do you remember?" She pulls back, grinning, looking me all over. She smooths my hair back and then holds my face. "You don't look like you were harmed." She looks down at my hands, and then her brows dip.

She grabs my arms, bringing them up and studying my wrists. "What happened here?"

"Happened when I was taken," I tell her.

"What did he do?" she asks with way too much sympathy in her voice. I almost want to cry, but I keep it together.

"What he had to do," I murmur.

"Well," she sighs, dropping my arms. "You don't have to be worried anymore. My dad has guards who live only a house away—not that anyone will do anything around here, but still. You are safe here. We'll protect you."

I force a smile at her. "I appreciate that."

"Jen, why don't you go show Gia to her room. Get her settled in, while your mother finishes up dinner," Uncle Jack suggests.

Jen nods eagerly, stepping back. "Sure. Come on, Gia."

I look back at Aunt Minnie, who smiles, and then at Uncle Jack, who bobs his head. I follow Jen out of the kitchen and up the stairs.

"You'll love it here," she says as we make our way up. "We have a hot tub, which feels so good when it's not too cold. The chill and the heat feel so amazing."

"Does anyone know you live here?" I ask.

She thinks on it. "Besides our guards, no."

"Any other family?"

"You mean the family members who would have tried to ship you off to another evil bastard?"

I look up at her as we meet at the top of the staircase. "You know about them too?"

"They tried to bribe my dad into marrying me to some Italian guy. I saw the letter he left in his office. He has a P.O. box in Utah. They think he lives there. Our guys used to go every month to check it, stay up to date, until we got those pictures of you months ago—heard about you and saw you were still alive. We started sending the guards every week then. Every week we got a new picture. Helped us sleep a little better at night." She starts down the hallway until we're at the third bedroom on the left. "I...don't want to seem like I'm all in your business. I know you probably don't want to think about it right now, but . . . did he try to kill you? He kept making threats."

I look her in the eyes. "He did once."

"And what happened?"

"He found out who I was. He was close to my dad."

"Yeah, they said that's the only reason he was keeping you alive."

Oh, but little does she know.

"Yeah. It was."

She opens the door and lets me in. "Are you glad to be back?" she asks.

I step inside, looking from the canopy sheets hanging over the queen-sized bed, to the french doors on the left. There is a balcony out there, and I sigh. Good. I can get air when I need to.

The floors are still hardwood up here too, a vanity on the west wall. The walls are painted a soft salmon, matching the quilted comforter on the bed, the white pillows, and the salmon throw pillows.

It's so basic.

So simple.

So beautiful.

So...different. All of this feels foreign to me now.

"I am," I answer, peering over my shoulder at her.

She smiles. "Well, good. You'll have fun with me here. We can go shopping. There's a ski resort only two hours away. We could go there. I have a few friends—but they know me by an alias. Chrissy Harrison. If you want, I can have someone make one for you, get you fake IDs so no one knows your real name."

"Sure. That'd be fun."

"Great. We can talk about names later." She points to the door on my left. "That's your bathroom. It's fully stocked. Like everything is in there. My mom and me went shopping for tampons, pads, body washes of all kinds for you to choose from, and I have some nail polish if you ever want to paint your fingernails or toes."

"You guys are very sweet. Thanks, Jen."

She nods. "I'll let you settle in. I know you've had a long trip. I'll come back when it's time for dinner."

I bob my head, and she walks out, giving a quick smile before disappearing and shutting the door behind her.

I sigh, looking around, up at the thick, brown beams, and then at the french doors. Walking over to the doors, I unlock them and grip the doorknobs, twisting them and drawing the doors apart.

The view is absolutely breathtaking.

The mountains stand tall, crowded with thick trees. The wooden guardrails lead down to a set of stairs that give way to the backyard. The backyard has a fire pit with cushioned lawn furniture set up around it.

Trees surround the home. It's like being in the middle of nowhere, where no one can find you. No one will bother you. I have a feeling they moved here for a reason—to escape the dangers of the world. To have a safe haven.

The sky is darker, the crescent moon coming into view. I stare up at the mountaintops, breathing in the crisp, clean air, wanting so badly to drown in this fresh start…take it in and accept it.

But I can't.

Because the only thing on my mind is him.

I can't get rid of my thoughts about him. I hope, after a few days or even weeks here, he'll become a distant memory that feels like it happened years ago.

But right now, with tears rimming my eyes, he is not that. My memories with him are fresh and deep, and it hurts to know that I'm the reason we can't create more.

I wonder what he's doing. How he's holding up.

He is self-destructive and angry, and those things don't mix.

An angry Draco is a dangerous one.

If only he'd given me another chance. If only he'd forgiven me… maybe things would be different.

I pick up my suitcase, tossing it on the bed, blinded by tears. I unzip it and shuffle through it for something—anything he may have left for me. There is the phone Emilio gave to me, with the voice recordings, but I don't think I can bear listening to that again. It'll only break my heart all over, and I need to keep it together.

I dig deeper, wrenching out the shoes and dresses and even the makeup bag until, finally, I'm at the bottom of the suitcase. My hands stop when I see the hard black case there. It's leather, all black. I pick it up, weighing it in my hands, caressing the smooth, cool surface.

And then I slowly unzip it.

Something shiny and silver appears. I open it all the way, and my heart races. It's a black-handled, silver-barreled 9-millimeter. I told him this kind of gun was my favorite.

There's money inside the case as well, and a sheet of paper tucked beneath it. I start to pull it out, but someone knocks on the door. "Gia? Getting settled in well?" Uncle Jack calls.

I zip the case quickly, shoving it back in the suitcase and picking up some of the dresses to cover it.

"Yeah! Great!" I call. "Just about to take a quick shower."

"Okay. Don't take too long. Dinner will be ready in about thirty."

"Okay!"

I listen hard until I can no longer hear his footsteps.

Shit. They're too concerned, breathing down my back.

I'll have to check later when things are quieter.

15

GIANNA

Dinner is quite simple.

And by simple, I mean completely informal…and I love it. It's not like how Draco would set it up, where butlers would bring our food out in an orderly fashion and bow before leaving.

No.

Aunt Minnie is a great cook, and she cooks for her family because she loves them.

All the food is set up on the table, hot and fresh. Grilled mixed vegetables and grilled chicken on top of fettuccini pasta and creamy Alfredo sauce. The bread rolls are piping hot, the tea sweet at first sip.

All the bowls are passed around, everyone talking amongst each other. I'm not quite sure how to slip into each conversation, so instead I sip my tea until the bowls come my way.

"So, Gia," Uncle Jack starts, placing the last bowl down and then picking up his fork. "I have a few rules I like to keep in place under my roof."

I meet his eyes, swallowing the chunk of bread in my mouth. "Yeah? And what are they?"

"One of them is for everyone to get along. If there is ever conflict or misunderstanding, you go to the source and figure it out like adults. Everyone at this table is older than eighteen. I expect you all to act like it."

After he says that, I look over at Clark, who looks me over twice before biting into his Alfredo sauce-covered bread roll.

"Okay. That sounds easy enough," I sigh.

"My second rule is if you ever need to go out, you let me know. Same goes for Minnie and Jen and even Clark. I need to know your whereabouts in case anything ever happens." I glance at Clark, and he rolls his eyes, slouching back in his chair. "Our Nicotera name is always a threat to someone."

I nod. "Right."

"And my last rule: no guns under my roof. It's plain and simple. If I see any trace of a gun, I will take it, and you won't see it again." He looks me hard in the eyes. "I have a place for guns that's nearby, but it ain't here. The only person that'll be carrying guns around this home is the man paying the bills. In other words, your Uncle Jack."

I pick up my tea, nodding. "Sounds fair."

"It's a bullshit rule," Clark mumbles.

"Clark, I've told you about cursing at the dinner table," Aunt Minnie scolds.

Clark digs into his pasta again, but his eyes are hard on mine. Like he knows something. Like I'm an enemy.

"Other than that, you are free to do whatever you want. Free to roam, free to go for walks on the trails. Free to make use of the hot tub. Free to cook whatever you want. You can do anything you see fit, just as long as you clean after yourself and as long as you don't set my house on fire by meddling with the fireplace."

Aunt Minnie and Jen laugh.

"It almost happened once with Jen," Uncle Jack chuckles, and Jen sucks her teeth.

"It was one time, Dad, and it was only a sheet of paper that got caught on fire."

"Yeah, yeah," he laughs.

"We're really glad to have you here, though, Gia," Aunt Minnie says with a soft smile. "We wouldn't want you anywhere else. If there is anything—and I mean anything—that you need, it's all yours. Don't even hesitate to ask."

"Yeah." I smile, doing my best to show my appreciation. "I'm glad to be here. Thank you, guys, again. I know having me around is a huge risk."

"We're always at risk, sweetie," she teases, waving a hand. "That'll never get old. Why do you think we live out here, in the middle of nowhere?"

Everyone at the table laughs—well, everyone except Clark. Clark smashes his lips together.

"Wouldn't have it any other way." Uncle Jack rubs his belly. "It's quiet. Peaceful. Every room has a great view. Don't plan on moving from here any time soon."

"I hear that." Aunt Minnie stands, grabbing Uncle Jack's empty plate. "Hope you guys have saved room for dessert. It's my favorite walnut and caramel cheesecake from Heidi's!"

"Oh, I love that place!" Jen squeals, hopping out of her chair with her plate in hand. "I'll grab more plates, Mom."

A hand grips my shoulder, and I tense up, looking up to see Uncle Jack hovering over me. He notices my reaction to his touch and pulls his hand away quickly. "Hey, you have nothing to be afraid of, Gia. You won't get hurt again. Not on my watch."

I swallow thickly.

"I'll be watching you, too," Clark says. "There isn't anything that can get past me. If they come here, they're asking for a death wish."

I expect Uncle Jack to say something in disagreement, but he doesn't. Instead, as I look back at him, he gives me a small nod. "The Jefe won't touch you ever again."

See, months ago that comment would have given me hope, but instead, it only fills me with despair. Suddenly, I'm not hungry, but I force myself to eat Aunt Minnie's favorite cheesecake anyway.

As soon as we're allowed to leave the table, I head back to my room, shutting the door, climbing on the bed, pressing my back to the headboard, and drawing my knees up to my chest.

I want to cry, but I don't.

Instead, I think about ways to get back.

Ways to fight.

Ways to be there for him again.

I'm at a loss. All of it will require help, and a plane ticket, and even a cellphone. All of that is traceable, and it will only put Uncle Jack in danger if he tries to come after me again.

I need another way out.

I need to get back to Jefe.

By nightfall, the house is way too quiet.

It's not eerie. It's not awkward.

It's just . . . way too serene. Though I know I don't need to look over my shoulder every single second, I can't help myself. Every little noise sends me into survival mode. Every creak, drip, rustle has me on edge.

Sighing, I roll out of bed, turning on the lamp beside the bed and then going for my suitcases. I unzip one of them, taking out the black case inside of it.

Opening the case, I take out the wads of cash and then draw out the small handgun. Inside the case is a note—one I couldn't read earlier because I was interrupted.

I pick it up and read it.

Por si acaso. Just in case.

I sigh, knowing the handwriting. He did promise me a gun.

After counting the money from the case and the money in the large pocket of my suitcase, which totals to $350,000, I go to the vanity with the gun in hand, shutting the light off and then walking to the terrace, but not before grabbing the coat Uncle Jack gave to me. I wrap it around my shoulders, stepping barefoot onto the cold cement.

The moon seems much closer.

Crickets chirp and owls hoot.

Like I said, too serene.

I drop my gaze to the gun, studying it. It's small, like a pocket gun.

Fits my hand perfectly. I would have gone with something bigger, with way more power, but I guess beggars can't be choosers. If Uncle Jack or Aunt Minnie knew about it, I'm sure they'd have taken it.

My eyes prickle and sting, but the tears don't bother reaching the surface.

Because something clicks behind me and then there is something hard and cold pressing into the back of my head.

16

GIANNA

"We have one rule," the familiar voice says. "No guns in the fucking house. Went through your bags. You should have gotten rid of that gun as soon you saw it."

My heart doubles in speed, but not out of fear. A thrill—a rush I haven't felt in a long, long time consumes me. *A challenge.*

"That's obviously a bullshit rule. You're holding one to my head right now."

"Put it on the ground."

"No."

"Now," he demands, pressing the gun into my head. "They don't want you dead, but I don't give a fuck if you die. Won't shed a fucking tear. I don't trust you. Put the gun down."

I sigh and slowly start to squat with both arms stretched. He pulls back just a fraction, and that's when I turn, pointing my gun in Clark's face, just as he points his at mine.

He smirks. "You don't fucking listen."

I cock a brow. "And you're easy to kill. Wouldn't be the first time a gun was held to my head, either."

His eyebrows draw together. I notice he's wearing all black, and I suspect he was planning this ambush, just waiting to sneak into my room and intimidate me.

"Why the fuck did he let you go?" he snaps.

"You don't even know who *he* is."

"Oh, trust me," he laughs. "I know who he is."

We both still have our guns aimed, arms straight.

"Who is he, then?"

"I watch the news. I'm updated on everything that involves a cartel, and he's a fucking kingpin. Everyone is out for him, but they can never seem to find him. The whole world knows who the hell he is… and I bet you know *where* he is."

"No, I don't. And even if I did, why would I tell the person who's holding a gun to my face?"

"Because if you don't," he presses the gun into my forehead, "I'll shoot you."

I don't even bat an eyelash. "'Kay. Go ahead. I'm waiting."

His frown grows deeper, his finger wrapping around the trigger, the gun pressing harder into my forehead. I don't waver. Don't sway.

He won't do it.

I know he won't.

He's not stupid.

He finally grumbles something and drops his arm. I lower mine too, but not completely.

"Why did he let you go? He's risking his entire life by having you out here after keeping you hostage for so long."

"He knows I wouldn't snitch."

"What are you? His fucking pet?"

I glare hard at him before stepping around him and going for my suitcase. "I am not his fucking pet."

"Then what are you to him? A spy? His sex slave?"

I roll my eyes. "Now you sound like a fifteen-year-old boy."

"Fuck you," he bites out. "I need to know this shit! They don't want to ask questions, so I will. I don't trust you. I don't believe he just sent you here without some kind of agenda. What does he want from us?"

My eyebrows stitch together. I'm utterly confused by his paranoia.

"He has everything he could ever want. Why would he want anything from you—or my family, period?"

Clark's finger wraps around his trigger again. He stares hard at me, nostrils flaring. "I know everything that happens, Gia. Every fucking thing. Even what happens in Mexico. *Hernandez*," he says, and a chill hits me hard, my spine stacking. "I heard she's taking over, and The Jefe is about to be in the dust. He's losing people. Is it true?"

"I don't know what you're talking about—"

"Oh, bullshit," he scoffs. "I know you know. I heard he dropped everything just to get you back from her. I heard she killed his cousin."

I swallow hard, looking away. "How are you hearing this stuff?"

"I have eyes and ears everywhere. I run a business, too, only mine is much simpler. Cleaner, although I don't mind getting my hands dirty when I have to."

"Is Uncle Jack still involved in it?"

He gives me an obvious look. "What? You think he's selling cupcakes and cookies now? Once you're in, you're in. It's hard to back out of something this big. He won't work with the Mexican cartels anymore after what happened with Lion and the Ricci clan, but I'm willing to. I want to expand. Become bigger, with or without him."

"Do you have a jet? A plane? Anything?" I ask, stepping forward.

"For what?"

"If you have one—or anything that can get us to Mexico—you might be able to meet The Jefe. You meet him, talk things over, maybe expand your business. But *only* if you get me there—and only if I know I can actually trust you by the time we're there."

Clark laughs, a deep laugh that grates my nerves. "Are you fucking kidding me? I've heard the stories about him. He'd kill me on the spot. You aren't that important to him, otherwise he wouldn't have sent you away." He looks me over. "Did he give you a number to call? An email? Anything for you to stay in touch?"

"No," I mutter.

"Then that settles it." He walks to the door, twisting the knob and pulling it open. "You mean nothing to him."

I rush for him, pushing the door shut, not giving a damn if the slam of it is loud enough to wake the whole house up. I glare up at him as he hikes his shoulders.

"You don't know him," I snap, getting closer to his face. "And you don't know me. I can be just as lethal as him. Don't think I can be stepped on or looked over just because I'm a woman. I'm not a fucking doormat. I need to get there, and you're going to make it happen. Do you have anything to get us there?"

"Why do you want to leave so badly?" he asks, suddenly annoyed. "Why put yourself in danger again?"

"Because he needs my help. His head isn't clear—he doesn't trust anyone—and he's not safe. He's going to get himself killed if he keeps going down that path."

He gets closer to my face. "That man will *never* be safe. The best thing for him right now is to die. He'll never be at peace, at the rate he's going."

I'm getting annoyed now. I know he has a way out. Our family always does. "Find me a way out," I say through clenched teeth. "Get me back to Mexico and help me find him. If he hears I'm back, he'll show up."

"What makes you so sure?"

I take a step back. "I just know."

I feel him looking at me. When I meet his eyes, I can see a million questions in them, but instead of asking them, he says, "We have a jet, but the men around here report everything to Big Jack, aka your Uncle Jack. If we take the jet, he'll know, and he'll send someone for us."

"Then we'll make sure he doesn't find out right away."

"How?" he asks, brows drawing together.

"Just take me to the pilot. I'll convince him to take us."

17

DRACO

We're in the middle of fucking nowhere.

The wheels of the SUV dip into potholes, running over large rocks and branches on the dirt road. I stare out of the window, a gun tucked in my waistband, a smaller one hidden under my jeans, strapped around my ankle.

The sun set a long time ago.

It's dark now.

I got a lead from someone I know and trust. As soon as he sent me the location, I made a plan: catch her by surprise and kill her. My men have worked hard for this. I have worked hard for this.

My driver continues driving for nearly ten minutes before coming to a stop. I draw my gun as he shuts the headlights off.

"*Ve allá*," I tell him, pointing to a darker area, surrounded by trees. *Go over there.*

It's pitch black. About a mile ahead of me is a small brown house, the lights on inside. Two cars are parked in front of it, flashy. Expensive. They belong to her. I know it.

One of my men, Sebastien, looks back at me from the passenger seat for assurance.

I bob my head, and he and Guillermo open their doors, sliding out and shutting them quietly, their dark clothes blending into the shadows. We watch them hustle ahead with newly imported AK-47s in hand, searching the area.

My eyes shift from them to the house.

A figure walks by the window. I can't make out who it is.

I look back at Patanza. "I'm going in. You wait here with Diego. If I take longer than ten minutes, you leave."

"But Jefe—"

"Do you understand, Patanza?" I demand. I tell her in English. So she'll know. I trust her the most, out of all my guards.

She narrows her brows, eyes intense, but sighs and says, "Sí, Jefe."

"Good. Hand me an AK."

She looks to her left, at the cart of guns, and picks one up to hand to me. I take it, turning the safety off while I look for the two guards I sent.

Sebastien is beside a tree, waving a hand, the signal that the area is clear.

I don't glance back at Patanza, who I know is dying to come. She wants her revenge too, but I want mine more.

My black boots hit the ground, my gun held high. I shut the door behind me quietly, and then walk down the path that leads to the house. My boots crunch on the gravel, nostrils flared, back straight, eyes right on the fucking prize.

I want to lift my gun and blast the house with bullets. I don't give a fuck who I hit or who dies. Anyone associated with her gets no mercy.

But I don't.

If she was just a person who owed me money, maybe I would. If she'd stolen from me, then maybe I would make it that easy. But that isn't the case.

She's done much worse, and for that she will fucking pay. I want to watch that *puta* die—shoot her once then feel her blood running through my fingers as I choke the rest of the life out of her.

Sebastien and Guillermo trail close behind me, their guns aimed forward. I lift mine, aiming too, walking right up the stoop.

If they betray you: Move fast. Think quickly. Take them the fuck down.

My father's motto. The Molina motto.

And it will be followed.

I rush up the stoop and kick the door in. A lamp falls over and someone screams. A naked woman is kneeling in front of two guards who are seated on the sofa. I raise my gun and shoot the girl, blood spraying the walls, some landing on the guards in front of her.

They shove her lifeless body away, scrambling for their guns, but my men put an end to them in a millisecond, blasting them several times. Their bodies hit the floor, crumpling over, blood leaking onto the dingy hardwood floor.

"Search the house," I command in Spanish.

I lift my gun higher in the air, pointing at every opening. A door creaks open to my right, and I shoot at it before anyone can step out. Something thuds to the ground, and I go for the door, rolling it open with one finger, my gun aimed inside. There is only one guard in this small room. Now he's dead.

I walk back down the hallway, toward the dark kitchen, stepping around the corner with my finger on the trigger. It's so quiet I can hear the faucet leaking. The floor creaks behind me, and I spin around, ready to pull the trigger.

"Just me, boss," Guillermo says, holding one hand in the air.

I lower my gun.

"Searched the whole house and outside. This box was out there."

I frown down at the box, looking it over. "Heavy?"

"No ticking. I don't think it's a bomb."

I dig in my back pocket, pulling out my pocketknife and slicing through the tape on the center of the box. Pulling open the flaps, I carefully take out the crumpled newspapers. For all I know, it could be a bomb, triggered by the faintest touch.

But it's not.

When I see what it is, my chest caves in.

This is something much worse than any bomb or set up.

It's cold and hard, with dark stains of blood on it. Bitch couldn't even clean it properly.

Jaw pulsing, heart racing, I clutch it in hand, my throat thickening as I flip it over and take the note out from between the teeth.

Family can be just as useless, right, Jefe?

Thiago.
His skull.
THAT. BITCH!

My nostrils flare as I study the skull. My cousin's skull. Her cursive handwriting. I remember it well, along with the many notes she'd leave behind, begging me to love her. Begging me to only be with her. Begging me to marry her.

She knew I was coming here.

She wanted me to find this.

"This lead was from a trusted source," I growl.

"Well, maybe we can't trust that motherfucker anymore," Sebastien mutters, stepping around another corner, peering down at the skull. "This place was a decoy. Doesn't even seem like they were here for more than a day. It was a set-up. I don't know what the fuck she was planning, but we need to get the fuck out of here before more of them show up. Now, Jefe."

I walk past Guillermo, back down the hallway, kicking the screen door off the hinges before getting back outside.

Just as we hop into the truck and the driver starts to pull off, a loud explosion catches us all by surprise. A bomb has just gone off, flames lighting the sky, the whole place on fire now.

My teeth grit at the sight of it.

She tried to kill me.

Enough of the fucking games.

This bitch is fucking with the wrong man.

18

GIANNA

The next morning, there is a soft knock on my door.

I roll over to the sound, fully alert, pushing the gun under my pillow when the door creaks open, and Jen steps in.

"Good morning," she chimes. She's fully dressed in a thick, soft pink sweater, khakis, and knee-high brown boots. Her dark hair is parted at the crown and gathered behind her in a low ponytail. "I just wanted to let you know that my mom had to run a few errands today, but she left me the car in case you want to go for breakfast in town." She twists her fingers into knots, smiling a little. "Maybe we can have a girls' day and get to know each other a little better? Get our hair done and maybe go shopping afterwards? If you want…"

I press my lips to smile as I sit up, rubbing the sleep out of my eyes. "Uh, yeah. Sure. That would be nice."

A sigh of relief escapes her. "Oh, thank goodness. I thought you were going to reject the whole thing. I may or may not have scheduled hair appointments for us—not saying your hair looks bad or anything, I just figured you might like a new look for your fresh start…" She trails off, chewing on her bottom lip. "Please tell me if I'm annoying you. I can totally call and cancel the appointment if it's too much."

I laugh, sliding out of bed and walking to meet her. I grip her shoulders with a warm smile. "Stop it, Jen. You are not annoying me. I appreciate you doing this. I always loved getting my hair done and going shopping."

She beams. "Mom told me your mom would take you to the hair salon with her every other Saturday and then to the mall to pick a new outfit to match your hair. I just wanted to do something nice."

My smile almost collapses just hearing about Mom, but I keep myself together, my smile never fading. "Which is exactly why I am eager to go. I'll get dressed and meet you downstairs."

She nods and then steps away, walking to the door. I get freshened up and dress in jeans and a chunky ivory sweater that was hanging in the closet. The closet was full of sweaters, but the jeans were either too big or too small. Luckily, whoever packed my suitcases put a few pairs in one of them.

I brush my hair up into a ponytail and loosely tie a brown scarf around my neck, then I'm out the door with one of the designer tote bags from the closet.

In the bag is the pistol Draco gave to me, tucked neatly at the bottom and wrapped in a scarf.

I walk down the stairs, doing a quick scan for any sign of Clark. He's nowhere in sight, which leads me to hoping he's actually out making something happen. He has to figure out a way to get me back to Mexico.

Jen trots down the stairs behind me, smiling hard with the keys in hand. "You ready?"

I nod, following her to the door. "Let's get this girls' day started."

After catching breakfast at a pancake house, Jen drives us ten minutes to a salon in the heart of town called Jills. Even while out in the small town, I can't help but watch my back.

It feels like someone is watching me. Maybe I'm just being paranoid. Maybe someone is. Either way, I've been keeping my eyes peeled.

Jen parks in front of a brick building with glass windows casing the front, giving full view to the stylists and their clients inside. I look to the left, spotting a black SUV parking on the side of the street in front of a bakery, the vehicle's windows tinted. I narrow my eyes at the SUV.

"Come on. They're nice here, I promise." Jen's voice cuts through my thoughts as she pushes out of the car, shutting her door behind her. I grab my bag and follow her lead, making way to the entrance, taking one last glance back at the truck.

I'm being really paranoid.

No one knows where I am now. He said I was safe.

Unless he has someone watching me from a distance to keep tabs for him...

As soon as the door to the salon swings open, a bell chimes above and all eyes shift to us. All of the women smile. Literally, *all of them*. I would say it's creepy, but it's not at all. It's warm and welcoming, making me forget all about the chilliness outside and the stupid SUV.

The smell of mint and eucalyptus surrounds me, a cooling, comforting aroma.

Jen stops at the front desk, where a woman with blonde hair accented with lavender streaks stands. Her nose is pierced, and the sleeves of tattoos on both her arms are beautiful works of art. Her nametag says Dalia.

She checks us in, and since we're a few minutes early she leads the way to the waiting area.

The waiting area is quaint and trendy, the sofas upholstered in a black and white pattern with turquoise throw pillows. The table set up in the middle of the area is piled with several fashion magazines. To the right of one of the couches is a water station, the water infused with oranges, lemons, and raspberries, along with a box of donuts.

"Please help yourself to the fruit infused water and donuts. They are always on the house for our clients, and there is plenty more in the back," Dalia says with a full smile.

"Thanks, Dalia," Jen responds.

Dalia walks back to the front desk and logs something into the computer. My eyes shift over to the display cases filled with all sorts of things, from hairsprays to shampoos and conditioners. There is even handmade jewelry for sale.

Someone sneezes, and I jerk my head up, focusing on the culprit. A woman in a chair getting highlights wipes her nose aggressively, and then mumbles something to her stylist.

I clutch the handle of my bag tighter, breathing as evenly as possible.

Jen stands up to pour two cups of water, handing me one when she spins around. She takes the seat beside me, blowing out a breath.

"You should try and relax," she murmurs. "I promise, no one here knows who you are except the family."

I take the water, lowering my gaze to my tote bag, steadying my breathing. My heart is pounding. I can't believe I'm so on edge. It's been so long since I've been out alone like this—no guards. No one breathing down my back. No Jefe.

I set my tote down on the spot beside me and then bring the rim of the plastic cup up to my lips, allowing the cool water to fall through my lips and sink down my throat. It's refreshing, and enough to make me sit back.

"Can I ask you something?" Jen asks after several small sips of her water.

I glance up at her. "Sure. Anything."

"My dad told me not to bring it up...but I'm just really curious about what happened there. With you and the man that had you."

My eyes are wider, my pulse skittering now.

"I heard you making noises while you slept last night. I'm kind of a night owl—always sneaking down at like two in the morning to get a snack or watch Netflix on Dad's big screen in his man cave." She laughs a little, but then her face is serious again. "But when I walked by, I heard...whimpering. Like you were crying, maybe?" She whispers the last part. I swallow hard, my eyes darting away from hers.

"I remember a lot of things," I murmur. "Things that were...terrifying. I have nightmares about it sometimes. I don't think they'll ever go away."

"What things? If you don't mind me asking?"

No, I don't mind her asking. I'm stronger than what happened. I'm better than it. It will not rule me.

I twist to face her, grabbing her hand. She looks down at it and then back up at me, her eyes cloudy with concern now.

"If I tell you, Jen, you have to promise not to tell anyone. Not even Aunt Minnie. And definitely not Uncle Jack."

She bobs her head. "I swear I won't. I'm good at keeping secrets, I promise."

I mash my lips together, releasing her hand to turn and place my water down on the coffee table.

"I was there for about two months. It got better after a while, but when I first arrived, I was treated like shit."

She blinks, but says nothing. Her eyes are begging for more though.

"I was locked in a cell—it felt kind of like a dungeon. It was dark, damp, and it smelled awful. They didn't even let me use the bathroom. I was tied up with these thick, hard ropes—" I hold up one arm and pull the sleeve of my sweater up, showing her the scars. "That's where these marks came from. I was trying so hard to get out of them, but it was impossible." I wipe the sweat off my forehead. "There were these guards there—his men. They would watch me, either in person or on cameras. They would switch out every few hours. Two of them were bad. Really bad. They always threatened to...*do* things to me, but the guy that was in charge of them didn't know about it."

"The Jefe," she says, loud and clear.

And I hold her gaze, nodding. "You know about him?"

"I know a lot of things about him. I hear Dad and Clark talking about him a lot. He's a big deal. Everyone's afraid of him. That's why we didn't think we'd ever see you again."

I sigh. "He can be cruel and controlling. He also likes to punish... but I got to know him, and he got to know me, and eventually things changed."

She gives a sincere nod.

"Anyway, I've been told I make noise in my sleep. *He* told me, actually. I don't even think I can help it. I get images of what they did to me—I won't go into detail, but picture the worst things that could ever happen to a woman, happening to me. There was no mercy for me there. No one gave a damn about me when I first arrived. I... wanted to die, that's how bad it was. But when I realized that he knew exactly who I was, I knew I had to do something about it. I had to get The Jefe to trust me."

"Well, he must have trusted you a lot. Look at you. You're here now. Free from him."

"Yeah." I sigh. "Trust me, he is *not* a good man. He's vicious, Jen. He's cold and deadly, and right now he's hurting, and that's the worst thing for him. He's not thinking clearly, and I'm afraid he's going to end up either hurting himself, or worse...end up dead."

"Don't you want him to die? After all he's put you through?"

Her question hits me hard, so hard I don't even blink. My breathing falters, heartbeat stuttering. I stare at her, unsure how to answer, until she fidgets, curiosity burning deep in her eyes.

"When I first met him, all I could think about was killing him. At one point, all I wanted was for him to die and for me to get my old life back...but now, after all that time, I don't know anymore. When I was there, he fueled me—inspired me. He revealed a side of me I never thought I'd be brave enough to own."

She looks at me, and I can't tell if she's baffled or terrified.

Her mouth clamps shut, and she places her cup of water down.

"Chrissy and Olivia?" a woman calls and Jen looks back.

"Oh—here!" Jen tugs on my sleeve before standing. I grab my bag and follow her and the stylist to two empty chairs.

"Olivia?" I whisper over her shoulder.

"I didn't want to use your real name. Oh, and by the way, you're not my cousin. You're my friend from Aspen, Colorado."

I bob my head as we sit. "Okay, friend."

She smiles, and the stylist asks us both what we'd like. I decide to go with a basic blowout, though the highlights the woman across from me is getting are tempting.

"I'm glad you told me, Gia," Jen says my way, her voice low. Her lips twist. "I hope to find someone who fuels me too—maybe not a kingpin mafia leader, but someone who still makes good money the legal way and wants a big family. Like a lawyer or an architect or something." She sighs looking into the mirror in front of her. "I think that's what I want."

She's so innocent and naïve. Jen is so...*pure*—the complete opposite of what I am. I'm worried having me around will only taint her. I am not good. Hell, I'm far from it, but she seems to be drawn toward me like a magnet.

Some of us Nicoteras should stay that way. Innocent. Pure. Sweet.

Not tainted, vile, and vicious. Not sold off to the highest bidder as a virgin Nicotera, scrambling around to save our own lives.

But I guess with a name like ours, things like that are usually bound to happen. Someone will come along and snatch that innocence right away. They will eliminate all the good left inside you until you are nothing but a vessel, with veins full of ice and a heart as black as coal.

I was afraid of becoming that...but now that it has happened, I don't see it being any other way. Being what I am now makes me strong. It keeps me on my toes. It gives me something to fight for—and I'm fighting to feel good again.

To *be* good again.

Get rid of all of my enemies and no longer having a target on my back. I just want happiness, even in the midst of all this darkness. I want to get away and be free—literally free of all the worldly troubles and all the violence.

The only problem is, the person I want to share this happiness with is Draco. That's why I have to find him. I have to be with him. I have to tell him how I really feel before it's too late.

I have to be his reina, so I tell my stylist, "You know what? I want what she's getting." I point to the woman across from me. "Give me highlights."

19

GIANNA

We get home just around lunchtime.

There are warm, lip-licking aromas drifting through the house, and Jen groans, like it's the best thing she's ever smelled.

"Gah, I love it when she cooks." She steps to the side to kick her boots off. I untie my shoes and place them on the doormat in front of the coat rack. I follow Jen upstairs, and we put our bags in our rooms, then we head back down to the kitchen, where Aunt Minnie is standing over a pot on the stove.

There are freshly sliced baguettes on the table top, bowls already set up there for whatever she's preparing.

"Hey, Mom. What are you making?" Jen asks, stepping up beside her and peering over her shoulder. "It smells amazing."

"My famous autumn chowder soup with toasted baguettes." She announces the meal with pride, and I smile. I can't believe it's fall already. Though it was only two months of being captured, tortured, beaten, and then treated like his reina, it felt like years.

I hear the front door shut, and I step back, taking a look down the hallway. I expect Clark, but it's Uncle Jack. He walks my way, smiling wide with open arms. He wrangles me up into a big bear hug, and I let out a small wheeze before laughing.

"Might as well get used to those. Everyone under my roof gets hugs when they first see me during the day," he laughs, letting me go. "Everyone but that crazy son of mine."

"Another one of your uncle's ridiculous rules," Aunt Minnie adds in.

Jen and I laugh, and Uncle Jack scoops Jen up in one arm, wrapping his other around Aunt Minnie's chest and kissing the top of her head.

"Like the hair, girls," Uncle Jack notes, smiling at us.

I return a smile. They are the perfect little family.

They seem so normal and nice. I'm certain they can get down and dirty if need be, but I don't think they've had to in long, long time.

A slight pang of envy strikes me. Why couldn't it be this simple and quiet for me? Why couldn't Daddy take Mom and me to a secluded home, away from all of the madness?

Why couldn't he keep his mafia life and his personal life separate? Everything he did, I ended up knowing about, either by an argument between him and Mom, or from overhearing my bodyguards.

It was never this easy. I could never really fall asleep until I knew Daddy was home safe. I always worried that he wouldn't make it home. That someone would kill him…and, eventually, someone did.

We all eat lunch at the dinner table, and during our meal, I pick up on Aunt Minnie asking Uncle Jack where Clark is. Uncle Jack tells her he'll be back, but nothing more. By his dismissive tone, I assume he has no idea where Clark is either.

After helping Aunt Minnie clean, Jen takes off to her bedroom to look for ski resort tickets, and I walk out to the deck with a cup of chamomile tea. Though it's a little windy, it blends perfectly with the warm, buttery sun. I sit in one of the rocking chairs, drawing my legs up so my feet touch my bottom, staring up at the mountains.

As I sip the tea, I catch sight of the scars on my wrist and I sigh. I place my tea down on the table beside me, looking down at the scars, running my fingers over them. They circle all the way around now, bold, pink scars that will never go away.

Scars that are a clear reminder of where I was. Memories that will never fade—that will always haunt me.

The door behind me creaks, and I look over my shoulder, spotting Aunt Minnie. She steps out with a warm, close-lipped smile, her eyes falling down to my wrists.

I drop my hands and tug my sleeves down, picking my tea back up again and sipping.

"Nice out here, right?" she asks with a small sigh. She takes the rocking chair to the left of me, looking up at the mountains, too.

"It's beautiful," I murmur.

Sitting back, she rocks slowly in the chair, breathing evenly. The wind tousles my freshly done hair, gold tendrils curling around my face. I tuck it back, and Aunt Minnie stops rocking. I feel her looking at me, so I look up. Her head is tilted, eyes slightly narrowed, like she's trying to read me.

"Can I ask you something, sweetie?" she asks.

"Sure," I answer. "Anything."

She sits up higher in her chair, her eyes shifting down to my hidden wrists and then back up at me. "While he had you, did you by any chance, happen to fall *in love* with him?"

Her question catches me completely off guard. My eyes grow a little wider, my heart slithering to the pit of my stomach. All I can do is look at her.

How can she tell? How does she know?

I let out a tattered sigh, glancing around. "What makes you ask that?"

"Oh, trust me. You can't fool me." She smiles. "I know heartbreak when I see it. I've been through it way too many times not to know when I'm in the presence of it. You...cared about him—about the man that abducted you."

I press my lips, focusing on the amber liquid in my teacup.

"You love him," she states.

I shake my head, my eyelids sealing. "No." How can I love a monster? How can I love a man who killed my husband? How can I love a man who kidnapped me, punished me like an animal day and night—who didn't take me seriously until I was completely demolished and torn down, beaten and raped?

"You don't have to hide the truth from me, Gia. I promise I won't tell your Uncle Jack—or anyone for that matter."

Fiery tears threaten to fall, but I squeeze my eyes shut and sigh again. "I . . . don't know what it is I feel for him, Aunt Minnie. It confuses the hell out of me, honestly." I open my eyes and laugh again.

When I meet hers, she's smiling.

She stands up, eyes gentle, face soft. "What you're feeling, my sweet Gia, is this crazy, wild thing called being in love. It will make you think you're insane, but when it lures you in, it takes over all of you. And once you're hooked and trapped, there is no going back." She presses her lips, like she's thinking about something.

"Maybe he was a monster to you, maybe he wasn't," she continues. "Maybe you want to hate him, but all you can see is the good—the positive traits. The sacrifices, like the one he made by sending you here, risking everything just so you could live on. He had to trust you in order to do that. He had to know you wouldn't speak or lay out his secrets. I don't believe what your Uncle Jack tells me about his loyalty to your father being the only reason you were sent here. I see right through it. A man that powerful, no matter how good he had it with your father, wouldn't just send you away—not unless he knew for sure you would keep quiet about what you know about him."

I don't know to respond to that. Hell, what do I say to that? She's read right through me, and even though they are my family—a part of my bloodline—I can't talk about him much. He wouldn't want me to. He would want me to move on. He wouldn't want to be figured out. He wants to be known as The Jefe and nothing less.

Cruel.

Cold.

Handsome and deadly.

On top of the world.

I shake my head and say, "Aunt Minnie, The Jefe is a monster. He's brutal and cold and strict. He didn't like to take the word 'no' for an answer. Maybe I did care a little. Maybe it was some kind of messed up Stockholm syndrome for a while, but there is no way in hell I am in love with a man like him. He's no hero. He's a villain. And villains only look out for themselves."

She lets the words sink in, but the word she says to me next makes the smallest, most genuine laugh bubble out of me. It's the first time in a long time that I feel it—a strong laugh that comes from deep within my core. A laugh so comforting and rich that I hope it helps me sleep better tonight.

"*Bullshit*," she says. "You're in love with him. Plain and simple." She walks away like nothing even happened, leaving me sitting there with a stupid grin plastered on my face.

After soaking up enough rays, I head back up to my room with another cup of chamomile tea. I place the teacup on top of the dresser, and then lock the door behind me, taking my gun out of the tote bag sitting on the bed and sliding it beneath the mattress.

With a deep sigh, I grab my teacup and saucer and walk to the double doors, pulling them open and stepping onto the terrace. The view is spectacular. I inhale deep, and exhale before taking a sip of the hot drink, just as a windy chill nips at my skin.

I don't mind the chill. It feels good.

I sit, cradling the hot cup in hand, watching as the sun sets behind the tall mountains.

I'm surrounded by nature.

There is solace here.

Peace.

It's the perfect place to escape from all the madness in the world and actually think and accept. It's the perfect way to start from scratch and actually live a normal life.

Some people would kill to have a home like this. This kind of tranquility is enough to savor and make you never want to go back to the real world...so why do I keep trying to go back to the cruelty when I'm better off here?

Long after dinner, and when the house is mostly quiet, I hear light footsteps drifting down the hallways. It's around one in the morning. Jen told me Aunt Minnie is always asleep by 11 o' clock, and Uncle Jack is usually right behind her.

I push out of bed, walking to the door and pulling it open as quietly as possible. The hallway is dark, but I see the familiar silhouette walking down the hallway, the opposite way of my bedroom.

I pull the door open, taking a step out. "Psst," I hiss, and Clark stops, peering over his shoulder. I wave a hand, signaling for him to come to me.

He turns, walking my way with an exaggerated exhale. I open the door and he steps inside, shutting it behind him quietly. He's barefoot, most likely because he's sneaking in and doesn't want to be asked questions by his parents.

"You were gone all day," I whisper-hiss, taking a step back. "What took you so long?"

"I had other shit to do besides getting in touch with the pilot, woman," he says snidely.

"Well, did you get in touch with him?"

"Yeah." He plucks a cigarette from behind his ear, walking past me to get to the terrace. He steps out into the cool night, the milky moonlight shining down on him, placing the cigarette between his lips. He draws a lighter out of his front pocket and brings it up, sparking it and lighting the end.

Once he takes a long pull and releases a chain of smoke, he says, "He's out of town. Won't be back for two days. I told him I need to see him as soon as possible."

"Did you tell him why?" I ask, stepping up and gripping the guardrail.

"No. He wouldn't have agreed to meet me if I'd told him."

"Good. We don't need him telling Uncle Jack."

Clark side-eyes me. "How the fuck are you gonna get him to take us anyway?"

"Guns aren't just for protection. They can be used to threaten, too. You should know that."

"I'd never threaten my own fucking pilot unless I have another one in line and we fucking don't right now."

"Then I'll be sure to get you a new one once everything has blown over."

He huffs a laugh, pulling from his cigarette again. "He really gave you a swelled head," he says through a cloud of smoke, voice thick. "I heard they called you Patrona. *Boss* . . ."

"Yeah. So?"

"They respect you? Enough not to kill me on sight if they see me tagging along with you?"

"They won't shoot at me. If you're by my side, they won't kill you either." I step forward, getting closer to his face. His nonchalant mood makes me not trust him. His eyes meet mine, his entire demeanor unwavering. "Don't make me regret this," I say through partially clenched teeth. "I know you know about the warrant and the prize for The Jefe's capture. If that's your plan, to turn him in, then—"

"Oh, please, fucking spare me," he says, interrupting my sentence. "If there's one thing I am good at, it's keeping my business afloat and watching my own ass, not ruining my entire fucking reputation. Turning in The Jefe or even telling anyone where he is, is like me asking to die." He steps back, shaking his head. "If you can't trust me, why not just do this yourself?"

"If I had my own way there, I would."

"There are trains, buses, taxis . . ."

"They aren't fast enough, and they're easily traceable. At least with a jet we can fly fast, ditch it, and run with a head start."

"Our pilot could get arrested, fired, or even tossed in jail for flying there without permission." He scoffs. "And all this because you want to run back to your master."

"Oh, fuck you," I spit at him. "Listen, I owe him this. I did something wrong, and I need to make up for it. I want to get back to him, and I'm not letting anything stop me, *especially not* a wannabe kingpin, Nicotera cousin of mine."

Clark hisses through his teeth, a jeer that only annoys me. "Damn. Now that— that was a harsh one. A good one, but harsh as fuck."

I roll my eyes and scoff. "You have to be high or something."

"Just a little drunk." He shrugs.

"Ugh." I walk back inside, sitting on the bench at the bottom of the bed. Clark takes a few more puffs from his cigarette before putting it out. He shuts the doors and walks my way when he's done, stopping in front of me.

"Look, I'll get you to Mexico and to your precious Jefe, but only because every second you spend here puts my family at more and more risk. He started a fucking war, and my family isn't going to pay for his mistakes if someone decides to come after you during it. If you're there with him and they know it, they won't come looking here. Trust me, I want you gone as soon as possible, but until that pilot gets back, we have to fucking wait. Threaten him all you want when you see him, but he has to get out of all of this alive." He stares hard at me, his eyes glassy, serious. "Agree to that, and I'll do everything I can to get you there."

I stand up, holding his gaze. "Fine."

He looks me over before walking to the bedroom door. Before he goes, he says, "This whole fucking arrangement better triple my income when it's over." The door clicks shut behind him, and I release a ragged breath, slouching back down on the bench, formulating the rest of my plan.

20

GIANNA

The next two days are a fucking drag.

Jen does her best to try and keep me distracted from the past, either by taking me for walks on the trail behind the house, or even making use of the hot tub at sunset. She even convinced me to make sugar cookies with her. Our ski resort trip is supposed to happen Saturday, but I'm afraid I won't make that.

I feel awful, knowing she enjoys spending time with me. Skiing would be fun.

But I can't.

I won't settle.

Every single hour, I'm wondering what he could be doing. Is he even thinking about me? Was what he said in those voice recordings true? Does he love me? And if he does, why send me away so quickly? Why send me away without asking me what I truly wanted?

Around midnight, the second day after talking to Clark, there is a knock on the door of my terrace. I shoot to a stand, digging beneath the mattress for my gun. I walk to the door and pull the curtain aside.

No one is there . . . at first.

Clark steps from around the corner and into the light. I release a soft breath, unlocking and opening the door.

"What the fuck, Clark?"

"Pilot is home," he says. "If we're doing this, we do it now."

"Why now?"

"He has a flight scheduled for my dad at 10 to go to Utah. We gotta get him and leave as soon as possible, before that flight."

"Fuck." I turn, putting the safety back on my gun and rushing for my suitcase. I pull out a pair of yoga pants and a T-shirt and get dressed quickly, all while Clark stands on the terrace with his back to me, sparking a cigarette and waiting.

I brush my hair and then go for the leather jacket hanging on the single recliner in the corner. Dropping the gun into a backpack, along with several wads of the money, I slug it over my shoulder, walking to the doors and stepping up beside him.

"Let's go," I breathe.

He looks down at me, eyes hard, face serious. "You're sure about this? Because if we go, there's no turning back. You won't be able to come back here if things don't go as you plan."

"Then I guess I'll be on my own." I walk around him. "Let's go," I call, already hustling my way down the stairs.

Clark follows behind me, hardly hesitating. When he meets up to me, he grabs my elbow and pulls me to the side, where the trashcans are. I frown up at him, but he holds up a finger, a silent command for me to wait.

He lifts the lid off the can and digs into it, pulling out a black pistol. He digs for something else and it's a gun magazine. He slams it into the bottom of the gun, loading it up and then cocking it.

He digs for another pistol, a silver one, and does the same thing.

Just as he pulls out a leather gun holster and straps it around him, the back door creaks on its hinges, and Jen appears.

21

GIANNA

My eyes stretch wide when Jen steps around the corner and looks right at us.

I can only see her from the moonlight, but the worry on her face is clear.

"I could hear you guys talking from my room," she murmurs.

Clark groans, tucking the second gun into the holster. "Fuck, Jen, just go back inside and pretend you didn't hear anything. We don't have time for this right now."

She ignores him, focusing on me. "Are you really leaving?"

"Jen." My head shakes and my mouth clamps shut. I don't even know what to say. Suddenly, all words are lost, and I feel awful—just awful and so fucking ungrateful.

"I guess I saw this coming," she sighs, tucking her hair behind her ears. "The way you talked about him...like he was everything to you." She steps up to me, and Clark sucks his teeth, turning around and flipping his wrist to check his watch.

"Jen, I will try to see you again," I tell her, taking a step forward.

She looks down at the ground. "You're worried I'll tell my parents." Her sad eyes flash up to meet mine. "I won't."

"You won't?" Clark asks, looking over his shoulder.

"No. You clearly love that man, Gia. I'm not going to stand in the way of it." She picks her head up and smiles. "I told you I want love, too. One day...hopefully."

I walk up to her, holding her shoulders tight, locking on her eyes. "You're still young. Your time will come. Travel. Be happy. Use that silly Chrissy name so no one knows who you really are." She giggles softly, but then chokes on a sob.

"Shh," I coo, wrapping a hand around the back of her head. "I will stay in touch."

"What if something happens to you or even Clark?"

"Nothing will happen. We'll be fine," I tell her.

She lets out a ragged breath. My heart aches when her glistening eyes meet mine again.

"Gia," Clark calls brusquely. "We have to fucking go."

I don't look away from Jen. She holds my shoulder, nodding. "I hope he makes you happy, Gia. I hope he forgives you and gives you the world when you find him."

My eyes burn, but I nod my head, reluctantly pulling away. She steps back, and I turn, snatching my gaze away and meeting up to Clark, who has already walked off.

"Get back inside, Jen," he orders over his shoulder. "And keep your mouth shut. I will be back in a few days."

I glance back at her, but she hasn't budged. She's still standing in the same spot in their backyard, watching us go. Her innocence kills me. It kills me because I was that girl, once—watching my Daddy leave and having him tell me to go back inside and wait for him to come back. I wanted to beg, plead, and cry. I wanted to protest and lash out—do whatever I could to make him stay.

But I never did.

I never did, because I knew when he left, he was leaving to handle business and to make things right.

And that is exactly what I am doing now. I'm going to make things right.

22

DRACO

I wish I could stop myself from doing what I am about to do, but I can't.

I was fucked over, and I have made it very clear to never fuck me over and never think I won't show my wrath, no matter who you are to me.

A line wraps around the nightclub in the heart of Cancun, the bass of the music rattling the supposedly vintage building. They say it's vintage, but to me it's a piece of shit that needs updating and remodeling before the roof falls on their heads.

The stench of cheap weed and cigarettes floats around me as I walk past the line and to the entrance. When the bouncer sees me and the two men trailing behind, he immediately steps to the side to let us in.

People shout and protest, demanding to know why they can't go in, too.

I ignore it all, my eyes ahead, my chin held high, and a pistol with a silencer hidden under my suit jacket, tucked away behind my back.

It's a completely different atmosphere when I enter. It's much darker, strobe lights pulsing, but hardly giving any actual light.

The bar is surrounded with bodies, waitresses rushing around with trays above their heads, wearing skimpy leather skirts or dresses and way too much hairspray.

There are people everywhere, either dancing, drinking, or sitting because they can't hold their fucking liquor. It's way too hot and way too crowded.

I walk through the crowd, toward the spiral staircase not too far ahead of me. The DJ shouts something into the microphone, making the guests scream and cheer even louder, some even rushing to the dance floor when the song changes.

I hustle up the stairs with my men behind me.

I know he's here.

He thinks he's safe. He is sadly mistaken.

I walk past each curtained VIP section—past the men getting lap dances from idiotic American girls and a group of women squealing as they down shot after shot of tequila, sporting bridesmaid ribbons and glittery white shirts.

I start to get annoyed, sweat prickling at my forehead…until I finally hear him.

That motherfucker's raspy, dry laugh can't be mistaken.

I look over my shoulder, holding a hand up, signaling for my men to keep watch of the hallway.

"Don't let anyone through," I order, and they nod, turning with their arms folded in front of them, keeping watch.

I draw my gun, walking toward the sound of his voice. I meet up to a black curtain and don't hesitate. I yank the curtain open, ripping most of it off the rod.

A bitch with long black hair, wearing only a thong, screams as she scrambles back, her body hitting the sofa. My teeth grit together when I hear him curse, and stumble back.

"Oh, shit!" Morales yells. "Je—Jefe, what's going on, man? W—what can I help you with?"

My jaw clenches tight as I step toward him, towering over him. "Get down on your fucking knees," I order in Spanish, and he drops down, eyes bloodshot and watery as he stares up at me. He throws his hands in the air. I bring my gun up, gripping his face with one hand and lifting the gun to his face with the other. "Open your fucking mouth."

He blinks quickly. "Jefe—"

"I said OPEN YOUR FUCKING MOUTH! NOW!"

He groans in defeat, his chin falling. As soon as his mouth is open, I cram the barrel of my gun into his mouth. I grip a patch of his hair with one hand, my finger weighing on the trigger.

"I think you forgot exactly whose bitch you really are," I snarl, glaring down at him. He blinks rapidly, making muffled noises around the gun. "You lied to me, Morales. She wasn't where you said she would be. You set me up."

He tries to shake his head, but I squeeze the patch of hair in my hand, tugging harder.

I pull the barrel from his mouth, pressing it into his cheek.

"No, Jefe, please!" he pleads. "You have to understand—she told me to tell you she would be there because she wanted to talk! She said you wouldn't be harmed!"

"And you believed that shit?" I snap, jerking his hair again and forcing his head back. "She tried to fucking kill me! She sent a message with my cousin's skull . . . and you didn't know?"

"Ahh!" he cries out, tears lining his eyes. The bitch in the thong whimpers from her corner, her hands shooting in the air when I look over at her.

Towering over him, I grab Morales by his thick throat, eyes boring into his. "You are nothing but a piece of shit, Morales. I have no idea why my father ever trusted a sloppy, no-good, traitorous motherfucker like you." I shove him away from me, and his body hits the floor. "Fat, lying, greedy pieces of shit like you don't deserve to fucking live."

"No—wait! Please, Jefe!" He crawls on his knees toward me, begging with his hands clasped. "Please! If you just give me another chance, I'll find her. I—I'll get her to you."

He can beg all he wants. It's too fucking late. He works for her. He's sold himself out. That's why he's here. He was celebrating. He thought he was never going to see me again.

He was fucking wrong.

The Jefe won't fall that easily.

My gun goes off.

One quiet, seamless bullet through the brain. Two more through his chest. He falls backward, eyes stretched with horror, landing hard on the dirty floor, body slumping like the sack of worthless shit he is.

The bitch he had with him screams at the top of her lungs. Her scream doesn't last for long. I shoot her in the head, too, for associating with a worthless fucker like him.

Her body falls forward, crashing onto the glass table, her face landing in the pile of coke.

One of my guards appears behind me, his gun out, ready to fire.

I turn, walking out of the room. My guards follow suit without a single word.

Everyone is too drunk or high to notice us. I bet they won't even find the bodies until morning.

See, that's the thing about places like this.

This is why they've never intrigued or enticed me.

A person can die right up under their noses, and they still dance and party and get drunk, completely unaware of their surroundings. A bomb could be getting placed in one of the stalls in the bathrooms. The bartender could be spiking the bottles, drugging the women and dragging them off to be shipped and sold, and not a fucking soul would notice.

Only the weak-minded need things like this to feel alive—parties, and drugs, and drink after drink after drink.

Anything could happen, because they aren't paying any fucking attention or staying aware of their surroundings. Because they think this world is safe and that nothing will ever happen to them.

That was Morales' problem. He thought he was invincible. He never took me seriously. He never paid any fucking attention to what I was actually saying, even when my threats were perfectly clear.

Even when he's witnessed my wrath, he still betrayed me. He celebrated before he even found out if was I still alive.

He was weak, and being involved with the weak has never fucking suited me.

23

GIANNA

My heart is pounding, my lungs filled with the cold, night air as Clark and I jog through the woods, shoving branches and thick pines out of the way.

"Remind me why we couldn't take one of the cars," I huff, trying to catch up to him.

"Traceable," he pants. "He has trackers on them, and the guards keep watch of them, just in case one is ever stolen or if we're running a deal. An alarm goes off at our station when one is in use. It'll wake them up, and the first person they'll alert is my dad."

"Of course." I keep jogging by his side until a clearing opens up ahead. Streetlights filter through the thick pines, and Clark picks up his pace, trooping ahead.

We step onto asphalt, and he comes to a halt, looking to the left, where a black Subaru is parked on the side of the road. He pulls out a set of keys and unlocks it, yanking the door open and hopping into the driver's seat.

I load myself into the passenger seat, the scent of stale cigarettes and expensive cologne closing me in.

"Let me guess?" I say, catching my breath. "Your getaway car?"

"Only way he can't figure out where I am all the time." He starts the car up and puts the transmission in gear, gripping the stick and pulling off with a loud purr from the exhaust.

"Why does he want to know where you are all the time?" I ask him. "Does he not trust you?"

He shrugs, switching lanes and changing gears again. "He has his reasons not to trust me."

"And what are they?"

He side-eyes me briefly before focusing on the road, the streetlamps flashing on his face. "A year ago, I killed someone he thought he could trust."

My eyebrows draw together. "Who?"

"His best friend." He pauses for a second, most likely debating whether he should continue with the story. I'm glad he does. It helps distract me from the fact that I'm walking away from ultimate bliss and right back into the fire and chaos.

"His name was Louis," Clark continues. "He was mine and Jen's godfather. We thought we could trust him. He'd always told me that if I ever needed to get away, to come hang with him at his place. I always did. He never bothered me, and I never bothered him or got in his way. But one day while I was at his place, I eavesdropped. I'm nosy as fuck, and I don't care to admit it. I want to know everything." He shrugs like he's trying to prove a point. "I heard him talking to someone on the phone, saying how he was going to bring Big Jack with him to some warehouse and that 'it' could happen there. I couldn't figure out what the fuck 'it' was until I came home and heard my dad on the phone ordering some of our men to pack the trucks with guns that had just been shipped in.

"I did what any nosy-as-fuck mafia son would do. I followed him —in this car—to the warehouse. Saw Louis with some man and instantly got a bad vibe. The man was trying to bargain or cut a deal, but Big Jack wasn't having it. He wanted all the money upfront, since this man was a new buyer. So the man pulled a gun on him. And then Louis pulled a gun on him, too. His own best friend." He smiles, like he's remembering something. He makes a right turn, gripping the steering wheel a little tighter now.

"But as it happened, an idea struck me. I had my gun on me. Two guns, actually. He didn't like guns in the house, so I always kept them in this car. I came out of my hiding spot and shot both of them in the head. I've always had a good aim. Big Jack didn't see it coming. He was stupid for going alone, thinking Louis could be trusted. Thinking anyone could be trusted."

"Wow," I murmur.

"He was pissed," he chuckles. "He shouted at me all the way home, saying how it was going to be a mess to clean up and that he was disappointed in me for following, but I think he was really disappointed in himself for falling victim to Louis' bullshit. And I also think he was proud of what I'd done." He runs a hand over his hair. "The thing about Big Jack Nicotera is that he thinks he can be what his brother was, but he can't. He thinks he can go to meets and deals alone like Lion could—because Lion was respected enough—but he can't. Because he's not Lion. He wants to live up to what Lion was, but he never will, because he trusts too easily and his gut isn't hard enough. That's why we're here—in the middle of fucking nowhere. Because the threats are everywhere, and unlike Lion, who knew how to handle his threats, my father is never bold enough. Or maybe he's just fucking lazy now. Whatever the reason is, he lays low. Only comes out when he has to. Hired more men. More bodies. Stopped dealing with supplying drugs altogether. It's just guns now."

"Having a soft gut doesn't necessarily make you weak," I say.

"In our world, it fucking does. I learned young," he tells me, voice harder now. "I was fucked over one time, and I swore to never let that shit happen to me again." His jaw flexes, brows furrowing.

I inhale and then exhale deeply, looking out of the window. "If it makes you feel any better, I've killed someone too."

He doesn't even look at me. "I know you have. That cold look in your eyes is very familiar to me."

I look over at him, about to question what he means, but the car slows down, pulling onto a rocky path. He shuts off his headlights and parks in front of a small brick house.

There is a garage off to the left, the lights on inside it. He hops out in a matter of seconds. Before I get out, I fetch my gun and then push the door open, following him to the garage.

He presses a button and it opens automatically.

First I see the athletic shoes, and then the jeans, and then rope around a striped blue shirt. When the gate is fully open, Clark steps forward with a crooked smile, and the man jerks in his chair.

"Here he is. The pilot," Clark announces with way too much pride.

I frown at him. "What the hell, Clark? Why is he tied up?" I hiss. "I thought you said he was home!"

"When I said home, I really meant that I took him from his house, brought him to a private garage of mine, and roped his ass in a fucking chair." He looks at me, and I throw my hands out, utterly confused. "What? He wouldn't fucking cooperate, so I dragged his ass here. Be glad that I did it. That motherfucker was heavy." He turns his back, and I sigh, twisting around and facing the pilot. I take my gun out and then place my bag down.

Walking up to him, I slowly peel the tape off of his mouth. He scowls up at me, breathing fast, eyes full of panic.

"Please," he begs. "Don't kill me, please. I swear, I didn't do anything. I've only been doing my job!"

I stand up straight. "What's your name?"

"Travis."

"Well, I only need your cooperation, Travis. That's it. We take you to the jet, you get it running for us, and get me to Mexico. When you get me there, this will all be over, and you can go back to doing your job."

"Mexico." He blows a breath. "I—I would have to make a pit stop for gas, and I can't do that without checking in. He told me I can't check in anywhere!" His eyes dart over to Clark.

I glance back at Clark, who rolls his eyes.

I bend over, pressing my palms into the tops of my thighs. "Listen, I don't care if you check in. By the time anyone catches on, we'll be too far ahead for them to do anything about it. Yeah, they may come after us, and yeah they might catch you, but if Uncle Jack asks, just tell him Gia Nicotera wanted to get back to Mexico, and she forced Clark to come along with her. Tell them I had guns to both your heads, if that'll help. You'll be in the clear and so will Clark." I walk behind him, pulling at one of the knots in the rope.

"Why would I lie for him after what he did to me?" he demands, glaring at Clark. "He took me during the middle of the night, while my family was sleeping. They could have seen what happened. My wife is pregnant!"

"Uh, I think if you want to keep your fucking job, Travey boy, then you'll say exactly what the fuck she told you to say, and go along with it. Your kids won't be feeding themselves, right? Your family relies on the money we give to you."

"Oh, don't you dare bring my kids into this," Travis seethes.

"Oh my God. Seriously?" I roll my eyes. "Just shut the hell up and help me untie him. You two can argue later."

Clark turns with a ghostly sneer. He pulls a pocketknife out of his front pocket and pushes a button on the side of it, slinging the blade out. Travis freezes up as Clark walks toward him with the knife. He grabs the top of the rope and slices through it, staring down at Travis the whole time.

Once the rope is undone, I step back, and Travis stands up, still wary.

"Better not give us any trouble, Travey boy. I've got my eyes on you."

"If I get fired—"

"If Big Jack fires you, then I will make sure you get enough money so that you never have to work for anyone ever again." They both look back at me. Clark's eyes scream his doubt, and Travis is flat-out stunned. I wave a hand. "I have a soft spot for kids. Can we go now?"

Clark walks past me, to the exit. I point at Travis with my gun, motioning with it for him to move along. He gives me a nervous glance before walking out.

When we're outside, Travis says, "I try to stay out of the loop on these things—what goes on in the mafia family—but you must be her. The girl they all kept talking about. The one who was abducted and then set free by some kingpin in Mexico. Now you're trying to go back there?"

I really am getting sick of everyone wondering why I want to go back. Maybe when they see Draco and me together, they'll understand. Until then, I'll keep my mouth shut and let his actions speak for themselves.

We meet up to Clark's car, and I open the back door for Travis. "Get in," I order, ignoring his statement.

He climbs in without hesitation, and I slam the door behind him.

"Hey, take it easy on the doors, Tomb Raider," Clark snaps as he starts the car up.

"Just drive." I shut the passenger door and place my gun on my lap. "How long to get to the private strip?"

"About twenty-five minutes," Clark answers.

"Is the plane fueled?" I ask, looking over my shoulder at Travis.

"Yes. There is a full tank and it was already checked, inside and out, by a mechanic."

"And we'll only need to make one stop to fill up?"

"Yes," he answers.

"Good."

Travis slouches back in the seat, and Clark puts the car in motion. We ride mostly in silence, but my mind is screaming. I have no idea what the hell I'm doing. This is a suicide mission, for sure.

For all I know, as soon as I cross that border, someone will recognize me and inform Yessica, and she'll come for me again. I'm praying the opposite happens, and they inform Draco instead.

Clark parks in an abandoned lot, leading us to the private runway on foot. I can see the jet. It's white, with a thick black line across the middle. It's not as big as Draco's, but it's nice. Simple. Just like Uncle Jack and his family—well, all of them but Clark.

There is no one around, to my surprise. There is a booth a couple yards away, but it doesn't look like anyone is in it.

"Did you tell security to go home? The guards?" I ask.

"Yes. Paid them off so they wouldn't ask any questions or report to Big Jack. No one's watching."

I hustle beside him, trying to keep up my pace while also keeping an eye on Travis, who is on the other side of Clark. We finally reach the jet, and Clark grabs a handle, drawing down the stairs that lead up to it.

He heads up the stairs, turning on several lights, and then popping his head back out, gesturing with two fingers for us to come inside.

"You, to the cockpit," he says, pointing at Travis. "How long to get this thing warmed up and ready to fly?"

"Um, give or take, twenty to thirty minutes," he answers.

"What?" I drop my bag on the seat. "We can't wait that long. We need to go now. Anyone could come out here!" I throw my hands in my hair, pushing it all behind me.

"Just chill, Gia. No one is around. Trust me."

"I don't trust anyone," I grumble, snatching up my bag and slouching in one of the chairs. Travis enters the pit, and Clark sighs, following behind him, watching his every move.

The smell of leather and spice surrounds me, my leg bouncing as I hear Travis complaining about something and then pulling a few knobs and twisting some levers.

Twenty minutes pass, and the engine starts, but they're still up there, trying to figure something out.

I pick up my gun and look out of the window, my heart catching speed again. The strip is empty. Vacant. We're the only ones here. I have to keep that in mind.

With a deep breath, I stand, going for the mini-fridge bolted to the wall. I take out a water bottle and crack it open, guzzling most of it down.

I sit back in my seat when their voices become calmer. My pulse settles, and I loosen my finger from the trigger.

Just as I start to relax, headlights flash on my face through the plane window, and a black truck with flashing blue and white lights appears, parking a short distance away from the plane.

I know that SUV.

I saw it earlier.

My heart drops at the mere presence of it.

A man in a black suit steps out, his hair parted just at the temple, gelled and combed in style. He adjusts the collar of his jacket, but I hop out of my chair, clutching the gun.

"Clark—who the fuck is that?" I hiss, shoulders hiking up, tense now. Every muscle in my body grows tight, my breaths thicker, becoming harder to pass through.

Clark spins around with his eyebrows drawn together, drawing the cover of one of the windows up and peering out. "Shit."

"I thought no one knew we were here! Is that a cop?"

I look back out the window, and the cop digs into the inside pocket of his jacket, pulling out a gold badge and holding it in the air.

"DEA! I need everyone on the jet to step off right now!" he commands.

My pulse becomes sluggish. I can hear it whooshing in my ears. My finger tightens around the trigger, eyes as wide as saucers.

"Gia, be calm," Clark murmurs. "We don't have any drugs. Just guns. And I have permits for mine. We can easily hide yours."

I don't speak.

I can't.

All words are lodged in my throat.

A fucking DEA agent is standing outside the jet. He could arrest us all and throw us in jail for the hell of it.

"I'm not here about the drugs, or the money, or any of that shit you try to do under the radar!" he yells, taking a small a step forward. "I'm here for Gianna Nicotera."

When he says my name, my sluggishly beating heart slithers to the pit of my stomach.

Clark looks over at me with a slight grimace. "How the fuck does he know you're here?"

I pull my lips in, taking a step to the side. I don't know. I have no clue how he knows. He shouldn't know…Draco was smart. He did it quietly. There's no way in hell…

"How long until we can take off, Travis?" Clark demands.

"Almost ready. Just—just two more minutes at least. Everyone has to buckle in."

I ignore them, staring harder out the window.

"She knows where you are, Gianna," the agent yells, pacing in front of the jet. "You can't run. She'll find you, wherever you go. Just turn yourself in and end this. Give her what she wants."

My heartbeat is all I can hear now.

A slow, deliberate thump.

Thu-thunk.

Thu-thunk.

Thu-thunk.

I can't breathe…

I can't…I can't talk. One moment I'm gasping for breath, listening to Clark shout my name, and the next, I'm seeing red. So much fucking red. I feel my teeth smash together, my gun tighter in hand.

I don't give much thought to what I do next.

My feet move faster than my brain can function.

Even though I hear Clark shouting at me, probably telling me not to go out, I don't listen.

Before I know it, I'm standing in the cold, hustling halfway down the staircase with my pistol aimed high and a bullet flying directly at the agent.

24

GIANNA

He hits the ground with a loud groan, and I rush for him.

Another agent hops out the car and I shoot him too, before he can draw his gun on me.

When I meet up to the first agent, who I shot in the arm, I pounce on top of him, gripping his throat. "Why are you here?" I shout.

"You know why I'm here," he says with a small laugh.

I press the barrel of my gun to his forehead, teeth bared. "I swear to God, I will kill you right now. Who sent you?" I ask the question, but I already know who. I know exactly who sent him.

He continues his stupid, devious smile. "She was right. You *are* fierce. Shooting a DEA agent. That's life right there, *slut*."

"Why are you working for her? What the fuck does she want!" I press harder, gripping his throat tighter. He struggles with his words now, trying hard to squeeze them out behind my hand.

"She…wants…you…found…" He runs his tongue over his lips as footsteps pound into the asphalt behind me, and the engine of the jet grows louder. "And *dead*."

My vicious scowl fades, my features collapsing. I stare into his eyes, and just as he starts up a crackly chuckle, as if he's gotten under my skin, my gun goes off, and his blood is leaking from his skull and onto the ground.

"Fuck, Gia!" Clark grabs my arm, yanking me off of the agent. "Your fucking DNA is going to be all over him!"

I glare up at him. "I don't give a shit! He worked for her! He was on her fucking payroll! If I hadn't killed him, he would have killed me!"

"Shit. Well, we can't just leave those bodies out here."

"I know we can't, that's why they're coming on the jet with us."

Clark's eyes nearly pop out of his head. "Their blood is going to be all over my dad's jet—on the private air strip only he and a few other businessmen use. They'll come for him eventually, when they see these agents missing."

"Send someone to ditch the car, Clark. We'll take the bodies over the border and ditch them, too. We'll burn the jet. He can always get a new one. My dad always told me material things are easily replaceable." I turn around and grab the agent's wrists. "Help me carry him."

Clark stares down at me in utter disbelief, but he doesn't speak on it anymore. Instead he bends down, grabbing the agent's ankles and walking backwards with his body.

We bring it onto the jet, dropping it into one of the empty seats. We do the same with the other agent, who is a little heavier, but we make do, strapping their bodies into the seats.

The second agent's breath snags.

"This one is still alive," I murmur.

Clark dashes off the plane and hops into the SUV. He drives toward a tree a few yards away and parks. He returns with a burner phone and sends someone a text, and then he looks up at me. "Someone will come for the truck."

I nod, sitting on the opposite side of the breathing agent.

"Are we ready to take off, Travis?" I call.

"Yes. All clear."

Good.

Clark straps in, and I do the same, but I don't take my eyes off those guards, especially the dead one. His blood still leaks, dripping onto his jacket and the leather seat.

I finally pull my eyes away when the wheels of the jet leave the runway and we ascend, the turbulence rocking me about.

My finger doesn't let up around my trigger. My heart is still banging like a drum. I don't know what the hell I've just done, but if anyone important finds out, I'm sure I will become a wanted woman after this.

"People will investigate," Clark warns.

"Then let them investigate. If your people are good, they shouldn't find a trace of that truck." I look at the one who's unconscious. "They're dirty agents, Clark. You really think they filled people in on their whereabouts?"

Clark runs a rough hand over his face. "Big Jack loves this fucking jet, Gia. I hope your master Jefe makes it right by buying him a new one."

I roll my eyes, looking out of the window, where the mountaintops and clouds are not too far below. "He will. We just have to get to him first."

25

GIANNA

Travis informed us that it would be a six-hour flight.

After making a subtle pit stop on a private strip on land owned by a man Big Jack pays off, we are on our way to Mexico City.

"Do you even know where to go to find him?" Clark asks, pacing back and forth now. He's nervous. He's been pacing ever since we were given the opportunity to walk.

"He has a home in Los Cabos," I answer. "I was there for a few days. If we can get to Cabos, I'm hopeful he'll have someone around, and we can get them to take us to him."

He stops walking, looking me hard in the eyes. "They're gonna shoot us on sight if they see us. You don't just pull up to someone's private home—a kingpin's home at that—and expect to not get shot at."

I sigh, looking at the barely breathing agent. His face is paler now, his hand pressing into the wound just below his chest. I push out of my seat, taking the one across from him and crossing my legs. His hooded eyes sluggishly drag up to meet mine.

I study him carefully; his breaths are heavy, labored. Sweat sprinkles his chalky white forehead and the side of his face. He's literally fighting for his life right now, clinging to every breath.

"It's better if you let go and let yourself die, rather than letting one of us take care of it." I watch the crimson leak through his already bloodstained fingers. "That's what will happen in the end, anyway. Either way, you'll have to go." I sit forward, and he flinches, nostrils flaring. I blink rapidly. "Are you afraid?" I ask.

"Are you taking me to The Jefe?" His voice is gruff and dry.

My head goes into a slight tilt. "Why would I do that?" He doesn't answer me, turning his head to look out of the window, so I place my gun down on top of the dead guard's lap beside me, looking him hard in the eyes. "I don't need The Jefe to fight my battles. You two came for me, thinking I would just give in and go to her." I cluck my tongue against my teeth. "You were wrong. If there's one thing he taught me, it was to fight for myself. End all threats. I couldn't let you stop me, and I damn sure wasn't going to let Yessica prevent me from doing what I need to do."

He breathes harder. "I have a family," he grunts. "I—I was just doing this for the money. I want to get back to them. I—if you let me go, I will never come for you again. You will never see my face, and I'll even say Matt, here, went off the grid and disappeared on me. I'll be a ghost to you."

My head lifts, air filling my lungs.

I look over my shoulder at Clark, who has his arms folded, his brows strewn together, and his lips pinched tight.

"Have you ever met Yessica?" I ask.

"Only once, and it was to give us our pay to find you."

I huff a laugh. "Where did you meet her and when?"

"A motel close to the border," he answers hurriedly, head bobbing. "I—it was called La Grandioso. About a week ago, she reached out to us—that's it."

Silence reigns, and I push out of my seat.

"Wait—please," the agent begs, sitting forward and then moaning in pain, squeezing his eyes shut. "I swear, I was only doing this for my family. Please. You two are family. You can understand, right?"

Clark scoffs. "Desperate move, asshole."

"If we keep him alive and hold him hostage, he might be able to get us to her," I murmur. "She won't question an agent on her payroll if he says he has a lead on me. We can use that against her."

"What?" Clark's frown deepens and he drops his arms. "Are you kidding? He's just saying this shit to get out alive. He has to fucking die, Gianna. Look at him—you can't trust a piece of shit like him. Like you said, he's a dirty agent. He'll say anything to get out clean."

I glance over my shoulder at the agent, whose eyes are wet and desperate, and then I see something familiar—something that should have been a clear sign to me from the very beginning.

This has happened to me before.

This is exactly why I was sent away.

For being lenient. For trusting. For thinking there are actually selfless people in this world who want to do right.

Images of the bombs going off on Jefe's cars and killing his men, the guns sparking, and the blood splattering on me, resurface.

Thiago, shot. Gone. Dead. Just like that. All because of a man like this...

A tunnel vision of what I thought was true and real hits me so hard my gut clenches, and my mouth fills with moisture.

I lift my gun, aiming it at his head. "Where's your wallet?" I demand, and his eyes stretch wide, full of horror now.

"M-my back pocket," he answers, voice panicked.

"Get up." I grab his shirt, yanking him up, not giving a damn how much pain he's in. Clark steps up to my side, assisting me. I dig into his back pocket, retrieving the hard, square wallet.

With my gun still pointed at him, I place the wallet on top of the seat in front of me and open it with my free hand. I sift through it, finding IDs, hotel key cards, and cash. I see everything that belongs in an official DEA agent's wallet—all but one thing.

Family portraits.

Every family man has at least one picture in his wallet.

"If you love your family so much, why aren't there any pictures of them in here?" I ask, frowning now.

"I—I have some! They're in the truck—back in Colorado!"

"He's lying," Clark grumbles.

"Please—I'm not! I—I have family!"

My lips smash together. "I am so *sick* of men like you lying to me!" I grip the collar of his shirt, yanking him close, causing a hard, anguished cry to escape him. "Why shouldn't I kill you?" I press the gun to his cheek.

"Because I can help you," he says. "I can get Hernandez to you. I can help."

I shove him away.

"She has many places that we meet—she's waiting to hear back from us. I can set it all up—I can get her to you and end all of this and never look back. If you let me go, I will—" Before he can finish his sentence, Clark is stepping past me, bringing the butt of his gun down and slamming it across the agent's head.

The agent passes out from the blow, and I whip my head up to stare at Clark, who grumbles "What? He was talking too fucking much, and I need to think." Bringing a hand to his hip, he walks past me again, slouching down in an empty seat. "Well, now that we know he's in deeper than he said, you may have been right about one thing. We can use him to lure her out when you're ready. Get him to call and say he found you when we land."

I pull my eyes from the agent. "So we have to keep him alive for now?"

"If he even makes it there alive."

I sigh, taking the seat beside him.

"Bet you didn't think shit would get this bad, huh?" he chuckles, leg bouncing. "Fuck, I need a smoke."

"How much longer?" I ask.

"An hour, give or take." I sigh, and Clark shifts in his seat, fingers tapping on the arm of his chair. "You know what your problem is?" he asks, giving me a hard, thorough sweep with his eyes. "Your problem is you trust too easily. You're just like Jen. She believes anything she hears, which makes her vulnerable and weak at times. She's too damn gullible. Now I get why he sent you back. You were a danger to his business. You can't believe everything you hear, Gia. You can't trust every man you meet, no matter how honest they seem.

That motherfucker right there is a prime example of a wolf in sheep clothing."

I meet his eyes briefly before dropping mine to my lap. "I don't want to be a danger to him anymore. If I don't prove my worth to him by taking Yessica down, he'll never forgive me, and sending me away again would be the nicest thing he would do. That, or he'll disappear and make sure I can never find him."

He releases a hard breath through his nostrils. "I just don't get it. Being with The Jefe comes with a heavy price. You'll be risking your life, for the rest of your life. You'll always be on the run. You'll never be safe, and you'll probably die before your fifties. Is that really how you want to live? What you want your future to be?"

I study his face, how serious he is. I never thought of it that way. I wanted to be with him so badly that I didn't even think of the consequences. How can I raise a baby in that environment? How can I raise a child, knowing he or she will never have a stable and happy home? How can I raise a child with the most ruthless man I have ever known?

"Let me tell you something," Clark goes on, voice low but firm, leaning over the armrest and toward me. "You really want to be a boss, show the world what you're capable of, then show them what you *really* are. Show the world that Gianna Nicotera should *never* be fucked with, and when they all know it, own that shit and never lose sight of it. Having power and respect always comes with a price. There will always be someone around, wanting to take you down, wanting to be you, and you have to be ready to end them before they can even finish speaking your name. Stay on your toes, keep your eyes open, watch your fucking back, and stay loaded. Don't trust this world. This world will fuck you over in a million ways with no apologies. Always be ready, Gia. Always make your statement. Never take shit from anyone. Instead, *handle* that shit and shut—it—the—fuck—down. Be the Patrona he needs you to be. The fearless woman your father always knew you would become. We both know that shit is in you. You just need to claim it."

26

GIANNA

We're landing.

I gain view of the red dirt surrounding the private airstrip, and my heart bangs around in my ribcage like a rattle. The wheels of the jet hit the ground, and Clark clears his throat, unclipping his seatbelt and walking to the cockpit.

He pushes the door open and says something to Travis. I look down at the pale agent. His lips are chapped, eyes sealed. He's still breathing—just barely.

"Get up," I tell him, but he doesn't budge.

Clark comes toward me, looking down at the barely breathing DEA agent. "He's worthless, Gia," he mumbles. "He won't make it off this plane. He's lost way too much blood. "

"We have to take our chances." I tuck my gun behind my back, reaching down and grabbing his arm." Help me get him up."

"Before I do that, you have to agree to let Travis go back home."

I frown up at him. "How?"

"We need to find him a way. We meet some of The Jefe's men and see if they can torch and get rid of this jet, but we have to get him back. He did the job; he got us here. Now we have to let him go. My father will ask him questions, but he'll do what you told him to do.

He'll say that you made him do it with a gun to our heads." Clark shrugs. "Not like it isn't the truth."

My eyebrows pull together, gaze shifting over to Travis standing near the door of the cockpit. He's already looking at me, lips pressed thin, eyes stretched as he drops his gaze to the barely breathing DEA agent.

"Fine," I grumble. "But once we find him a way back, he's on his own from there."

"That's fine." Clark walks away, murmuring to Travis, whose automatic response is a sigh of relief. Clark digs in his bag nearby and hands Travis some money, clapping him on the shoulder before turning to come to me again.

After Clark and I strap on our bags, Clark picks up most of the agent's weight. We struggle carrying him off the jet, Travis trying to help from the back, dragging the agent's mass and our own luggage toward the barbwire gates.

Outside of the gate is a security booth, and from where we are, I can see a man standing in it, wearing all black. He sees us and immediately comes sprinting out of the booth, a handgun pointed our way. His eyes drop to the bloody agent, and he panics, coming to a halt and shouting for us to stop in Spanish.

When we don't stop, he shouts even louder. He points his gun up in the air and shoots, trying to scare us off.

"Damn it. Wait here with him," I grumble, slipping from beneath the agent's arm. Clark grunts, cursing at the agent to stay steady as Travis rushes around to keep the balance.

I hold my hands in the air, marching ahead as the man continues shouting obscenities, demanding that I stop now before he shoots.

"You can't shoot me!" I yell in Spanish.

"Why the fuck not?" He steadies the gun, aiming it at my head. "This is private property, and without a code and proper paperwork, you are not allowed to use this airstrip!"

"The Jefe!" I shout, and his eyes go round, gun still aimed.

"What about him?"

"I'm with The Jefe. You can't shoot me. You shoot me or hurt any of them, and he'll be pissed."

The man's bushy eyebrows dip beneath his black cap, his mouth a narrow line. "You're lying! Anyone can say they're with The Jefe to protect themselves! I let you get through, and it's my head on a fucking platter!"

"Call his people—the ones who work most with you and this private strip! I know you have their numbers. Tell them La Patrona is here! They'll understand!"

I glance back at Clark and Travis, who are now struggling with the agent. He's a big man, probably both of their weights combined, and Clark may have been right. He won't make it far. Not in his condition.

"Wait there!" the guard commands, stepping back slowly. He hustles to the booth, still glaring out the window. In seconds, he has a phone pressed to his hear, lips moving rapidly as he speaks.

I see his eyes get bigger as he stares at me and then, in no time, his mouth clamps shut, and he places the phone down. He steps back out again, this time without his gun aimed at me.

"La Patrona." He rubs a hand over his face "His woman. I am so sorry."

I ignore his apology. "What did they say?"

"They are on the way here, Patrona."

"Who did you speak with?"

He shrugs. "I'm not sure. A man."

I groan. He has many men working for him.

"Is there anything I can do for you?" the man asks hurriedly. "You can understand that I was just doing my job—protecting the strip. Doing what I'm paid to do."

I step up to him. "I understand." I glance back at Clark, Travis, and the agent. The agent's head bobs and his knees buckle.

Shit. He's done for.

Clark curses loudly, dropping his heavy body on the red dirt and then bending down, pressing two fingers on his upper neck to check his pulse.

"I told you, Gia!" Clark yells. "He's fucking dead!"

I sigh, looking at the guard again. The guard looks perplexed and stunned, eyes a little wider now. "Do you speak English?" I ask.

"Yes," he answers.

"Have any men who know how to make two dead bodies and a jet disappear?"

His lips smash together as he looks around me at the agent on the ground. "I know people, yes."

"Then call them. Tell them we want the jet to be untraceable and for the bodies to never be found again. There is another body on the jet."

"They'll expect pay," he says. By his tone alone, I know he's not just talking about the men he'll call who, I know, will expect to be paid. He wants to be compensated for this, too.

I sigh, taking my tote bag off my shoulder and slinging it around. Unzipping it, I snatch out a few rolls of the money I packed. "It's $50,000. All I've got right now." That's a lie. I have more on me.

He bobs his head, taking the case. "It's more than enough. Gracias, Patrona."

"How quickly can you get it done?"

"I'll make the call now. It won't take long for them to get here. Maybe thirty minutes or so. Your people aren't too far away. Close to the border, which is a little over forty-five minutes from here. You are welcome to wait inside the booth. It's air-conditioned."

"It's fine. I'll wait out here. Make the call to your people."

He nods and turns, marching back to the booth and picking up his phone to call. I make my way back to Clark and Travis.

"We'll get you out of here soon enough," I tell Travis.

"What did that motherfucker say?" Clark asks, pointing at the booth. "And did I just see you give him *money*?"

"Yes, I gave him money to take care of the bodies and the jet. We have to cover our tracks and make sure nothing links back to your father. Right?"

He sighs. "We could have gotten him to handle that shit without pay. He knows the Jefe doesn't fuck around."

"The money means nothing to me. There's more where it came

from." I look down at the agent, blowing a breath. Swiping a hand over my sticky forehead, I bend down and take the badge off his holster. I place my bag down next, taking off my leather jacket.

It takes about forty-five minutes for the guard's "cleaners" to show up. They pull up in a brown vehicle, speak to him briefly, and then come right for us.

"This one of them?" one of them asks.

I nod.

He bends down, grabbing the agent by the ankles and dragging his body through the gate and toward the jet. Another man comes hustling after him, climbing on board first and tossing things out. Mostly papers and folders.

Once they have the agent's body on the jet, they come back down, dusting their hands off and walking toward us. One of them hands me a paper. I look it over—Big Jack's registration for the jet.

I hand it to Clark who folds it up and tucks it into his back pocket.

The man who dragged the agent's body says, "We'll fly the jet to an abandoned strip—not many know about it. If it is vacant, we'll pour gasoline and burn it. Once we burn it, we'll send the pieces to a dump to smash and compact them. Then," he grins, like this truly excites him, "we'll burn it again, just to be on the safe side."

"All with the agents inside of it?"

"Oh, we were going to chop and burn them, but if you want us to just torch the bastards while they're on board, we can do that too. Either way, you'll never see them or that jet again."

I bob my head. "I don't care what you do with them. Just get it done please. Make it seem like they and the jet never existed."

"You got it, Patrona." They take off for the jet, climbing back on again and starting it up. As the engine of the jet warms up, I hear the crunch of tires over rocks and dirt, and when I look to my left, I see a white Chrysler driving toward us rapidly.

Clark snatches his gun out, holding it at his side as the vehicle swerves and parks sideways, blowing a gust of dirt in our direction.

When the car parks, it's just my luck that Patanza bustles out of the car, brows stitched, pointing her gun at Clark, swaying it between him and Travis.

"Put your fucking gun down!" she roars in Spanish.

Clark scoffs. "What? I'm sorry! No hablo Español!"

"NOW!" She barks the order in English.

"Patanza! He's with me!" I step in front of Clark. "You don't need to shoot him—either of them!"

"Fuck that, Gia! No one told you to bring them! They know about you—about Jefe! He's already a fucking liability, now get the fuck out of my way!"

I don't budge. Instead, I pull my gun from behind me and point it at her. Emilio steps out from the driver's side, his hands at his waist, like he's exasperated from the ordeal already.

"He cannot come with us, Patrona. The Jefe won't like it," Emilio says to me in Spanish.

"I don't care. He's my cousin. He comes with me."

Patanza paces forward, raging. "What if I shoot you, huh? He doesn't give a shit about you anymore, Gia! You never should have come back! You're the last thing on his mind!"

"I don't believe you." I steady my gun, the anger seeping to my fingertips, ready to pull the trigger. I can't shoot her—*won't* shoot her. She's like family to him, but she doesn't know that I won't shoot. She thinks I'm a threat to them both now—that I'll do anything to stay alive. And maybe I will. "Take us to him."

Emilio sighs again. "You know we can't do that, Patrona."

"Yes, you can. This is not a request. It's a demand. I need to see him. Immediately."

Emilio shifts on his feet, head shaking. Patanza keeps her gun pointed my way, mostly trying to get at Clark.

Emilio murmurs something to Patanza, and she glances over at him, grimacing. Finally, after several expletives, she lowers the gun, and Emilio pulls out a burner phone, turning his back to us and walking a short distance away to make a call.

Strapping the gun around her, Patanza storms toward me, getting in my face. "If you do anything stupid, I will end you myself, Gia, and I mean it. Don't fuck with me right now," she growls through clenched teeth.

I challenge her stare, narrowing my eyes. "I'm here for Draco. That's it. Don't hurt me, and I won't hurt you."

Her nostrils flare and then her gaze shifts over to Travis. "Who the fuck is he?"

"My uncle's pilot. He flew us here."

"He can't come with us to Jefe's territory," she spits out.

"We know. We'll find a way for him to catch a ride home. You won't have to worry about him."

Her eyes finally shift over to Clark, who has a smirk on his lips. "What the fuck are you looking at?" she snaps.

"Never seen a woman so aggressive," he chuckles. "Or that good with a gun. Makes me wonder what else those hands can do."

"Fuck off." She turns her back to him, walking to Emilio, who wraps up on his call and then turns with a loud, tired-sounding breath.

"All right, Patrona. Get in the car," he says.

"What?" Patanza steps in front of him, her back still to us. "Is he sure about this? We don't even know the men she's with! For all we know they're trying to turn him in! We can't take her to him!"

"The Patrona I know would never do that," Emilio responds. "He may be angry with her, Patanza, but even I know she would never do that. When I described the dark-haired one, it's like he knew exactly who I was talking about. He's a Nicotera."

She huffs, turning back around and looking Clark and Travis over. "Whatever. But we're taking the guns." She comes to us again, demanding them.

I don't hand mine over. She challenges it, holding her hand out, eyes furious. I keep mine gripped in hand.

"Perra estupida," she spits.

Clark willingly hands his guns over, winking at her in the process. He's getting under her skin, something he knows how to do to anyone all to well.

"Your bag, too," she demands. He hands it to her and she takes it, heading for the trunk of the car and opening it. She tosses the bag inside and then puts the safety on the guns before putting them in too.

She comes back and pats Clark and Travis down, then orders us to get in the backseat.

I lead the way, letting Travis in first. I climb in next and Clark follows, slamming the door behind him. After Emilio talks to the guard in the booth, he and Patanza hop in the front and buckle in, leaving the private airstrip immediately.

"What makes you think I can't just take one of Gia's guns and shoot you both in the back of the head?" Clark asks, like he's truly curious.

"I fucking dare you to try it," Patanza grits through her teeth, glaring back at him.

"Clark, please just shut the fuck up," I mutter, shaking my head.

He laughs. "It was just a question. Are we not allowed to ask questions around here now? I know it's not a free country, but damn."

I sigh.

Patanza's jaw flexes.

"Either of you got a cig?" he inquires, and they both look at each other before focusing on the dirt road again and deciding to ignore him.

"Mexicans," he mumbles, laughing to himself and staring out the window. "Always gotta be so fucking serious."

27

GIANNA

We take Travis to an airport close to the border. After Emilio talks to someone, working privately to get him through without his passport, Travis is on his way with the wad of money Clark gave him earlier and nothing more.

To be honest, I'm not sure if Travis will keep his word. For all I know he'll tell Big Jack everything that went down instead of what we told him to say: that I forced him into doing it. I'm hoping that's all he says—that he had no choice. That I held a gun to his head. That he only did it for his family's sake, and to save his own life. It's the truth, anyway.

Minus Clark's annoyed grunts, shifting on the leather, and sighs, we drive mostly in silence. For the most part, Patanza keeps her gaze ahead. I see her glance over her shoulder every once in a while, but not fully.

Maybe she trusts me a little. Maybe she doesn't.

I don't know. She's become a lot harder to read lately.

I ride in the backseat for what feels like hours before we finally stop, reaching the same factory I saw before boarding Draco's jet and flying to Los Cabos.

There is already a jet waiting there. Emilio parks the car and hops out, hustling toward it, where a man in a black cap and black suit is already standing.

They nod at each other and then Emilio points at the car.

"Get out," Patanza orders, pushing her door open and stepping out.

Clark blows a heavy breath. "Here we go."

Emilio jogs back, popping the trunk with the car's key fob and taking out Clark's bag and his guns. We follow Patanza to the jet, Emilio behind us, and board quickly.

She steps aside, letting us on first to sit.

I take a window seat, and Clark sits across from me, rubbing his face. His leg bounces as soon as he straps in, and then he grips the arms of the chair, knuckles turning white.

"I need to take a smoke before this jet takes off," he tells Patanza.

"Too bad," she mutters, slouching down in her seat. "Cigarettes are bad for you, anyway."

Clark fists his hair. "Fucking bitch."

She looks over at me. "Buckle up, *Patrona*." She says the name with disgust, mocking it.

"Where are we going?" I ask in Spanish when the seatbelt is clipped.

Emilio takes the seat beside Patanza after tucking everything in the cabins above his head and then they both buckle in.

Meeting my eyes, Emilio says, "Puerto Vallarta."

"What's in Puerto Vallarta?" I question, still speaking his native language.

"A safe place," Patanza responds. "So just shut up and ride."

I ignore her, focusing on Emilio. "Will he be there?"

Emilio gives a slight shrug, eyes mellowing. "No se, Patrona." *I don't know, Boss.*

I sigh, slumping my body in the seat, staring out of the window as the wheels of the jet begin to roll.

The flight takes less than two hours.

After everything is collected from the bins, we follow Emilio off the jet and through the gates of the runway. This one isn't private. There are many jets and people around, but they're all minding their own business.

All of them seem rich, the men wearing expensive suits and sunglasses and the women wearing tight, silky dresses or blouses, red-bottomed heels and their hair styled to perfection, despite the dusty wind around them.

Emilio leads the way to a building. It's like an airport, but much, much smaller and fewer security guards around. He bobs his head at one of them and they nod back before looking away.

He reaches another door and heads out. A white van is parked up front and he goes for it, swinging the back door open as a man in the driver seat steps out.

I know this man.

It's Diego, one of his best guards.

He spots me and looks me over twice before murmuring, "Patrona."

I nod back.

Apparently he told them to keep their respect. That's good. I know how easy it would be to yank the authority right from under me.

Diego pulls the door open, and I walk forward, climbing inside. Clark starts to climb in, but Diego stops him with a firm hand to the chest.

"Hands up," Diego orders.

"You've got to be fucking kidding me," Clark scoffs, but puts his hands on top of his head anyway. When Diego starts to pat him down, Clark says, "I'm annoyed as fuck, and no one wants to let the gringo take a fucking smoke break. Get too close, and I might bite your fucking face off."

Diego keeps a solid face, nudging him when he's done. "Get in the fucking van."

Clark slides across the bench, sitting next to me. "I swear they're testing me," he grumbles.

"Be patient," I murmur. "You'll have your cigarettes soon. The Jefe doesn't cut corners. You of all people should know this."

"I know. I know. Just over this protocol shit."

When all the doors are shut, the van peels off. We ride on cobblestone streets with the front windows down. I can smell the ocean before I can see it. A few minutes later, we're riding on a quiet dirt road with a clear view of the sapphire water, the waves crashing to shore.

There are hotels crowding the area below, tourists and locals on the beach. Children playing. The sun blazing.

The van slows down, and we ride up another dirt road. At the box is a security guard who sees Diego and nods once, letting us ride through. We ride a little more until reaching a castle-like building.

It's a villa, made of creamy stucco with a brown clay and cement roof. A trained fuchsia bougainvillea tree borders part of the rooftop and the thick stucco walls of the villa.

Diego parks in front of the home, and Emilio springs out of the passenger seat, Diego following suit.

They open the doors from both sides, and we step out, Patanza following behind Clark from the very back row.

As soon as I step out, I know the ocean is close. The air is thick and damp. I taste the salt on my lips, shut my eyes for a brief moment, and breathe. I know I'm far from safe and far from being okay, but this is liberating.

I can breathe, despite the humidity and the heat.

I finally made it back.

There's something about these exotic places that make me feel free. I guess that's why I wanted my wedding to be in Mexico. Here, the water is blue and the palm trees whisper sweet, soothing melodies.

"This way, Patrona." Emilio walks by me, leading the way to the front door.

He unlocks it, and as soon as we step inside, I'm in love.

This place is huge—not like the others. It's spacious, and I'm sure it has many, many rooms. The floor tiles are ivory, waxed so well I can see my reflection.

The wide glass doors to the left let in the salty breeze, giving a clear view of an infinity pool with an immaculate waterfall coming from brown stones, and of course the roaring ocean beyond it.

The east wall of the living room is made of the same stone as the waterfall, a fireplace built into the bottom center. The furniture—tan leather with a mix of wicker pieces and orange and brown throw pillows—looks comfortable enough for a nap, which I definitely need.

"If you two would like to come with me, I will show you to your rooms," Emilio says, pointing at the staircase.

I nod, looking over at Clark, who doesn't understand the Spanish words, but follows my lead anyway. As I walk up the stairs, I feel eyes on me.

I think it's Patanza only, but I'm wrong. It's her and Diego. Both of them are watching. Hard. Patanza mutters something to him before storming off.

I pull my gaze away, following Emilio to my assigned bedroom after he shows Clark his room.

"Now this is what I'm talking about!" Clark laughs. "Finally some fucking luxury!"

Emilio takes me to another room. It's beautiful. A canopy bed with sheer white sheets curtaining it. They're drawn back, as well as the curtains above the wide glass door that reveals the sparkling ocean and a part of the infinity pool.

"Your bag will be brought in shortly, Patrona." He smiles at me. "He wants us to check it first."

"That's fine, Emilio." Before he takes off, I stop him and he looks back, eyes inquiring. "You don't have to give my cousin the guns or his cellphone. I know Jefe won't allow that under his roof, but can you at least make sure Clark gets his damn cigarettes? He's a true asshole without them."

Emilio smiles with a curt nod. "Of course."

"Gracias, Emilio."

He pauses, looking me over once. "Is there anything else, Patrona?"

I shift on my feet, taking a long look around the room before meeting his eyes again. "Just…thank you, I guess. For bringing me here—trusting that I would never bring harm his way. Not intentionally."

He presses his lips. "I know an honest person when I see one. Like I said before you left, we all make mistakes. None of us under this roof are perfect."

"I know."

I give him a small smile, and he takes off, the door clicking shut behind him.

I walk to the balcony and grip the rail, shutting my eyes and breathing in before exhaling.

I know it's not freedom.

I know there is work to be done.

But I'm here.

I made it back.

It won't be long before I see him again.

28

DRACO

She's back.

I don't know why I was foolish enough to think she wouldn't try to find me. Only reason she's with my people is because having her out there alone would have gotten her killed.

People are still looking for her.

Her face is familiar—all over posters in the cities. It puts me in a position where I have to protect her, but only because I can't stand the idea of Yessica putting her hands on her again.

I assumed Gianna would think about all of the horrible shit I'd done to her—things that I'm sure have traumatized her—and stay right there in Colorado with her family. The months with me, I'm sure, have changed her. Made her fearless but still broken...just like the person I am.

She knows I'm not innocent.

She knew how big of a risk it was to come back to me. She could have been killed as soon as she stepped off that jet with her cousin, but still, she returned.

She doesn't know what to expect from me. For all she knows, I could kill her as soon as I lay eyes on her, or have her suffocated in her sleep.

She's stupid for coming back.

She's always been so damn reckless.

I can't go to her—won't go to her.

I tell myself this—that she's worthless. Unimportant. Irrelevant and a waste of time…but only I know it's all a fucking lie.

She's wormed her way in. She did it to me a very long time ago, when we were children, and again during our deadly reunion in Lantía when she was locked up in my shed.

Fuck her.

She fucked up.

Maybe she'll take the sign and leave once she realizes I'm not coming.

That I owe her *nothing*.

29

GIANNA

Three fucking days.

Three long, weary, annoying days, and not one sign of him. Not one message or phone call. I've kept my eyes open and my ears peeled. I haven't even heard his men speaking to him on their phone calls.

I'm starting to think he's not going to show up at all—that I gave up a life back in Colorado to get nothing in return.

On top of that, Mrs. Molina came here yesterday. She still can't stand to look at me. She hasn't spoken one word to me since her arrival. She looked me right in the eyes then passed right by without a single word.

Instead of eating breakfast at the table with her—something she's done each morning while here—I tell Emilio to bring mine to my room.

Of course Clark doesn't give a damn. He enjoys the buffet breakfasts at the table with Jefe's mother. She doesn't speak to him much either, but I can always hear him trying to start conversations and getting dry responses in return.

I also hear him trying to get Patanza to open up.

Today he's swimming in the pool, Patanza keeping watch of him, her gun tucked in the holster at her waist, arms folded.

"Come on, mamacita!" I hear Clark call to her from my room. "You look hot, and I don't mean that in the physically attractive way. I mean you're sweating and shit, your hair all damp. Jump in the pool with me. I'll cool you off…or warm you up even more. Whichever way you want it, baby."

"Shut the fuck up already," I hear her snap at him, but I'm almost certain I hear a dip in her voice, like she doesn't fully mean it. Like she…enjoys it.

I know for a fact that he's getting to her in some way, because when I walk out to the pool, needing a word with him, he steps out and winks at her. She jerks her gaze away, muttering something in Spanish, but I see the color bloom in her cheeks. She turns her back so we can't see, but I notice it.

Clark is not an ugly guy. He's a Nicotera, and Nicoteras are far from ugly. I'm certain she finds him attractive, but she'll never admit to it. Not an American man. Not for Patanza.

Later that night, I think I've had enough. I go out to the pool, not even changing clothes. One of my guns is in a lace holster strapped around my thigh, beneath my skirt, just in case.

I'm becoming more and more paranoid with each passing day. Sooner or later, I'll start to wonder where his men's loyalties lie. They won't be with me. I have to be prepared. *Por si acaso.*

Emilio brings out the tequila I requested, placing the tray with a shot glass, a full bottle of tequila, and a water bottle on top of it, down on the table behind me.

"Gracias, Emilio."

When he's gone, I pour myself a shot, but instead of drinking it, I stare at the amber liquid, my stomach churning.

I can't drink. I'm too bothered. Too nervous.

Sighing, I place the shot glass down and walk close to the edge of the pool, studying the wet stones of the man-made waterfall.

The water trickles from high above, pouring into the pool below. My eyes drop to the crystal-blue abyss, focusing on the calm ripples.

I have no idea what the hell I'm doing anymore—no idea why I'm even here. I should have thought this through. I should have considered the peace I had there, in Colorado—maybe started over—but Clark was right.

I was a threat to his family.

They don't deserve to die because I'm a target of one of the most powerful women in this drug industry.

He needs to show tonight, otherwise I'll be making plans to leave and be on my own. I can't stay here forever. It's not safe to be in one place for too long.

It's well past midnight, and no one has heard from him since the call Emilio made before we flew here.

I pick up the water bottle and open it.

I take a few hard gulps before placing the bottle down on the table, but as I lean over, I hear footsteps behind me.

I pause, spotting the familiar silhouette. Broad shoulders. Large chest. Thick legs, clad in black dress pants. Through the corner of my eye, I see him stop several steps away, his fingers sliding into his front pockets.

"You still haven't learned, have you?" His deep, husky voice does something to me.

For a split moment, I can't tell if the rush coursing through my body is due to my masked excitement, or because he just does this to me—swirls everything up inside me and twists it, making me loathe and adore his voice all at the same time.

It's been days since I've heard it. Listening to those voice messages over and over again wasn't the same. I couldn't feel the warmth of his breath on my skin. Couldn't see his eyes dilate as he spoke. Couldn't smell his breath, which always seems to smell like a hint of mint and traces of weed.

He takes a step forward, and out of instinct, my hand touches the gun tucked in the lace holster strapped around my thigh.

"Don't be dumb, Gianna. Why else would my hands be in my pockets?"

"How should I know?"

"You should know I'm not walking with my hands tucked away to make you feel *safe*."

I turn slowly to face him, my fingers still touching my thigh. I feel the hard edge of my gun, finally meeting his hard brown eyes.

He draws a pocket-sized pistol from his pocket as soon as our eyes bolt, taking several steps closer.

When he lifts and aims it, my breath falters, but I don't let him see my worry. I conceal it, holding his gaze as he takes the final step toward me, pressing the gun under my chin. The coolness makes the hairs on the back of my neck prickle.

"The one thing you should have learned while in this country is to *never* let your guard down. Whether you knew I was coming or not, you should have been prepared." His voice is gravelly, heavy. Almost foreign. He watches my face, looking for any sign of weakness. His face hardens, the skin tightening around his eyes when I don't budge or flinch. "Why are you here?" he asks, voice low, keeping the gun steady.

"To help you," I answer, voice soft.

"Does it look like I need your help?"

I look him over, mainly his face. His eyes are tired and red-rimmed. They've always been cold, dark, and empty, but not *this* cold. Not this vacant. There is no thrill, drive, or fire in them. There is only…darkness.

"I don't care if you need it or not. I'm here, and I'm not going anywhere."

"You brought a family member into this. One I already don't trust." He presses his body to mine, lips on the shell of my ear. I can smell the liquor on his breath, strong and pungent. "Should I go kill him? You know, *primo por primo.*" *Cousin for cousin.*

My eyebrows draw together in an instant.

I shove him hard enough to make him stumble, snatching my gun out of the holster as soon as his hand shifts. He already has his pointed at me by the time mine is in the air, but I don't let up. I aim mine right back at him.

"Go ahead and do what you want to me," I say through clenched teeth. "Get it out. Punish. Slap. Punch—do whatever you need to do. It wouldn't be the first time. I don't care what you do to me, but you aren't touching a hair on my cousin's head."

A very faint smirk tugs at the corner of his lips, but his eyes remain the same. Black. Icy. "You think I don't want to kill you? That I won't?"

My finger remains steady around the trigger. "You can't fool me, Draco. I heard the voice recordings. You're trying to prove something to me—that you aren't vulnerable to me—when I know the truth. You thought I wouldn't show after hearing that, but here I am." His smile fades, grip tightening around the handle of the pistol again. "How could I not?" My voice cracks on me, making me sound so damn weak. "Why couldn't you just tell me how you felt in person? We could have worked something out."

I take a small step forward, but he tenses up, keeping his gun pointed directly at my head.

I don't care.

I lower my gun, tucking it back into the holster.

His breathing picks up. He pants through flared nostrils, the rims of his eyes glistening as they hold mine. With his lips pinched tight, he steps toward me, pressing the gun into the center of my forehead.

I lift my free hand, grabbing his forearm.

He doesn't waver.

Doesn't flinch. The gun barely moves an inch.

I hold his cold, empty gaze, pressing on his arm, forcing it down.

He lowers it inch-by-inch, lower and lower, until the gun is at his side.

Those vacant eyes become cloudy. They glisten. They're heavier.

"You didn't give me a chance to say what I had to say," I whisper, and my throat thickens with want. With need.

"Back away from me, Gianna," he growls. "I swear I will rip you to fucking shreds."

I ignore him and clasp his face in my hands, forcing his eyes on mine. "I'm sorry, Draco. I'm sorry for not trusting you. I'm sorry for setting Henry free. I'm sorry that I made your life worse. I—I'm sorry about...Thiago. It was all my fault. I know it. I'm so sorry. I should have listened to you. I know you hate apologies, but I'm telling you now. I'm so, so sorry about everything."

He stares so hard, I feel like he's looking right into my soul. He's do damn quiet that I panic inside, begging him to say something with me eyes.

Then something happens.

Something that both terrifies and relieves me.

Something I didn't think could ever happen.

A wet trail slides down his cheek through that blank stare. I'm sure it's the only tear that has left him since his father died.

He vowed to never look weak—to never reveal. To always be like a vault.

Guarded.

Solid.

Hard to break.

The Jefe doesn't cry.

He doesn't show weakness.

He doesn't...he *can't*...

"I want to hate you," he grumbles, grabbing my face, holding it much tighter than I expect. One of his hands wraps around the back of my neck, the other clutching my ponytail. I gasp when he yanks on it, exposing my neck, forcing me to look at the sky. The tip of his nose starts at my collarbone and trails up to my earlobe. "I want to fucking kill you just as much as I want to love you."

My heartbeat goes unsteady, my breaths a tattered mess when his lips touch my chin. On his breath, I smell the liquor even more now. It's strong, like he drowned himself in it before finally coming to face me.

He eases up on my ponytail, and I lower my head, eyes dropping to his. Our lips are close. So close.

His warm, familiar scent is way too comforting to me. His lips touch mine, just a soft, feathery-light touch.

"I want to fuck you. Kill you. Hate you...love you." He frowns, looking me deep in the eyes. "Do you see what you do to me? You confuse the fuck out of me." He releases my hair and pushes me away.

My breath comes out winded, chest working hard as I focus on him.

He stares right at me.

"Well, hate me first," I say, breathless. "Hate me for as long as you need to, just promise to love me just as much as I love you later."

His chest works harder, his breathing uneven.

I take a step, and so does he.

And before I know it, I'm rushing to him, my body slamming into his. I'm wrapped up in his strong arms, my legs hooking around his waist.

His groan is heavy and solid, humming through my body, sparking the illicit flame inside me again. He spins around, marching away from the pool.

My back slams onto a cold glass table, and he shoves my skirt up. I sit up, clawing at his belt buckle, unzipping his pants in the process.

He shoves my hands away, reaching down and gripping my blouse, ripping it apart at the collar. The buttons fly, scattering on the ground.

He forces my back down on the table, drags my hips to the edge, and maneuvers between my legs, bringing a hand up to my throat and gripping it. His hot, thick cock presses on my thigh, eyes fierce—blazing with hunger.

Ah, there it is.

The fire.

The power.

That sweet, sweet domination.

The Jefe I know and crave.

No words are spoken as he uses his other hand to lift me up, getting a better hold around my throat—just enough for me to breathe, but not too much. It's like he wants to strangle me, but by the way his thumb caresses the crook of my neck, it's like he wants to keep me forever.

He holds the back of my neck tight, and then he's inside me, filling me up.

His strokes don't start light and easy. No, they are hard, quick, almost frightening. The hand around my throat moves up to lock my face between his fingers, eyes still trained on mine. His nostrils flare as he thrusts powerfully, hips propelling, pounding so hard the legs of the table rattle.

Soft, sweet moans escape me.

I shouldn't be so pleased.

He's not fucking me with love.

He's fucking me with pure, violent hatred.

He hates me right now, but if this is how he wants to own and handle what he hates, then so be it.

He can own it. He can own *me*. He can hate me as long as he stays buried inside me.

He picks me up off the table and starts to bounce me up and down on his thick cock. Not once does he pull his eyes away. I don't bother looking away. His face is solid, serious. Other than his flared nostrils and the tight grip he has on my ass, I wouldn't be able to tell he's enjoying it. He's holding on tight, breathing heavily.

"Fuck your hate out," I tell him.

"Shut the fuck up," he grumbles, but I hear the strain in his voice.

I hold him tighter around the neck, bringing my face down, pressing my lips to his.

He tries to resist, but the groan that rips through his body is proof enough that he's obsessed with the idea of this.

He can hate me all he wants right now, but by the end of this, he will love me again.

He will trust me.

He will be my king, and I will be his *reina*.

He snatches his mouth away, lifting me up high enough to remove his cock from my pussy.

He places me on my feet, twisting me around and forcing my face down on the table. He grips my hip with one hand, using his other to clutch and wrap my ponytail in his hand.

Each thrust fills me up.

Every plunge is powerful, and met with a swirl of my hips and a tight, hungry clench below.

"I want you to hate me," he growls, slamming his cock deep.

"No," I pant.

"You should be afraid of me, Gianna," he says through clenched teeth. "You have no idea how bad I want to choke the life out of you right now."

"I'm not afraid of you." After I say that, he pulls the band out of my hair and my ponytail falls, my hair curtaining my face.

"You are heaven and hell," he rasps. "Peace and chaos."

He holds my hips tight, and another hard groan rips through his chest. He's coming. Knowing that pleases every fiber in my body.

He stills inside me, his forehead dropping down on my spine.

He picks his head up and pulls out rapidly, as if realizing his body's betrayal. He zips himself up as I sit up. My shirt is a shredded mess, revealing my lacy nude bra. He looks me up and down, like he knows I'm a beautiful, dangerous mess and can't help being addicted to me. Like he hates me so much, but loves me all the same.

"You are not helping me. I have this handled." He gives me his back. "You came back for nothing. Waste of time."

I walk up to him, but don't touch him. "I'm helping you, Draco. Fuck Yessica. She doesn't scare me. We can take her down."

He walks away, shoulders hunched. I chase after him, clutching his wrist and spinning him around. "Draco!"

"Fuck off, Gianna! Just go back to where you were!"

"No!" I grip his arm tighter. "I'm not going back, Draco, and you can't make me! If you want me there, you'll have to drag me back yourself, but trust me, I will put up a fight this time."

His jaw pulses, brown eyes sweeping my body, trying to make me feel puny. Insignificant.

Screw that. It won't work. Maybe it did before, but not anymore.

"What the hell can you do that I can't?" he challenges, getting closer to my face.

"I can be myself," I answer. "Be what she's always wanted to be—*La Patrona*."

He tips his chin, studying my eyes. "She will kill you as soon as she sees you. All of Mexico is on the hunt for you."

"Then let them look. That doesn't scare me." I step, pressing a hand on his cheek, the pad of my forefinger running over his cheekbone. "Let me fight with you, Draco. You aren't alone anymore. Let someone you care about be there for you." I narrow my eyes as he does his. "I know you're thinking you have to get to her immediately, but you don't. Sit. Plan. Think things through. She will not make a fool out of you again, do you hear me? Not while I'm alive and breathing. You will get your revenge. She will pay for what she's done and so will Henry. You just have to be patient."

He pulls his eyes away, removing my hand and adjusting the collar of his shirt. He rakes rough fingers through his hair, sighing hard. He's agitated. I get it.

With stitched brows, he says, "If you die, it will not be on my conscious. You wanted this, not me, so fight all you fucking want, but you won't be doing me any favors. I don't need your goddamn help." He turns sideways, giving me one last look before storming away, right to the wide open entrance.

This time I don't chase after him.

He needs space.

He'll have it tonight, but tomorrow, I refuse to be ignored.

30

DRACO

I can't remember the last time I slept.

It's never been for longer than an hour or two. Tonight, I am completely restless. I can't even get comfortable in my bed knowing she's here, under the same roof.

I was weak out there.

So fucking weak for her.

But how the fuck was I supposed to resist her after all this time? It was only a few days that she was away, but it felt like an eternity.

Her skin on mine, after what felt like fucking years, was euphoric as hell.

This is why I didn't want her to come back. I'm only weak for her. I only buckle beneath her touch. Only she can do this to me—make me lose control of myself.

She owns way too much of my body, has claimed my fucking soul, and she knows it. She fucking knows it.

The night shifts into day, the sun creeping over the horizon. The house is mostly quiet, giving me time to think.

I spark a joint, standing on the balcony, inhaling deeply and letting it cloud my lungs.

I hear a door slide open and look up. From where I am, I can see

Gianna stepping onto her balcony, looking at the ocean. She inhales deeply, and then exhales, opening her eyes.

Her fingers push through her thick, wild curls. Those fucking highlights. I don't know why she did that to her hair. She was fine without them. Natural looks best on her, not that she isn't fucking sexy right now, wearing only a white robe, her hair damp like she's just gotten out of the shower.

Her eyes drop and she looks to her left, down at me. Our eyes latch, only for a brief moment. Her lips part like she wants to say something, but I frown and pull away, putting out my joint and walking back into my room.

I spend most of my time in the office, looking over maps, making calls, trying to get any fucking lead that I can. All of it is a fucking dead end. No one has seen or heard from Hernandez in days.

Just when I feel like giving the fuck up, Guillermo comes rushing into the office.

"Jefe," he pants, stopping on the opposite side of my desk.

"Yeah, Guillermo?"

"Nito said he saw a man in a wheelchair being pushed around in Lantía. No arms or legs. He thinks it's Henry Ricci." Just as he says that, Gianna steps into the office.

My jaw clenches when she asks, "When did you hear that?"

"Just got off the phone with him," Guillermo answers.

Gianna looks over at me. "We should go. It takes about an hour and a half to fly there, right? We might be able to catch him."

"You don't know why he's there. It could be a brief visit—a waste of time," I tell her, waving a dismissive hand.

"That doesn't matter. He's around. He can lead us to her. Tell the guy who saw him to keep an eye on Henry."

I look at Guillermo who is silently agreeing, his head doing a simple nod, like she's right. Of course she's fucking right. It's a quick flight, but I don't trust it.

It makes me skeptical. Why would Henry return to a city he was captured in? What game are he and Hernandez playing at?

"Load up. Get ready," I command, and my men take off in a flash.

Gianna comes closer and Patanza waits at the door, watching her. "I'm coming to help," Gianna insists.

"I told you I don't need your help."

"I don't care. I'm going anyway, and Clark is coming with us. He's resourceful."

I cock a brow, opening the top drawer of my desk and taking out a pistol and a carton of bullets to load it. "You trust Clark?"

She swallows hard. "I didn't at first, but now I do. He's had my back ever since we left, hasn't made me doubt him since."

"Emilio spoke to the security guard who had the DEA agents taken care of. Gonna tell me about that?"

"Yessica sent them after me."

I stop what I'm doing, frowning up at her.

"They came on her behalf. Ordered me to get off the jet when we were about to leave Colorado. I got off, and I just…blacked out. I shot them."

I don't give a fuck about any of that. "Wait—she knew where you were…

I feel my blood running cold now, my pulse picking up in speed. How the fuck is that even possible? I covered my tracks. I made sure she would never even find out I sent Gianna out of the country… unless the DEA was keeping tabs when she landed in Colorado. Found out about Big Jack. Found out where he lived and how close he and Lion were as siblings…

"Emilio has already let Clark call to tell Big Jack to pack up and move to the safe house until this is over," Gianna announces, her voice cutting through my thoughts.

I blow a breath, placing a hand on my hip. "Goddamn it, Gianna."

"What, Draco?"

"She could have found you there."

"Good thing I didn't stay then, right? She won't find me here."

"No one can be trusted. Don't you get that?"

She looks at the open window. "I'm here. You're here. If she tries to come for me, you and your men will be around. That's all that matters, right?"

I stare her down. She thinks she's so fucking smart. I can't stand it sometimes. "Patanza, get Gianna ready."

Patanza nods and turns, marching down the hallway, bobbing her head at Gianna before disappearing. Gianna gives me her back and walks to the door. Before she gets away, I call her name and she pauses, looking over her shoulder.

"You and your cousin will fly there with us, but only so I can keep an eye on you both. Try any shit, and I won't have a problem slicing your throats."

"Won't you?" she responds, and I swear I see a smirk tug at the corner of her lips before she walks away, her full hips swaying in the process.

When it's time to go, she walks downstairs in black cargo pants and a sleeveless, dark gray shirt. Her hair is pulled back into one single braid, her face clear of all makeup.

Even without it, she's still so goddamn flawless. I can't fucking stand it. Her bold green eyes are set on mine, sparkling from the sunlight streaming in through the skylight windows.

She walks down the stairs in calf-high black boots, and strapped around both her thighs are leather holsters, guns tucked away inside them. Around her waist is a leather belt, a smaller pistol inside the holster.

It takes everything in me to look away, not gawk like some fucking love-struck idiot.

I can't stare at her, no matter how badly I want to. I can't let her know I still want her. What happened last night was a fucking mistake. I shouldn't have fucked her. It made me look stupid and weak, and I can't afford to be that around her.

Not anymore.

When she's down the steps, I give a hard look at Patanza, whom I'm sure told Gianna what to wear and how to strap herself up. Patanza is just as loaded, if not more, with holsters, knives, and guns.

Clark trails behind them, pleased, I'm sure, to have his guns in his possession again.

It's only for now. I need all the men I can get. I don't know what I'm walking into going back to Lantía. If he's willing to sacrifice his own life by helping me, then fine, but just in case he pulls some bullshit, Patanza has her eye on him. She's my best shooter.

"We're ready," Gianna declares, and I lower my gaze to hers.

Turning my back and marching for the door, I tell them, "Let's go."

Guillermo pulls up to the curb with the van, and Sebastien hops out, pulling the back door open. I step aside, letting Patanza and Gianna in first.

Clark follows behind them, peering up at me on his way. Before he can get inside, I press a firm hand to his chest and grip his shoulder, stopping him. "Only reason you're alive right now is because your cousin wants you to be, but if I see you do anything shifty, I will end you."

His mouth twitches, eyes hardening as they hold mine. "Trust me, if I was stupid enough to stand against El Jefe with no backup, I might as well kill my fucking self. Fret not, kingpin." He claps my shoulder. "I've got your fucking back. You'll see." He jumps into the third row, right beside Patanza. Gia is on the second row, where I have to sit, and an exasperated sigh falls through my lips.

I climb in anyway, avoiding her eyes just as much as she avoids mine.

Sebastien is back in the driver's seat, and Guillermo puts pressure on the pedal, taking off.

The ride to the runway is quiet.

Everyone, I'm sure, is thinking, mentally preparing themselves to take action. Everyone is strapped with guns, loaded, prepared for the worst.

I feel Gianna look over at me, but I don't look her way. I keep my focus ahead, watching the road. In an hour and a half, Henry might be gone. But he won't get far. We'll track him.

"Make sure Nito sticks around the mansion. Tell him not to get too close," I tell Sebastien. He pulls out his phone and dials him, speaking in his native tongue when the line is answered.

"How long are you going to give me the silent treatment?" Gianna asks.

I look at her sideways before peering ahead again.

"It's getting old, Draco," she murmurs lowly, but I'm sure everyone in the car can hear her.

"No one asked you to come back."

"I wanted to," she says with venom in her tone.

"Shouldn't have."

"Don't act like you didn't want me back. I know you did. I can see it in your eyes."

"You spend less than two months with me and think you know everything about me." A dry laugh escapes me. "You are sadly mistaken. Now shut up before I send you back to the house."

Through the corner of my eye, I spot her fist clenching in her lap, edging to the strap on her leg where her knife is.

Her hand stops, and she groans, annoyed.

She knows better than to try me right now, but I'm a little amused that she considered it, however briefly.

We board the already running jet with haste, buckle in, and take flight in less than ten minutes. Gianna doesn't bother sitting next to me. Instead, she sits beside her cousin, and Patanza is seated across from him, keeping watch like the hawk she is.

After landing on my private airstrip, we load in another van and drive through Lantía, the city I have admired since I was a niño.

I grew up here during my teenage years. Back when my life was easy. I was always on the beach, always playing fútbol, living a careless life. But then my father got deeper into the business. Life became even more dangerous. We bounced from house to house like a game of ping-pong.

The threats started coming left and right. My freedom, as I knew it, was over. Just like that.

As we pass by one of the elementary schools, I remember the teacher my father had to take and beat down because he would constantly grip the back of my neck and leave bruises. He pulled me from public school and had me homeschooled that same month. To this day, I'm not sure if that was a wise choice for him.

My thoughts were always closeted. I had no one my age to talk to, besides Thiago, and I only saw him once a week.

Fuck.

Thiago.

Mi primo. My throat thickens, remembering his eyes that day. The blood. His words. He was a fool. He thought I didn't need him. He was wrong. We had our differences—I have differences with everyone— but he was family. The only family I had left, besides my mother.

I rub the back of my neck, looking out the window, at the children playing outside, some of their parents watching from the shade of their porches.

It doesn't take long to reach the path leading to my favorite mansion. If I thought the rides were quiet before, it's even quieter now. I don't hear a single breath, just the crunch and pops of the rocks beneath the tires.

The palm trees clear up and the home appears.

My home.

The creamy stucco was always my favorite, the roof a dark chocolate, offsetting the overall appearance. There are no lights on. The house looks completely vacant and dark inside. Every window is pitch black, the curtains drawn.

Guillermo pulls up to the front of the house and parks.

"No cars," Clark says, peering around. "Sure about that lead, man? Or are we wasting our time?"

"Yes, I'm fucking sure," Guillermo grumbles.

"Unlock the doors," I order. The doors unlock and I ease out, the bottoms of my boots crunching on gray and ivory pebbles. My eyes shift up to the open gate ahead. My men know never to leave my gates open. Someone has trespassed and may very well still be around. "Keep quiet. Don't shut the doors."

Gianna steps out of the car, leaving the door open for Clark to follow after her. Patanza comes out behind me, strapping her AK-47 around her. She looks up at me and then over at Gianna, who side-eyes me.

"Someone was here," Patanza murmurs, looking at the open gate. We get to the gate, and I look down when pebbles transition to sand. There are thin, straight tracks of a wheelchair, along with footsteps.

A noise sounds from a distance, a familiar one. The creak of my backyard bridge. Loud and rickety. Mamá has bugged me to get it fixed for years, but I kept it that way so no one could sneak to or from my house without me seeing them.

As a child, it would wake me up at night, and sometimes I'd see my father walking to the shed, going to handle business.

Gianna rushes ahead as soon as she looks up from the tracks and hears it.

"Gianna!" I snap in a low voice, but she ignores me, still running.

31

DRACO

"Shit!" Clark hisses. He takes off after her, and Patanza runs after them. I rush ahead, snatching the gun from my holster and hustling across the thick sand.

All I hear is the roar from the ocean and the howl of the wind as it whips against me. I see Gianna with one of her pistols in hand now, running through the sand, up the hill that leads past the shed.

What the fuck is she doing?

I gain some ground, running past Patanza and Clark, finally catching up to Gianna and gripping her shoulder. Yanking her around, I grip her face and force her eyes on mine. "What the fuck are you doing? Slow the fuck down before you end up killed!"

"No," she says through ragged breaths. "He's here. Let's settle the score." She snatches her body away from me and gives me her back, charging ahead again. Fuck. She never fucking listens.

"Both of you stay back. Patanza, tell Guillermo and Sebastien to keep watch up front. If you see anyone you don't know around here, you kill them."

Patanza bobs her head and takes off.

Clark throws his hands in the air. "Well hurry after her! She could be walking into a fucking death trap!"

My nostrils flare as I glare at him for a brief moment.

But he's right. He's fucking right.

She's being a reckless bitch, and she will die if she doesn't slow the fuck down. I turn, sprinting through the sand and jogging to the cement steps a few feet away from the brown bridge. Just as my feet hit the solid ground, I spot Gianna standing in the middle of the pathway.

"Gianna," I mumble, stepping up to her side, but she doesn't look at me. Her eyes are fixed on something else.

I look with her, and when I do, I can't believe what the fuck I'm seeing.

In my own backyard.

As clear as day.

A tall man with a straw cowboy hat is walking through my garden. He has on a plaid shirt, his hair pulled back into a slick, inky ponytail. He's tall. Lean. But not a fucking match for me. I could drop him in a second.

He isn't what surprises me either.

No. What surprises me most is the butchered man sitting in the wheelchair.

How he sits there, his back toward us, his dark hair shifting with the wind, barely touching the nape of his neck. He's looking down at something.

The man in the cowboy hat grips the handles of the wheelchair and starts to turn him in our direction, but I lift my gun and find my target, shooting him right through the fucking head before he can get the chance to see us.

I run up the hill, through my bed of flowers, as the no-armed motherfucker I had locked in my shed for over six months stares right up at me. His eyes are terrified, his face paling beneath the bold, golden sun.

My shadow hovers over him, and seeing him like this—alone, weak, and easy to kill—stirs something up inside me.

My blood boils, my fingers tightening around the gun.

This motherfucker is the reason I am here. He's the reason I lost Thiago. He got away and told that bitch *everything* he knew.

"Surprised to see me, *pinche cabron*?" I shove my gun into his cheek, and he breathes a little harder, dropping his eyes.

His head moves sideways, and when Gianna emerges from behind me, her pistol in the air and pointed at him too, he sighs.

"Just my fucking luck, huh?" He huffs a laugh, lowering his gaze to his lap.

"What the fuck are you doing here?" I ask through bared teeth.

"For all you know, I could be the bait for a trap." He smirks.

"For all you know, you could be dead within the next second," Gianna snaps back, breathing harder. "Where is she?"

"Oh, come on, Gianna. You know I'm not going to tell you that." He looks down at his lap again, and that's when I notice the skull.

Trigger Toni's skull. I see the initials from this angle.

My eyes shift over to Gianna, who is focused on the skull, too. Tears line the rims of her eyes, but she keeps her arm leveled and her gun steady.

"Why do you have that?" Her voice cracks with the demand.

"He was my cousin, Gia. Your *husband*—even if it was for less than thirty minutes. It's all that's left of him. I had to come and get it." He smiles sheepishly, looking at me again. "Your men? They talk a lot in that cell you had me locked in. It was my only entertainment, really— that and getting Gianna to trust me enough to eventually set me free. Toni always did say she was pretty damn gullible. I just didn't think, being Lion Nicotera's daughter and all, that she'd be that easy to fool. But I guess there's a reason he's dead now, too." He sighs, and Gianna nearly freezes up with the words he's spewing. "Anyway, your men mentioned you buried his skull in this garden, but not before going into great detail about what was done to him before it was buried. The finger cutting, eye gouging, head scalping, and teeth pulling. The *acid*."

I lower my gun and grip the collar of his shirt. "I don't have time for your fucking mind games." I growl. "Where the *fuck* is Hernandez?"

He shrugs. "I have no idea."

"I will find her. And when I do, I will make sure she feels every ounce of pain I deliver."

"What did she do exactly?" he asks, like he's truly curious. "For you to be so angry, I mean?" I see Gianna tense up through my peripheral. "So what, she killed your cousin. Is he enough reason to start a war? You killed my cousin, who was more important and more powerful than that piece of shit cousin of yours ever would have been. Trigger Toni was going to rule the fucking industry and then *you* came along and ruined everything—El fucking Jefe." He leans up, staring hard into my eyes. "You will go down burning with this stupid bitch at your side. And when you do, she will laugh. She will laugh her ass off and relish in her victory while sleeping naked on a bed made of money. After all, it's all she's ever wanted, besides power: for you to go down, for you to be forgotten. Forever."

The urge to grip his throat and crush it until he turns blue consumes me, but it's too late. Gianna steps beside his chair, points her gun to his temple, and shoots him. His blood splatters, some hitting my face. Most of it lands on my shirt and hand as his body slouches back in the wheelchair.

I blink hard and step back, brows furrowed, glaring up at her.

She grimaces down at his limp, bloody body, and then at the skull. Putting her gun back into the holster at her waist, she snatches the skull up and hurries through the garden to the double doors that lead to the basement.

She stomps down the steps, and I run after her, reaching the floor of the basement and watching as she rushes around, looking for something. She tosses the skull down on the floor and continues searching for something—I have no idea what—until she finds what she's after.

When she grabs the handle of a sledgehammer and lifts it up in the air, a shrill cry floods my eardrums. Her cry is louder than any noise I've ever heard come out of her, the hammer all the way in the air. It comes flying down with full force, crushing the skull into pieces. She does it again, and this time the hammer breaks the skull into many fragments.

Her breathing is wild, chest heaving, loose wisps of hair now hanging in front of her face. Her eyes are deranged, darker than I've seen them, and for a split second, they are foreign to me.

This isn't the girl who was terrified of me. The girl who looked like she wanted to jump a bridge and end her life while under my roof.

No.

This is a *woman*—a powerful woman who has finally found her strength. A woman who knows all about the dirty ways of this fucked up world and is tired of putting up with its shit.

"Fuck Henry," she pants, and the heavy end of the hammer hits the ground as she stands up straight. "And fuck *Trigger Toni*." Her eyes pull up to mine, still panting. She shifts sideways, swallowing thickly.

I want to tell her how stupid she is for doing what she just did—killing the only source that could have gotten us to Hernandez—but I don't, because she did exactly what I would have done.

She *killed* him.

And with no remorse in her eyes.

No fallen tears.

No regrets.

She pulls her gun out again and storms past me, rushing up the stairs.

Before I go, I look back at the shattered skull. The pieces of him. How he was whole before and had a little meaning, but now, he is nothing but a shattered, worthless pile of shit.

When I make it up the stairs, Gianna is digging through Henry's pockets. She fishes out his cellphone and his wallet.

"What the fuck happened?" Clark asks, trudging up the hill. When he makes it up to where we are, he looks down at Henry with a screwed up frown. Pointing at him, he says, "Whoa! What the fuck happened to him? He has no fucking limbs!"

I ignore his exclamation, focusing on Gianna again. She's scrolling through the cellphone now. Her eyes light up several seconds later, and she points at the screen.

"What did you find?" I ask.

"Someone just sent him a text, said they're on the way to get him. We have to go."

"Come on." I rush her way, yanking the cellphone out of her hand, sliding it into my back pocket, and then clutching her wrist, running down the hill and across the wooden bridge. Our feet drag in the sand with the weight of our boots, but I don't stop, not until we're all in the van, loaded up, and driving away from the house.

Guillermo takes the hidden dirt road I created for getaways. When we reach a safe distance, I release a sharp breath, pulling out the cellphone.

"There was something else. A message from her," Gianna murmurs without looking at me. "She told him to meet a carrier named David. Maybe we can call the number she messaged him from—distract her. Have your men track her location."

"My tech guys are in Sinaloa. We won't make it there fast enough, and it's way too dangerous for you there right now. They catch sight of you or Clark and they'll be onto us—they may even kill you on sight. Most of those men are not loyal to me there because they wish to *be* me. We'll have to ditch this phone soon."

"Shit," she hisses.

"Don't worry about it right now, reina. Her time will come. Trust me."

Her eyes hold mine, her teeth sinking into her bottom lip. "Reina," she says softly, but it sounds more like a moan than anything.

She is reina. Always has been, even during her stupidity.

She should know it—the power she possesses—and she shouldn't doubt it.

But I still need to keep my distance. Instead of giving her all my attention, I look down at the cellphone, retrieving mine and taking pictures of his previous locations.

Fucking idiot, using an iPhone like he was free of troubles. Once she finds out about Henry, she'll ditch the phone she's using. She'll be pissed, and I really don't give a fuck.

They thought it was over when they took my cousin from me. They thought they had the upper hand by gaining more territory.

Wrong.

This shit has just begun.

32

GIANNA

Halfway during the ride to the airport, Draco tosses Henry's phone out of the window.

After doing what I did, I expected to be trembling with paranoia. I expected myself to question what I'd just done—especially after crushing Toni's skull . . . but I haven't. Honestly, I don't think I ever will. I've changed. I realize that now.

I am not the woman who was kidnapped, tortured, and trapped in that shed. I am stronger. Smarter. *Colder.*

Power intrigues me. Death no longer affects me. The crown is so close to my fingertips—I feel like I can already feel the smooth gold and the precious jewels. Once we get rid of Hernandez and her crew, the crown will be mine. *Ours.*

We arrive at his villa in Puerto Vallarta again after a flight that was a little chattier coming back than when we left.

As soon as Guillermo parks, everyone climbs out of the car, I with a sense of triumph. I'm still pissed she wasn't there. We need to find her and get this over with already. Such a coward she is, hiding away.

I follow Draco's lead to the door. He retrieves a key from his pocket and sticks it into the lock, leading the way inside. I glance over my shoulder and Patanza is behind me, Clark only a step behind her, looking at her ass.

"Look away before I stab your eyes out, gringo." She rolls her eyes, entering the house.

Clark chuckles, but definitely doesn't stop his staring.

Draco walks into the living room, heading for a corner table set up with tequila. A heavy sigh escapes me, and as badly as I want to toss my body on the couch and rest, I don't bother. I need a shower. I need to think.

Draco pours himself a shot of the tequila, releasing a long sigh.

I start to walk to the stairs, to the bedroom I was staying in for the past four nights, but Draco calls my name, stopping me in my tracks.

I look over my shoulder at him. He's in front of the wide glass door now, shot glass in hand, ready to be taken in one smooth gulp.

"To my room," he commands without looking at me.

I could question it, but I don't.

His room means privacy.

All I can think about is how much we need it right now.

I turn and go up the stairs to my room for a change of clothes. I walk back down to his bedroom afterward, which is much nicer than mine, set up with a king-sized bed and draped with a Mexican-styled comforter and throw pillows to match. The headboard is wide and thick, and seems to be made of glass and wood.

The floor is made of copper Mexican tile, and there is a wrap-around terrace that overlooks the Pacific Ocean. A table is set up out there, topped with unlit candles and clean plates, merely for decoration.

There is a lighter on one of the nightstands and I pick it up, sparking six of the candles in the room.

I then walk to the terrace and let the wind sweep over me. It feels amazing. Too bad I can't fully enjoy these blissful moments. This paradise. I catch it when I can.

With a sigh, I turn around and walk to his bathroom, starting up the shower and scrubbing the blood off my body, the hot water soothing my sore muscles.

I scrub hard—so hard my skin starts to turn a light shade of red. I don't stop scrubbing until I hear a noise outside the bathroom.

I rinse and then grab a cotton robe, stepping onto the glossy tile floor and walking out to the bedroom.

Draco stands in front of the entryway of the balcony, his back to me. His hair is a mess—disheveled and wild. He's grown facial hair, which doesn't look bad on him at all.

I have never seen him like this. He always used to look so well put together. Clean, neat, and shaved. Now, it seems he couldn't care less. And maybe he doesn't. Maybe he's too focused and determined to worry about his appearance at the moment.

"Why did you kill him today?" he asks without looking back.

I study him for a split second. His breaths are steady. He doesn't seem hostile. When his head turns, eyes sparking and expecting an answer, I say, "He wasn't going to tell you anything useful. He kept his mouth shut for months because he was loyal to her."

"You don't know that."

"Draco, you had him tortured and dismembered, and he still didn't talk. Not once did he waver or crack. That's loyalty. He wanted to protect her until his dying breath. He loved her more than his own life."

He turns fully, looking me all over. Grabbing the hem of his shirt and tugging it over his head, he reveals his solid body. The beautiful ripples of his muscles glow from the candlelight, the curves and dips in his back impossible to look away from. He seems so soft, smooth, and perfect on the surface, but deep inside, he's a battered, broken-down beast with a thousand walls and a soul harder than steel.

After a brief silence, he says, "I know what you're trying to do, Gianna."

"What do you mean?"

"You're trying to gain my trust back. Believe me," he says, peering over his shoulder, "it'll take more than a few kills to gain that back. What you did was unforgivable."

I feel my throat tighten, my eyes shifting to the terrace. "How long?"

"How long what?" he asks, slightly irritated as he unbuttons his jeans.

"How long until you can trust me again?"

"Trust is not something I just hand out. I started to trust you, and you betrayed me. No matter what I feel, trusting you again won't come easy."

I don't know why that pains me so much to hear. My beating heart seems to slow in speed, the thumping a somber beat in my own ears as I study him.

Pulling my eyes away, I walk to the terrace, stepping out, the coolness of the cement kissing the bottoms of my feet.

I grip the rail and stare ahead at the ocean. The moon is perched at the end of the dark horizon, the milky light rippling with the calm waves.

Heat presses against my backside seconds later, and a strong arm closes around me. His mouth presses on the back of my neck, and he gives me a soft, simple kiss. Warm. Slightly damp. Enough to send a gush of heat tunneling through my entire body, pinging me right in the core.

"Like I said," he whispers, dragging his lips up to the back of my ear. "I want to hate you just as much as I want to love you right now. Nothing about that has changed."

"I don't know what else to do to get you to trust me, Draco." I turn in his arms, meeting his brown gaze. "I'm here with you. I came back; I found you." I press a palm to his chest and push a little to get a deeper look into his eyes.

"Forcing it won't make it any better." He tips my chin when I start to drop my gaze. "But what you did today made me proud."

A smile tingles the edges of my lips. "Me killing someone made you proud?"

"You did it for me."

"And I would do it again."

His face turns serious. He lifts his head, looking over me, at the ocean. "When we find her, she is mine to kill."

I nod, twisting to look at the moon. "I know." I sigh. "I would say

I'm sorry again, but like you said, apologies are useless. They don't help anything."

"That's right," he responds, voice husky, deep.

"I missed you," I whisper.

The pads of his fingers tickle the curve of my neck, his lips on top of my head. "How can you miss a man like me?" he asks in my hair, his fingers pressing into my skin. "After all that has happened to you because of me...*how?*"

That's a good question—one I constantly have to ask myself. I have no idea why I missed him. I should have left this world and never looked back.

Meeting Draco Molina changed my life drastically, and I really am not sure if it was for the better or for the worse. My life was once so simple, so stable, but now, at every turn, there is someone or something lurking. Someone will always be out for me. To the world, I will always be a target, because he loves me, and if anything ever happens to me, he will let it be known how important I was to him.

"I can't deny what I feel," I finally say. "We met before, as kids. Maybe it was fate. Maybe it was meant to happen this way." I pause, shifting on my feet. "Maybe you aren't a monster to me. Maybe you are my hero instead."

He breathes harder, and I hear the small groan bubbling in his chest. "I am far from a hero, Gianna. I am still the villain. You may see the good, but I am not a good man. The people have seen the damage I've done. They know it's me against the world. To them, I will never be a hero. To them, I will forever be the devil in expensive suits. A lot of innocent people have died because of me—because of what Yessica did to Thiago. And a lot more will probably die soon."

"We have to do what we have to do."

"Many months ago, you wouldn't have been saying this." He raises a brow.

"Things change."

His eyes drop to my cleavage. I almost forget I'm standing in only a robe. He runs his tongue over his lips, eyeing me briefly before focusing on my bosom again. Grabbing the loosely tied rope around my waist, he tugs on it, causing it to fall.

My robe falls open, but I don't waver. I don't cower or cover myself up. He takes a step back to absorb what he sees, and I stand there, letting him take it all in.

"Some things may have changed," he rasps, "but there is one thing that hasn't." He steps closer, cupping a large hand around the back of my neck and applying pressure to make my chin tilt.

"What's that?" I ask when his lips barely touch mine.

"Your body is still the same. Especially your pussy. Tight and so fucking wet."

I clench with need as he runs a palm over my hip, swiveling it around and sinking it between my legs. His middle finger presses into me, applying gentle pressure to my clit when he's found it. His eyes are locked on mine, lips parted, breathing deep and heavy.

"Do you want me to fuck you?" he asks, voice a near growl.

"Yes," I whimper when he slowly massages my clit with the pad of his finger.

"Beg me."

"You know I don't like to beg."

"Then you don't want me to fuck you."

I stare into his hard eyes, trying to challenge his statement, but I feel so weak. So vulnerable. So ready.

He stares right back, and before I know it, his finger is absent. He picks me up, forcing my legs around him and walking inside again.

Tossing me on the bed, he flips me over, bringing my ass up in the air. His belt buckle jingles, and when I look to my left, at the oversized mirror that gives full view of our reflection, I watch as he folds the leather belt in half and brings his arm in the air.

A sharp sting bites my ass, and I let out a soft cry.

"Beg," he demands.

I clutch the sheets, pressing my cheek to the comforter, studying him at this angle. He looks so hostile and angry, but still so wickedly delicious. The candlelight flickers, revealing his pulsing jaw.

He's still upset with me. I can see it—feel the quiet rage radiating off his already hot skin.

He grabs my ass with one large hand, lifting the folded belt in the air again.

"I won't ask again, Gianna," he growls.

"Please," I finally whisper, giving into his demand.

He tosses the belt aside, slowly unbuttoning and unzipping his pants. Through the mirror, I see his pants and then the briefs come down, his hard, thick cock appearing.

He fists himself and pumps with ease, using his other hand to grip my waist. He moves forward, barely an inch, his thick, heavy cock still in hand, and slides the head of it through my slit and up to my clit. He does it over and over and over again, making me writhe, ache—*need* so much more of him.

"Beg again," he groans.

My mind is spiraling now, my body overheated. Seeing him like this, how he stares down at me like he wants to own and dominate every inch of me, leaves me no choice but to beg.

I breathe raggedly, my damp hair falling over my face. His cock slides back and forth, toying with my clit. He barely dips the head into my entrance. He does it just so I can feel it—know he's there. Teasing me until I break.

"*Está panochita está bien mojada*," he groans, squeezing his eyes shut. *This little pussy is so wet.*

I breathe my pleasure, loving the way his native language rolls of his tongue.

"Say more," I beg. "In Spanish."

"*Ruégame*," he demands with bite in his tone. *Beg me.*

"Please," I beg again.

He lets out a sharp, stilled breath, still gripping his cock, lightly pumping. His other hand rides up my spine and clutches the back of my neck. The head of his cock presses on my entrance, and finally, he sinks into me, tightening his grip on my neck with each inch inside.

Nothing about this is gentle.

None of it is sweet or nice.

He holds the back of my neck so tight, I'm sure it will leave a bruise.

This is dangerous and angry. He's still not done hate-fucking me yet, and frankly, I don't care.

His hips thrust forward, and he slams into me, forcing my face down on the comforter, making my back arch.

"Ruégame," he commands again through clenched teeth. *"Ahora, niñita."* Now, little girl.

"Cojeme más fuerte, Jefe," I beg, my breaths rapid now. *Fuck me harder, Jefe.*

I throw my hair over my shoulder, but he catches it, pulling on it like one would the reins of a horse. His lips come closer to my ear. "Again," he groans, pulling out, making me ache all over again, more now.

"Fuck me, please," I sigh, plead.

And he has no problem doing so. He flips me onto my back, spreading my legs wider apart. His cock is buried inside me again in no time, and he folds my legs, clutching my hips as he stands in front of the edge of the bed. He lifts me up, angling my pussy just right, and as he holds me tight, he slams into me again.

Over, and over, and over again.

He watches me with fierce, wicked eyes, not once wavering. Not once does he pull his searing gaze away from me.

He wants me to know that he owns me—mind, body, and soul. He wants the whole fucking world to know I belong to him.

Him and only him.

He bends over, his mouth coming to one of my nipples, and he sucks it into his mouth until it's supple and pebbled, his hips still grinding. With the sensational tug of my nipples, and his cock hitting my most tender spot, I can't help what happens next.

My thighs shake around his waist, my eyes rolling backward. It's too much. He's too much. Too amazing. So fucking good.

God, I come. I come so hard around his delicious cock.

I hold him tight, my fingernails sinking into his skin as a hard moan rips right through me. He groans from the pierce of my nails, but he doesn't stop moving. "You are squirting all over my cock, niñita," he says in my ear, voice deep and raspy. So sexy. So bad.

He curses beneath his breath as his strokes become unsteady, a hand sliding down to hitch my knee up to my chest, plunging deeper, gripping the meat of my ass as he pounds away. Before I come down from the high of my orgasm, he's pulling out and sliding down, his mouth hovering over my pussy.

I look down and his eyes are trained on mine. He seals his mouth around my clit first and then slides his hot, smooth tongue down and around, licking up every drop.

My fingernails sink into the comforter, my back bowing. I beg him, "...please...*please*, Draco." It's too much. Too powerful. I feel like I'm going to explode and shatter by a million tiny orgasms.

But of course he doesn't let up. He eats me hungrily, sucking and licking my pussy, taking it all in, until I squeal so loudly I'm sure everyone can hear it.

It's impossible for my body to die down, especially when he's deep inside me again, his mouth claiming mine. I taste myself on him. My body is writhing beneath his.

His hand cups the back of my neck, and he presses my forehead to his shoulder, our bodies completely molded. Becoming one. Merging. Syncing. His other hand is on my hip, and as my orgasm continues shooting through me, his body stills, his head turning to look down at me.

I sink my teeth into his bottom lip before releasing it, holding on tight to him, his savage groan vibrating on my bosom.

His hips work hard with each spurt of release. When he finally collapses, I twitch and clench my walls around his satisfied cock, breathing way too hard. My hair is slick with sweat, as well as my body.

I don't know what the hell that was or how it happened so quickly. I don't know how he knows my body so well or how he did this to me —how he *always* does this to me—but it was exactly what I needed.

His hate and his passion: a mix of the two always leaves me craving more.

"*Eres toda mía, Gianna. Para siempre.*" *You are all mine, Gianna. Forever.*

I release my last sigh, shutting my eyes, and giving him a simple nod. "I'm all yours, Draco, for as long as you'll have me."

33

GIANNA

"I know what last Thursday was," I whisper on his chest. We lay in the bed, our legs tangled up, my ear on his chest.

I was about to leave the room after he fucked his hatred away—figured he still needed space from me—but he told me to stay. Now, here we are, breaths mingling, my fingers playing their own piano game on his ribcage to the Latin music coming out of the hidden speakers.

I can't say I'm not enjoying this. Surprisingly, I've missed this. Probably too much.

"What was last Thursday?" His voice is raspy, warm, as it flows through my hair.

"August 22nd. Your 31st birthday."

"You remembered." It's a statement, not a question.

"After that tragic birthday breakfast story you told me, it's impossible to forget that date."

"Hmm." His chuckle rumbles in his chest.

"How will you celebrate?"

"By killing Yessica."

I look up into his eyes. When I see them, I realize how serious he is. I sit up on an elbow. "You need to do something, Draco. Drink, breathe, relax—something."

"I'll do all of that after I handle what needs to be done." His lips press for a moment. "A man like me can never truly relax. I will always want to be wanted, taken down. Killed."

I sigh, feeling my chest squeeze tighter. "Promise me something?"

"What?"

"Promise me that when we find her and end this, we'll take some time off alone to celebrate properly—your birthday, and getting rid of her."

He smirks, the candlelight making him seem calmer, kinder.

"Maybe, niñita."

I stroke the hair on his chin, letting the silence sweep over us, thinking for a moment. "Those flowers," I murmur. "Death by Indigo. What if I hadn't read the note before getting close to them?"

"Then you would have died," he says, almost nonchalantly, but his grip tightens around me.

"How do you know about those? Are they in a garden somewhere too?"

"No. Those are too risky for any of my men to be around. I had them imported."

"Why'd you send them to me?"

He's quiet for a second, mulling it over. "I wanted you to see that even beneath their beauty, they are still deadly. Much deadlier than the Blue Betrayals." He pauses again. "I had to research the Indigos once."

"When?"

"Few years back."

"Why?"

"They were delivered to me personally. They were beautiful, but beauty can be deceiving as fuck." He swallows hard, adjusting his head, eyes focused on something across the room. "I never keep them out in the open. Only use them to intimidate. If you touch even a petal, and any of its gloss gets on your fingers, it can cripple those fingers, make them numb. But if you bring those same fingers to your mouth, say, after eating, and ingest it, your entire body will freeze up on you. Not right away, no, but every single part of you will turn black inside after only an hour. It will paralyze you to the core, but you can still feel and see everything. Death by Indigo." He blows a heavy breath. "What makes them so fascinating is that beneath the beauty, there is poison. And that poison makes it one of the most powerful, most vicious plants on this earth. Poison ivy doesn't have shit on them."

That makes me laugh, just a little.

He continues. "They are banned in the United States and even here, in Mexico. They can only be bought on the black market." He pauses. "When I first saw them, they were a gift from a woman I didn't know. It only took a few hours for me to learn she was the mother of a man I had ordered to be killed. So, before letting the delivery into my factory, I did my research. Found out all about them.

"And just as I found out all I could about them, the guard that delivered them dropped the vase, couldn't even move. Couldn't speak or respond to me as he laid there on the floor, but I could tell he was trying. It was so rapid—so swift. He seemed perfectly fine one minute, but in the short span of thirty minutes, his lips were shriveled and blue, his skin pale and chalky. His eyes, blood shot red. She was trying to kill me. So…" He sighs, like shards of glass are trapped in his lungs now. "I killed her."

I look up at him, but his eyes are still ahead, focused on anything but me. "She was a threat, and I'm certain she would have tried again if I'd shown her mercy. It's like she wanted me to know it was her. She didn't try to hide it. It was almost like she wanted me to kill her."

"Wow." I drop my head, focusing on the crucifix resting on his chest.

"I am not proud of the things I have to do, Gianna. It does not please me to kill women. Children are my weakness. No harm has ever been inflicted on a child because of me. Ever. Even during this war, I do my best to make sure there are none around before taking action. But sometimes...I can't help it. Sometimes, it just happens, and there is nothing I can do about it."

We're both quiet for a minute, absorbing the story, letting it sink in.

"You know if we do this," he says, shifting sideways, "we'll be making even more enemies. We are exposing ourselves. More people will die, and our lives will really be at risk. One of us might *die*, Gianna."

His words should intimidate me. They should make my heart leap and then pound down on my ribcage. They should terrify me, send me running... but for some reason, they don't. My heart hardly reacts.

"Well, if I die, it'll be a sacrifice I'm willing make." I turn and press my body to his, meshing, wrapping my arm over his shoulder. "I don't have much else to live for, Draco. Clark doesn't need me. He's been doing this on his own for years. The only person who needs me, whether he knows it or not, is Draco 'The Jefe' Molina." His eyes shimmer from the flickering light. "I'm not backing down, and I'm not afraid to die." I kiss him. Soft. Sweet. "I'm here, by your side. Let's get back to the throne *together*."

I don't think I've ever seen the spark in his eye that he has now. Not ever before.

Beneath that spark lies determination, passion, ferocity, and my favorite of all, *power*.

A growl rides through his throat, and before I can process it, he's between my legs again, consuming me with a kiss. Before it can register to my brain, he's fully inside me, stroking softly. Not rough.

No hate.

No anger.

It's gentle.

Sweet.

Sexy.

Perfection.

My moans ignite as he shudders, his cock pulsing inside me, lips on my neck, gripping me tight. My fingernails skate down his muscled back, digging into his hips, needing him to go deeper.

"It is *our* throne now," he whispers in my ear, and then he stills, coming for the third time tonight, groaning softly in my ear like it's the best thing he's ever felt. "And I'm glad you know it, reina."

34

DRACO

She's lying beside me the next morning, her brown hair stretched out on the white pillow, wisps of it over her face.

I push the gold strands of hair away from her face, watching her breathe. Sigh. Moan in her sleep. Her skin is a soft shade of tan, the sunlight sweeping over her naked body with each inch spilling over the horizon.

My skin is much darker in comparison to hers, my hands appearing too rough to touch someone who still seems so delicate. I lay my hand on her shoulder, my palm sliding down her arm, dipping into the curve that leads to her hip.

I wish I could say I hate her.

I wish I could just walk away.

I don't know when I became so fucking weak for this woman.

I shouldn't fucking love her this much—I shouldn't care.

Love is a fucking weakness.

Useless. Futile.

I will go to war for my business, for my deceased cousin—for my father's name, and my mother's freedom. I will set fire to anyone who disrespects me by letting him or her know who the king is...and she wants to do the same.

But if she dies...

If I lose her...

A sigh escapes me as I roll onto my back, staring up at the ceiling fan. It's the crack of dawn, a light breeze making the curtains flap. The breeze drifts over my sweat-dampened skin.

Sleeping didn't happen last night. It didn't matter how completely satisfied my body was due to having her precious pussy wrapped around me, I still couldn't close my eyes.

Too many thoughts are running through my mind. Too much I want to do, but can't just yet. Not until the time is right. Not until I find that spiteful bitch and choke the life right out of her.

Gianna sighs, and I look over at her, just as she twitches in her sleep and groans, brows stitching. She has nightmares. I know it. I have them myself. They're a grueling package deal that comes with wanting to be one of the most powerful, most dangerous people on earth.

I should send her away again, but she'll only come running back.

Like a moth to a flame, she won't be able to stay away from me.

And the truth is, I can't stay away from her, either. It's so fucking selfish of me. Instead of wanting her gone—back where it's safe—I'd rather keep her here, around me. Letting her risk her life for mine. Risk it all for me.

Now, I see that I am not only fighting my own battle—I am fighting hers too.

She deserves happiness. Deserves to be free. She deserves to win, for once, get everything she's ever wanted. And as soon as this is all over, she will.

I will give her the fucking world.

I will give her my all.

She will be happy.

Finally.

35

GIANNA

His side of the bed is empty when I awake. It's not too cold, so maybe he just left.

Running a hand over my face, I toss the sheets away and press my feet on the tile floor, making way for the bathroom. I take a quick shower and get dressed in white shorts and a loosely knitted summer sweater that hangs off the shoulder.

I walk to the patio door, drawing it open and stepping onto the balcony. The warm breeze runs over my damp scalp, so soothing. It's not too hot yet. The sun isn't fully in the sky, but something tells me that when it is, the day will blaze away.

I have another splitting headache, and I'm still so damn exhausted, even after a pretty decent night's sleep, but I won't let it stop me from enjoying this day. Enjoying what we have for now.

There are things he and I have to discuss. Last night was like a dream—I never wanted it to end. It made me think of the future. It made me think about us.

I walk out of the bedroom and down the hallway, smelling syrup, cinnamon, and one of my salty favorites—bacon. As I step around the corner, past the bar and kitchen, I enter the dining area, and the table is filled to capacity—all but one seat that is right beside Draco's, who sits at the head of the table.

I'm surprised to see Mrs. Molina is sitting with everyone. Her eyes barely linger on mine when she sees me. She drops her gaze and continues eating, putting her focus on her plate.

Clark is sitting beside Patanza, and Mrs. Molina beside Draco. Emilio has clearly pulled a chair up from the pool; it's wedged between Mrs. Molina and Draco.

All eyes shift to me when I enter—all eyes but Mrs. Molina's.

"Do you always sleep in late?" Clark asks, looking me over. "Early bird catches the worm, and all that other shit. Gotta stay on top, cousin." His forehead creases as he puts his focus on me. "You good?" He gives Draco a glance, like he'll lunge at him if he has to.

I smile. "I'm good, Clark. Just need some coffee to wake me up."

Draco lowers his newspaper to look at me, running his eyes from head to toe. "Come, Gianna. Sit."

A soft smile pulls at the corners of my lips as I walk behind the chairs, taking the empty one between him and Clark.

"Eat, reina," he murmurs, and I don't hesitate. I pile bacon and fruit onto my plate, but then my eyes land on the pancakes.

Pancakes? I quirk a brow, looking his way just as he looks at me.

"I had a taste for them," he says, and there is nothing more. No need for him to go into the back story, or how he's most likely trying to overcome his awful, bloody past.

I huff a laugh, biting into my bacon. Emilio fills my empty mug with coffee, and I thank him. He gives me a solid nod, but his eyes linger on mine longer than they should. I pull away, digging into my breakfast.

Forks scrape on china and lips smack as everyone devours their meals. For the most part, we are quiet, but the quiet doesn't bother any of us. It's...peaceful.

If only for now.

Draco clears his throat after taking a few hard gulps of his coffee. "There is something I need to say—and I will only say this once, and never again. I've already spoken to Emilio about it, so I'll tell you all in English, so you can understand."

Patanza straightens her back, giving him her undivided attention. I'm surprised she's even eating breakfast with us. She normally doesn't—would rather patrol and protect than waste time eating.

Clark lowers his glass of orange juice, and Emilio lowers his fork, still chewing. Mrs. Molina meets her son's eyes for a brief moment and then drops them down to mine. I start to look away, knowing she's probably still angry with me, but I catch a glimpse of something in her eyes.

Something I can't quite explain.

Like she's still wary of me, but still cares. Like she's accepting my silent apologies with her eyes, without uttering a word.

Draco's voice fills the room again, pulling my focus to him. "Everyone at this table has a purpose," he starts. "Every single one of you are important to me in some way." He looks at Clark. "You are important to Gianna, which makes you an important asset to me."

Clark smirks, slouching back in his chair, like he's proud of the status he's accomplished with The Jefe in such a short amount of time.

"I know I have been restless. I know I have done things—unspeakable things—that may or may not let you sleep at night. I know I have been working you all hard—harder than ever before. But out there," he says, holding a finger up and pointing, "is a threat that needs to be taken care of. And you all know that I will not rest until we find her. I will not rest until I see the breath leave her body. I don't care about the territory she's trying to take. That's nothing—land I can easily get back with a snap of my fingers. Right now, I'm letting her relish in it, but that will be mine again once this is all over."

He drops his hand, clenching his fist on top of the table. He shuts his eyes and starts to seethe like a wild bull. I drop my hand on top of his forearm, and he glances down at me, steadying his breaths, shutting his eyes briefly before opening them again.

"She took someone important from me—from us. He was important to many of us around this table. He left an impact, especially on me. Yes, he frustrated me constantly. Yes, he tested my boundaries—my limits…but that is what I loved about my cousin. I loved that he pushed me—drove me to do the things I needed to do. I loved that he tested me, because in this world, there is never a moment where I will not be tested. Whether he knew it or not, he was keeping me on my toes. He was keeping my power at its highest. He was doing all that he could, not only for himself, but for me to stay afloat as well." He drops his head, some of his raven hair tumbling onto his forehead.

"We will find Hernandez and trust me, I will make her pay. But if you're sitting at this table, it means I trust you in some way. And I am telling you now to accept who I am and how I do things, because it will only get worse from here. Things will only get dirtier until I win. I am not a man who begs, but right now, I am asking that you keep fighting with me. Keep going. We will get her. That is my word."

Silence consumes each and every one of us. I don't know how his words, even though they're still brutal and gritty, are so powerful. I don't know how he expects us to react after hearing that.

But, I do what I can. *Say*, what I can.

"I will always fight with you," I whisper, grabbing his hand on top of the table and squeezing it. "Always, Jefe."

"Sí, Jefe," Patanza adds. *"Siempre."*

"Always, hijo," Mrs. Molina adds softly.

Clark clears his throat, holding his half-empty glass in the air. "As long as I come out of this on top too, I will be by your side, Jefe."

"Good," Draco murmurs. He squeezes my hand in return, sighing. "Finish your breakfast and then go pack lightly. I have a few calls to make, but as soon as I'm done, we will be on our way to Acapulco."

"Acapulco?" Clark asks as Draco pushes back in his chair and stands.

"A lead was found by one of my tech men when I sent her the numbers and locations from Henry's phone. Her voice was caught on a satellite phone. Location says she's stationed somewhere in Acapulco."

With those words, no one is finishing breakfast. We all push out of our chairs, ready to start packing—ready for this to be over with already.

"I'll help you pack," Patanza murmurs to me.

Draco, Clark, and Emilio are already out of the dining room. Mrs. Molina remains in her chair, and I look back at her. She speaks before I can get away.

"Emilio told me what he did for you two nights ago," she says, her voice low.

I stop at the opening that leads to the hallway, turning to face her. My chin falls, words trying to escape, but I don't say anything.

"When?" she asks.

"When what?" I murmur.

"You know what I'm asking."

I press my lips, giving her the only answer I can. "Soon."

She sighs, pushing back in her seat, stacking the plates beside her. "I am too old to hold onto grudges, Gia. I've gone through my fair share of mistakes. You didn't trust him then, but you trust him now, don't you?"

"Yes," I answer.

"Good. Because he needs you right now. And that's something he'll never admit out loud." She looks me over, her eyes tense, focused. "Protect him and yourself. I want to see you both when it's all over."

I give her a light nod and nothing more.

"Come on, let's get your stuff packed," Patanza says over my shoulder. She takes off, her boots crunching on the tile as she drifts down the hallway and toward the bedroom. Before I can get around the corner, Mrs. Molina calls my name again.

"Yes?" I answer when she steps closer.

"Make sure you don't let him down again," she says. "Or it will be my wrath you have to face the next time. Not his."

She says it, and I know she means it. Her face is stale, but still soft somehow. Her eyes edgy, bordering on dangerous.

She may seem like a sweet, innocent woman, but I'm more than positive Mrs. Molina has gotten her hands dirty in the past.

Being with men like Draco, it changes you. You're forced to defend yourself. Your hands are dirtied up the instant you take interest in a Molina, but as soon as you fall for one, it takes no time at all for the same hands to be smeared with someone else's blood.

36

GIANNA

I thought we'd never fucking land.

When the wheels of the jet finally come to a stop, we all gear up, leaving the jet's cabin, the soles of our shoes clinging to the black asphalt as a wave of sticky heat wraps around us, a taste of salt in the air, stinging my dry lips.

I gather my hair up, wrapping it into a tight bun, watching as Emilio leads the way to a silver SUV. He hustles to the driver side and bends down, patting the front tire until he comes across a key fob taped to it. He then unlocks the doors and we all get into the vehicle, not even bothering to buckle in.

"Where is he now?" Draco asks, pointing his gaze to the left, at Patanza.

"Still at the old factory," Patanza answers.

Draco sighs, reaching down and pulling a gun from the holster strapped around his ankle. It's a silver pistol. He wipes it clean, studies it for several seconds, and then hands it over to me.

I frown at it before meeting his brown eyes.

"Can never have too many," he says, and I take it, looking it over. I run my thumb over the handle, but when I flip it over, that's when I see the stamp.

My breath falters, my thumb pressing into it. A lion with its mouth wide open, giving a silent roar with a wild mane around its large head.

Beneath it are the initials L.N.

Lion Nicotera.

I peer up at him, eyes burning, but he's already focused on me. "First gun your father ever gave to me. He sent me back home on a private jet with this, after Trigger Toni murdered my father. Told me to never let it out of my sight during my travels home. I clung to this gun like my life depended on it. Even when I got home, I kept it under my mattress for months. I still, to this day, have never used a bullet in this gun. I never wanted to, and maybe it's a good thing. They're your bullets now. Father to daughter."

I swallow hard, feeling like sand is trapped in my throat. I don't even know what to say.

He leans in, grabbing my chin between his thumb and forefinger. "Never hesitate," he says softly. "Just do."

We park in front of a factory that many would probably never give a second look. It's not big at all, made of what looks like old tin and wood. The windows are grimy and broken, and the area reeks of urine and vomit.

There are shacks not too far away. It's so dark inside them, I can't tell if they're occupied or vacant.

Draco walks ahead, and we all follow his lead. Emilio catches up to him, drawing his gun and then pulling open the raggedy, creaking door.

Draco already has a black pistol in hand. He steps right through them and looks around, until his eyes catch something.

I follow after him as he walks to a splintered door and pushes it open.

"Jefe!" someone shouts.

I follow him inside the room with Daddy's pistol in hand, and see a short, bald Caucasian man standing in front of five different computer screens. He wears glasses as thick as microscopes, has a salt-and-pepper moustache, and is wearing a plaid blue and white button down shirt. His khakis are dirty, like he fell recently and tried to dust himself off. He has a clumsy, geeky look about him.

His eyes shift over to mine when Draco bobs his head, and they expand into saucers.

"Oh!" He covers his mouth, looking between Draco and me. "This is—this is *her*!"

Draco's lips press. "It is."

"La Patrona," he sighs, like the name is a fantasy to him. "I have heard a lot of things about you. It's great to finally put a face to the name—and a pretty one, at that."

I smile.

"Good or bad things?" Clark asks, stepping up beside me and folding his arms.

The man shrugs and bluntly says, "A mix of both—which isn't necessarily a bad thing."

"What do you have for us, Allen?" Draco takes a step around him to look at one of the computer screens.

"Oh— you are in luck, Jefe." Allen sits in the chair and starts clicking away at one of the keyboards. "I've been tracking the phone number you sent me yesterday. It's a satellite phone. She's been using it ever since I called you a few hours ago about her location. She's been making calls every two to three hours, some to the same people. Her conversations aren't very clear anymore, and I also think she's left Acapulco."

"Where is she now?" Draco stands up, spine stacking.

"Sinaloa," the computer tech sings, typing something in. As soon as he does, he points at the screen. "See that flashing red dot? That's her location. Right now she's on a call."

"Can you listen in on it?" Draco asks.

"I can try." Allen taps a few keys, and then her staticky voice fills the room. The mere sound of it is like nails on a chalkboard, making the hairs on my spine stand up.

"It may be a little hard to hear at first," Allen murmurs, twisting a knob for the volume and then typing again. "I'll try and clear it up."

"Of course," Hernandez says. "My men will be there soon, depending on how my next shipment is handled with my new territory...Well speak to my men...I don't have time to meet up for this deal...Ugh. Fine. Since you leave me no choice. Respect is respect after all, and I need you to trust me." After several seconds, she scoffs. "El Jefe?" She then laughs. "I know he's looking for me. He's not going to find me. Right now, he's probably trying to figure out how to win his territory back without being seen...Trust me, he won't do a damn thing... once I do what I need to do, no one will give a damn about El Jefe. No one will respect a man who gave his position of power to a woman... No need to be afraid. Forget about him, okay? I was told we could work well together...I hope I won't regret it...Good. I'll have my men take care of him once this is all over, and you'll only have to deal with me from now on. You just worry about getting me the coke and the boat for clearance, okay?"

That. Bitch.

She thinks she's so smart—so bold and confident and invincible. If Draco hadn't already called dibs, I'd kill her my goddamn self.

Draco clenches his gun tight, fisting it until his knuckles turn white. His jaw is pulsing rapidly, eyes a shade darker as he stares at the screen.

"How long can you keep track of her?" he asks through clenched teeth.

"As long as she has that phone and continues making calls, I'll receive waves of it. If she ditches it then I'm not sure," Allen says.

"She'll most likely ditch it by the end of the day," Draco grumbles. "Like she said before, she learned from the best." Draco steps around the desk and looks at Patanza. "We need to figure out who the cocaine is coming from and who she's meeting for it."

"How, Jefe? She didn't mention a location. We don't even know who she was talking to," Patanza tells him. "Most of the men in the territories she took have boats and marinas. We can go through all of them, but it's going to be impossible to get to her on time if we sift through every single person you gave her access to. By that time she'll have everything she needs."

Draco breathes hard through his nostrils, turning his back to her and looking at one of the computer screens again, his hand on his hip now.

"She was talking to someone who seemed concerned or afraid," I mention. "Or maybe worried about you?"

"They're all fucking afraid of him," Clark gripes before pulling out a cigarette and sparking it.

"No, but this person seemed like he didn't want to do it and was only going through with it because you gave her the territory—like he is still hesitant and would gladly pass up the opportunity out of respect for you. Any of your suppliers still that loyal? Loyal enough to be worried about you?"

Draco peers over his shoulder at me, head shaking.

Patanza frowns a bit, like she has a clue, and right before she speaks, her cellphone rings. She snatches it out of her back pocket and looks at the screen. Draco turns fully to face her when she answers the phone.

"Who is it?" he asks.

When she looks up, her eyes are round and wide, and she murmurs a name I have never heard before.

"Ruben."

37

DRACO

Ruben Andrés.

A friend from private school who grew up with rich, part-time parents, anger problems, and always picked fights. Despite it all, he was a fucking bulldog and always had my back before I was homeschooled.

He's one of my biggest suppliers and transporters—always cutting deals for me, showing up for me. He's always been loyal, even though there are times when he has annoyed the fuck out of me by showing up late for certain drop-offs and pick-ups.

It has never mattered, though. He always shows. He never disappears, and every sprinkle of coke ever weighed is exact when imported and delivered to me.

Giving Ruben up to Hernandez was one of the hardest things I've ever done. His territory—his boats—play a huge role in my cartel.

I didn't think she'd go for Ruben so quickly, knowing the type of relationship he and I have. Either she's that fucking dumb, or thinks I'm too stupid to figure it all out and take action. She thinks she's doing this under my nose.

She's the stupid one.

I know exactly where he schedules his drop-offs and where he docks his boats for imports.

He's always respected me, just as much as I've respected him. I have other loyal men, men who fear me, but not as much as Ruben. Ruben both fears and respects me. I know working with her doesn't sit well with him, which is why he's just called Patanza.

One phone call, and he's already setting it up for me.

He will drop everything so I can do what I need to do.

Bingo, puta. You are mine.

38

GIANNA

I don't ask questions.

I don't say much.

It's the flight leading to it all.

Life or death.

Restoration or destruction.

The entire time, everyone has been preparing—looking at maps, taking calls, and filling empty chambers with bullets. Draco has been on several calls with different men, setting up for the arrival.

When he finally catches a moment to breathe, he takes the seat beside me.

"Everything has to go as planned," he says without looking at me. "If she finds out and gets away, that's it. I'm certain I won't find her again. She'll go so far underground, I'll never find her, and she'll keep growing her cartel. That is what I don't want."

"What if she sends someone else to do the talking and the dirty work?"

"The good thing about Ruben is that he's a face-to-face man. He gives his respect and expects it in return. He expects to meet the leader for each drop-off and pick-up every time. His number one rule, otherwise he's not up for working with you. Not to piss anyone off, but as a mutual respect. Lucky for him, I don't have a problem with mutual respect, and since Hernandez is new and wants to get on his good side, she'll have no choice but to meet with him." He drops his hand, placing it on top of mine. A heavy sigh escapes his body.

Patanza and Clark's bickering over which gun needs to be used for whomever tries to defend Hernandez is all I hear for a while.

"I don't want you out there, Gianna," Draco says.

"Too bad. I'm going. You can't make me stay back."

He drops his head. "There are ways of getting you to stay behind. I'm sure I have chloroform stashed somewhere on this jet."

I narrow my eyes up at him, and he tips his chin, a smirk playing on the edge of his lips.

"Jackass." I laugh softly.

He shifts in his seat, his hand sliding down so our fingers can weave. He squeezes my hand a little, focusing on my eyes. "I will let you go, but promise me that when I say something, you will listen. I don't need to be worried about you while all of this shit goes down. If I fucking lose you—"

"You won't lose me," I assure him, bringing my free hand up and gripping his chin. "I'm ready. I've *been* ready, Draco. This is our fight. I will do whatever you need me to do." I sit up in my seat, leaning closer to him. "Let's take that bitch down once and for all. I'm honestly so fucking tired of talking about her."

At that, he chuckles, slouching back in the leather seat. "We should be landing in about two hours." He holds my hand tighter.

A phone rings, and Emilio answers it, then points his gaze to Draco. Draco nods, but doesn't budge. He stays glued in his seat for a while, holding my hand, thinking, breathing.

He's so tired.

Utterly exhausted.

It's as clear as day.

I don't know how he continues to fight, but he does, and he does it well.

I know he's trying to get even for Thiago. I know he wants to get to her for his sake and for his soul to rest peacefully, but something deep in my gut tells me Thiago isn't the only reason he's fighting so hard anymore.

At first, that was his mission. Revenge.

But ever since my return, things have shifted. In the beginning, his fight was distant, cold, dark, and had no end in sight, but now it is full of fire, happening right before my very eyes, and so fucking brutal. And it will be coming to an end soon. Very soon, if all goes as planned.

I thought I knew what all The Jefe could do.

I thought I had him completely figured out.

I was wrong.

I see now that he would travel thousands of miles and set this world ablaze with each footstep when it comes to the people he loves. He will let the entire world know he's on the hunt—that a minor setback doesn't have shit on his comeback—and there is nothing this world can do to stop it.

He is the boss.

The king.

The fucking Jefe.

He is everything I crave and more, and when this is all over, I can't wait to be on top of the world with him.

I just pray we both stay alive long enough to enjoy it.

39

GIANNA

The sky is dark, the jet landing on a quiet strip.

Draco unbuckles his seatbelt and pushes to a stand, glancing sideways at me as he picks up an AK-47, strapping it around him. Patanza and Emilio follow suit, as well as Clark, who gives his gun an aggressive kiss before holding it close.

"Keep me safe, motherfucker," Clark says, clutching his gun.

I stand last, my guns already in holsters and strapped to me. We all have bulletproof vests on, but even so, I still feel exposed.

Emilio steps toward the exit of the jet, and when Draco bobs his head, he pushes the door open. As soon as he does, I see a man standing at the bottom of the staircase.

He's a buff man with a bald head, guns strapped around him. With his nod of respect, I assume he's one of Draco's men.

Draco asks him something when he meets up to him, and the man turns around, speaking rapidly and hustling at his side. More men appear from parked cars as we march, following in line.

"You good?" Clark asks, stepping up to my side and walking with me.

I glance over at him before putting my focus ahead, on the man I'm doing this for.

I'm risking my entire life. My future. For all we know, Yessica knows we're on the way and will end us before we even begin.

She's not stupid. If she learned from the best, she's going to take caution. *Right?*

"You're nervous for him," Clark mumbles.

"A little."

"No need to be," Patanza says, meeting on the other side of me. "Jefe has gone to war many times before. She isn't the first he's had to settle the score with." Patanza pauses, focusing on her boss with furrowed brows. "But she is the first *puta* to make him work this hard just to find her. I fear for her, because when he gets to her, he won't be lenient. Not even for a second."

Oh, I know he won't.

I know once he gets a hold of her, his wrath will be hard to witness. A part of me feels bad for her—for what she'll go through—but a part of me can't wait to see what he does.

We meet up to three different BMWs: one black, one silver, and the other white. Draco takes the white one, flicking his fingers at me to hurry. Patanza and Clark jump into the backseat of the silver car and Emilio and the new guard take the black one, Emilio climbing into the passenger seat. We follow the black BMW, and the driver of our car clears his throat.

"She deserves every bit of punishment you give her, Jefe," he says.

Draco doesn't even look at him. He's been so far gone and way too focused ever since landing, ready to claim his deadly prize.

The cars drive for some time—nearly thirty minutes—before we slow down, parking in front of a tall building. The windows are tinted black, shining from gold garden lights. We step out of the car, and it's quiet. Too quiet. The wind doesn't even blow. The air is stiff and hot, but I can smell the sea—the thick scent of salt.

Clark meets at my side, taking note of his surroundings with his finger on his trigger. Draco follows one of the drivers to the building. We don't hesitate on following him. I draw my gun from the holster in my waist—Daddy's pistol—and study the building. It's clean.

Shiny.

The offices are full of desks, computers, and stacks of paper. We pass by many cubicles. The only thing I can hear is the pounding of our boots on the linoleum.

The leading guard continues until he reaches a door with a SALIDA sign above it. He shoves it open, and we're in a dark, dank room. Another door appears, and he pushes it open as well.

This door leads to a staircase. We take the stairs down, everyone hustling, still not speaking.

My heart is rattling in my chest now, my adrenaline increasing by the second. My body wants to shake and throb. I want to be terrified, but I can't be.

There is a task to complete.

This task won't be over until we get to her.

After hustling down the stairs, we walk through a long underground tunnel. I keep my eyes on Draco, who hasn't bothered to look back or even around him.

Finally, after two minutes of walking, a ladder appears. The guard takes the ladder up, telling Jefe to wait just a moment. He props the square, brown door above open and takes a look out.

He then looks down, nodding with approval.

Draco takes the steps up. He's out in no time, and Patanza and Emilio follow suit. Clark looks at me, shrugging lightly before following too.

I take the stairs next, two of the guards still behind me. A hand comes in plain view, tan and large.

I grab it, and I'm hauled up rapidly, clashing softly into a broad, strong chest. It makes me slightly dizzy.

My breathing falters as I peer up into Draco's eyes. His head is tilted, his eyes remorseful, like something is wrong.

"What?" I ask. "What is it?"

"This is as far as you will go, Gianna. Clark will stay back with you. He's already agreed to."

I frown. *"What?"* I look at my surroundings. Ahead of us is very tall grass, and beyond it are docked boats in a small marina. Wet cement and wooden boards lead to each boat.

From where we stand, no one can really see us. We're beneath the roof of a broken down shack, hidden between shadows, the moonlight not even touching us.

"Do not argue with me, Gianna," he mumbles when a set of new men walk past him, loading up their guns, slamming bullets into chambers and gripping their Glocks. There are ten of us now.

Patanza and Clark stand at the edge of the roof, glancing back at me once before pulling away.

"You will stay here, keep watch. You see *anyone* or *anything*, you shoot and then you run."

"Draco, no. I can't just stand here. I want to be out there—I want to help you," I plead.

"I know you do but I can't risk it, Gianna. As soon as we walk past this field and to the marina, it will become dangerous. I can't promise to watch your back as well as my own. I need you here, where it's safe. You can still fight from here. If any shit goes down, put those guns to use. Don't hesitate. But don't come out and try to help. You hear me?" He grips my face between his fingers, breathing heavier now, eyes boring into mine. "*Do not* come for me, Gianna. You fucking run if you see or hear anything wrong, and you don't look back. Do you understand?"

"Draco." I grip his forearm.

"I need you to understand."

"Please," I whisper, the rims of my eyes burning now.

"Stay. For once, reina," his head shakes, eyes sealing, "fucking listen to me, and *stay*." When he opens his eyes again, they're glistening, cloudy with emotion.

My chest tightens, throat thickening with the same emotion. My grip slacks around his wrist. I lower my arm, keeping my head high, and finally nodding.

He needs me to stay. He wants to keep me safe. He wants this. More than anything right now. Honestly, he may be right.

"Fine." I whisper. "I'll stay."

"Bueno." He steps forward, gripping my chin. His lips fall down on my forehead, a soft, damp, warm kiss. And then his lips are on top of mine.

The kiss deepens, his other hand cupping the back of my neck. He kisses me hard and rough. It's both demanding and empowering. I kiss him back, clutching him tight around the neck, breathing raggedly when our lips are forced apart by a guard's whispered warning that they have to get moving.

Draco drops his hands, but his eyes don't pull from mine. He takes several steps away, holding my gaze. The rims of my eyes are wet and hot. He tears away before I can, turning and marching after one of the guards.

"Protect yourself, Patrona," Emilio says, eyes stern, serious. He leaves too.

Patanza follows Emilio's lead, glancing back at me and then at Clark, nodding once at him. They all disappear in the depths of the tall grass, and I squeeze the handle of my gun until it hurts.

"Let him handle this," Clark mumbles, stepping to my side. "He's keeping you safe."

I know he is, but . . .

"I've heard so many horror stories about that man. They made it seem like he had no heart—no soul. That he was the boogey man of the cartel world. But when I see him look at you—*touch* you—well, shit." He huffs. "There has to be a heart in there somewhere."

"What do you mean?" I ask, voice low. Soft.

"He looks at you like he would die for you, Gia. He holds you like he never wants to let you go. He kisses you like you mean *everything* to him." He sighs heavily, rubbing the back of his neck. "Now I see why he was so lenient with you when he sent you away. Now...I get it. He's in fucking love with you and that motherfucker is in deep."

40

DRACO

If I die…

If I lose…

If I never get to see her again, at least I know that I gave her a chance to get away from it all.

Even if my dying breath is used to take Hernandez's, at least I know that she'll be safe from her.

She will be Queen.

I prepared her.

Whether I live or die, nothing will stop her.

Whether she chooses to remember me or not, at least I know that I morphed her into the *real* woman she is.

A woman of power.

A woman of strength.

A woman who knows exactly what she wants and what to expect from this fucked up world.

My woman.

She's no longer the niñita that was shackled and weak.

She is strong.

She has risen.

She is Queen.
Mi reina.

41

GIANNA

It takes everything in me not to let my emotions show.

Instead, I do what he needs me to do. I keep watch, my gun at my side, ready to fire if necessary. It's so damn quiet I can hear my own heart beating, the bell of the buoy a short distance away.

Clark steps to the left, near a metal rail with a pair of binoculars in front of his eyes.

"Fuck," he hisses, and I look over at him.

"What?" I step toward him, peering ahead with squinted eyes.

"I can't see a fucking thing. I don't even know where they went." He looks some more, and when he finally catches sight of something, he holds a hand up. "Got them. I see a hand in the air. He's giving them a signal to get ready." He drops the binoculars and walks to me, handing them over. "She's arriving. Look by the black boat. You'll see them."

I pick up the binoculars and scan the perimeter. I see Draco and his men by a black boat not too far away from us. Patanza is standing with a cellphone, most likely texting Ruben, letting him know we're two boats down like Draco had planned.

They all crouch down when they hear a loud bell go off. I look toward the chime of the bell and see a yacht riding up to the marina.

It's a black yacht, and of course, I can see the cheetah print seats from here. There are several men on the boats, at least a dozen of them.

She has more than us, but with Ruben's men around too, we'll outnumber her. We'll have sixteen, double what she has…unless she has more inside.

Her hair flaps with the wind, her chin held high, like she rules the damn world. My jaw clenches, and I grip the binoculars tighter. I look to the left and see a thin man standing there, waiting for her, wearing a silk shirt and a gold necklace. A straw fedora covers his dark hair, his hands in his pockets, watching the yacht approach.

"She's getting closer," I murmur, dropping the binoculars.

Clark bends down where a black duffle bag is and unzips it, digging out a pump action shotgun and a box of shells, and then loading it. "I love me a good AK, but I dare a motherfucker to try and get past me with this baby." I see his teeth sparkle from the moonlight.

I bend with him, taking out a few of the pocketknives, just in case, as well as a dagger, sheathed in a red leather holster. I pull the blade out, and it's thin and sharp—not too long, but long enough to intimidate and even kill.

When Clark has the gun loaded, he stands up tall. I stand with him, looking into his eyes.

He glances over at me with a quirked brow. "What?"

I press my lips, wanting so badly to smile, but unable too. I look back where Draco and his men are waiting behind the boat, their bottom halves soaked from the water.

"Oh, don't even try it, Gia," Clark retorts, and I meet his gaze again. "I don't need your sentimental bullshit right now. We get out of this alive and then you can thank me. Sound good?"

I give him a half-smile. "Sure."

"Good," he smirks, "cause she's about to get off the boat now."

I turn, strapping the knife to my holster and gripping my gun. Clark has the shotgun in the air, aiming it where Yessica's boat is. I pick up the binoculars with one hand, watching as men in all black with M4A1s step off, glaring hard at Ruben.

When they've all stepped onto the wooden walkway, she comes off last, wearing cheetah-print heels and a red blouse. Her lips are a dark shade of red, almost the color of blood, and from the lamp above, her hair appears even redder now. She's impossible to miss—an easy target.

I get the urge to shoot her right where she stands, but she's not mine to kill.

Play it safe.

Keep it cool.

Her time will come.

I continue watching through the binoculars as Ruben extends his arm and offers his hand, saying something to her. She takes his hand, shaking swiftly, and then pulling away, most likely demanding something.

Ruben gestures toward the end of the walkway, and she bobs her head, following his lead, her men trailing behind her while Ruben's men in navy blue lead the way for him.

"That's right, bitch," Clark murmurs, following her with the eye of his shotgun. "Keep walking. Right into your little trap."

I keep watch with the binoculars. Ruben is doing a great job, smiling, pretending nothing is going on. I look where Draco and his men are. He has his hand up, all of them still crouched low, their guns lifted and ready to blast.

Ruben leads Yessica to two barrels in front of a white boat and has his men pull off the lids. One of his men pulls out a soaking wet package, slicing right through it.

Ruben steps forward, pulling out a knife, saying something to her as he digs the knife into the white powder and brings it up to her, flat and covered in white dust.

I imagine him asking, *"Would you like to give a try? See how pure it is?"*

She looks him over twice before stepping forward and taking the knife from him. She drops her head, her red hair curtaining her face, and sniffs hard right before pinching her nose and then knocking her head back.

"Wow," she mouths. Her lips move again, but I'm not sure what she's saying. She grips Ruben's shoulder, and he looks sideways at her hand before frowning.

Now.

Now is the time!

Ruben glances at one of his men, who steps forward and presses a gun into one of Yessica's guard's head. Her eyes grow wide as Ruben says something.

And when he says his final word, I know exactly what that word is. Even without the binoculars, I would know what he's just said to her.

With her eyes so wide and her face so struck with horror, there's only one word—one *name*—that will shake her so hard to the core.

"*Jefe.*"

42

GIANNA

Just as that name is said, her guard is shot in the back of the head and Draco drops his hand, shouting for them to go.

All of his men hop onto the walkway, and bullets start flying.

So many bullets.

So much yelling and barking.

Ruben dashes for the boat ahead of him, two of his guards covering his back and shooting down two more of her men. The rest of them are still out there, but three of them are taken down by Yessica's men, one keeping her behind him, making it hard for anyone to get to her.

"Fuck! I can't get a good shot! I need to go out there!" Clark barks.

"No—you heard what he said! They've got it!"

"Shit!"

I understand his urge. I want to do the same, but I'm safer here.

The bullets are loud, bouncing off the boats and echoing, drifting with the wind. I watch Draco the most. He's running behind his men, but several of them are shot down by Yessica's.

Draco keeps running, going for his target.

Going for her…until…

A gun goes off.

The bullet hits someone close.

Someone important.

A hat falls off, the body crumpling to the ground.

I panic, watching Emilio go down, too.

"Patanza," I hear Clark gasp. He drops his gun and makes a mad dash through the tall grass, his shotgun in front of him. "Run, Gia! Get back underground!" Clark yells.

My breathing accelerates, my fingers going numb around my gun. I keep the binoculars up, looking at Draco, who's glaring down at his best guard and then his manager, Emilio.

Draco picks his head up to find the culprit, and I look with him.

I see her standing next to two of her guards with a smoking gun aimed in his direction. A smile stretches across Yessica's lips and then…she runs.

43

GIANNA

He told me to run.

He doesn't' want me out there. I should know better. I can't do this to myself—to him. My future . . . my life . . .

But if I don't run . . . if I stay—everything could be at risk. I take a step back, breathing harder, my stomach churning. I peer through the binoculars, searching for her again. She's getting away. She can't get away! If she does, this will never end.

Fuck running.

I can't just stand by and let her go.

In a flash, the binoculars hit the ground.

My gun is in the air, pointed ahead of me as I push and shovel my way through the tall grass. Some of it slaps me in the face, but I don't stop, not until I reach the clearing. Breathing frantically, I look to my left and see Draco going toe-to-toe with two of her guards. He punches one in the throat and then shoots him in the crotch, turning rapidly to face the other one, who has a pocketknife in hand, swinging it and trying to cut him.

I look ahead, past him, and spot red hair flailing. She's running hard and fast in her heels, back to her yacht.

"Go! Go! Go!" I hear her shout to whoever's on board. "Start it up! Hurry!"

I run faster. Past Clark trying to pick a barely breathing Patanza up in his arms to drag her away from the shootout. Past Emilio who has a bullet in his head.

Even past Draco, who has just now taken down the other guard with the pocketknife he tried slicing Draco with. Ruben's boat has sailed already, now in the middle of the ocean with three of his men keeping watch.

Yessica's boat starts to pull away.

No.

Fuck that.

She is not getting away again!

I won't make it to the dock she's at. I spot another one with a longer walkway and I take it, boots clomping on wet wood, my gun locked in hand, my lungs tight and filling with air, working overtime, despite the clench in my gut and the rattle in my head.

Her boat is close. Bullets go off again ahead of me, but none hit me. I keep going.

Going.

Going.

Until I'm leaping in the air and crashing through glass.

44

GIANNA

My ears ring, and I groan, looking down at the cuts and gashes on my hands and arms. A shrill command is the first thing I hear when the ringing ends. I grab Daddy's gun just as one goes off, hitting the floor beside me. I roll the other way, hiding behind a wall.

Boots thump, and someone appears with their back to me, stepping around the corner. Lifting my gun, I shoot him in the back of the head before he can see me and his body hits the ground.

I wince, dropping my arm, focusing on the sharp crystal sticking out of my forearm. It's a small piece. I don't think it's caused much damage, but it fucking hurts.

I grit my teeth, holding back on a scream as I slowly pull the piece out, tossing the bloody glass on the floor.

Another gun goes off, shattering the window beside me. Close. Too close.

I run to the next opening, and it's the front of the boat. There is a man steering the boat. He spots me and tries pulling his gun on me, but I shoot him first, and he buckles forward.

The steering wheel snags, his arm getting caught on it when he starts to fall, making the boat jerk and knocking my body sideways.

I get back up and push him away, straightening the wheel.

I look around. It's darker now. Quieter. They're looking for me. The boat is only so big. Eventually they'll find me. I'm assuming there is only one guard left on this boat. I saw several of them out there, dead or about to die.

I press my back to the wall when I hear laughter.

"Oh, Gia. Gia, Gia, Gia." Yessica's heels click on the floor. I think she realizes they're giving her location away, because after several seconds, I don't hear them anymore. I look out to the left, seeing a slice of the marina. We're not too far away from it.

"Just give it up, will you! Draco is going down! He can't defeat me!"

I grip my gun tighter, pressing my back to the wall.

"You could be my colleague, join my side," she says, sweetening her tone. "Together, we can rise! Become the best bitches and bosses in the world. Untouchable. Irresistible." I hear the smile in her voice. "We can get whatever we want."

Glass crunches, and I look to my left, holding my breath. I lift my gun, pointing it ahead, a trail of dark-red blood leaking down my forearm. I can't see a damn thing now. They've shut all lights off on the boat.

The footsteps get closer and then I see a large body in dark clothing. His pistol is high in the air, his shoulders hunched, and when the person spots me, he picks his head up, eyes growing wide.

"Draco," I whisper as quietly as I can. I realize now he's soaking wet from waist to toe.

He holds a finger up to his lips, gestures for me to be quiet, but as soon he lowers that finger, glass shatters again, and he falls to the ground, body slamming down and rocking the boat.

Heavier footsteps start up and a large body comes charging toward him, scooping him up by the back of his shirt, his hand immediately wrapping around Draco's throat.

"Who's the Jefe now, motherfucker!" the guard laughs, and from this angle, I know exactly who he is.

The big man with the blind eye that abducted me. The one who thought he was intimidating me. Fucking Alonso.

I lift my gun, but I don't have a chance to pull the trigger. Someone knocks it out of my hand with all their might and then shoves me forward, my chest slamming into wall.

I turn around and look up. Yessica stands in front of me with a gun in hand, pointing it directly at me.

"Maybe you're just as stupid as he is," she murmurs.

I look to the left, and Draco can't get even. The man is dragging him around, tossing his body, throwing him through the glass windows and then charging him again like some kind of raging bull.

"He won't survive this." She laughs. "Look at him. Being tossed around like a cheap, worthless dog toy."

I glare at her.

"Join me, Gia. Become my colleague. Stop giving the men the glory and become a truly powerful woman on your own. You don't need him. You never have."

I clench my jaw, baring my teeth. "Fuck you. I'll never partner up with a psychotic bitch like you. Henry. What about him, huh? He was trapped for months, and you didn't do shit to find him. Trigger Toni? Huh? Who had his back then? You're not loyal. You're desperate. Stupid. A fucking *psycho*."

I hear Draco holler out in pain and then roar. Bones crack. More glass shatters. All of it makes my blood run cold and my belly clench tighter.

Yessica's face pales, her eyes becoming harder. She wraps her finger tighter around the trigger.

"You know what I remember most? How he used to pet me when I sucked his cock? How he ran his fingers through my hair and told me I was *so good* at what I do to him—how I made him feel."

My nostrils flare up, my heart catching speed again.

"His eyes would roll so far to the back of his head. God, I loved seeing him like that. It was the only time he made himself vulnerable for me. Especially when I rode his cock after a long, hard day. He would grab my ass and squeeze it. He would tell me what to do—like go faster, or slower. To grab his balls and fondle them. He'd pull my hair while I rode him in reverse, suck on my neck..."

She keeps talking, every word narrowing my vision, making her the only target. I'm seeing nothing but red now.

If there is one thing I know, it's that I'm a jealous woman, and when some other woman talks about what is mine like it is still hers? I. Get. Pissed.

Call it a Nicotera thing—or call it a Gianna thing. Whatever it is, I won't fucking have it.

So, no. I don't think about what I do next.

I don't care that it doesn't make sense, or that it could damn well kill me. I can't stand to think of him with anyone else.

Draco is mine.

Only mine.

My rage has blinded me tenfold, and I charge ahead.

I rush for her, tackling her to the ground, and her gun goes off, but the bullet doesn't hit me.

Her eyes are wide as she tries to shoot again, but the gun clicks this time. No bullets.

I snatch the gun out of her hand and toss it, bringing my arm in the air and dropping my fist, slamming it across her jaw. She groans, but I punch her again. And again. And several more times.

I punch until her face is bloodied, and then I yank her up, dragging her useless body off the boat and throwing her into the shallow water.

I jump off the boat and grab her by the hair before she can get away, pushing her under the water, my hands closing around her throat as I stare down at her. Her eyes stretch, mouth wide open, gurgling.

"He will never love you. He calls me his reina, something I know he *never* in his entire life called you. You're a worthless, stupid bitch."

I squeeze even tighter, wanting to end her right now. Desperate to see her take her last breath—but a deep voice calls my name.

His voice.

"GIANNA!" Draco barks, and I look back. He walks toward me, the water splashing around him. "She. Is. Mine," he fumes.

I let up, yanking her out of the water by the front of her shirt. She coughs hard, gasping even harder when she's finally claimed oxygen.

But it doesn't last long, because as soon as Draco reaches us, he wraps one large hand around her throat and squeezes it so tight, her eyes bulge right out of their sockets.

Her face turns red, then purple, then blue.

He's panting hard, growling as he lifts her up and stares at her. He's been shot in his left arm. It's leaking blood, but it doesn't seem to bother him one bit right now.

"I told you I would find you," he rasps. "I told you this wouldn't be pretty."

He finally lets her go, and she falls into the water, landing on her back. We both glare down at her, and she looks right back up at us, only this time, when she looks at us, there isn't power or authority in her eyes.

There is fear. Ultimate fear.

She's afraid for her life.

Good.

She should be.

Sebastien, Diego, and Guillermo come to us, pushing their legs through the water, pointing their guns at her.

"Yes! Finally got the stupid bitch," Sebastien says in Spanish with a grin, licking his lips.

"*Ahora que,* Jefe?" Guillermo asks, peering up at a battered Draco. *What now?* Draco's right eye is bruised, his bottom lip busted, and some of his face is scraped and scratched. He was shot, but he's alive.

He's alive.

"Drag her ass," he demands. "All the way to the tunnel. By her hair."

Guillermo wastes no time following orders. He pushes his AK behind him and grabs Yessica's wet, red hair. She screams for him to let go, but Guillermo and Sebastien get a kick out of it, sneering down at her, dragging her through the water and up the steps that lead up the wooden walkway.

"Where's Patanza?" Draco asks Diego, fully concerned.

"Clark took her back to the hideout. She was shot in the shoulder. He got the bullet out. She'll be okay, but we have to find a doctor quick to get her stitched up."

"Oh, thank God," I sigh. Patanza is a hard-ass, but she doesn't deserve to die. She deserves to live again. She needs another chance.

Diego looks at Draco's bloody arm and then mine. Mine is not nearly as bad as his. "Both of you need to see a doctor, too."

Draco nods, shutting his eyes for a brief moment. His knees buckle, but I catch him, wrapping my arm around his waist.

"We need to get you to a doctor," I say hurriedly. Diego starts to help, but I hold my hand up, letting him know I've got it.

"I'm fine," Draco rasps. "Motherfucker was strong. Took everything in me to get him down with one good arm." He looks down at me, gripping my chin, fixing my gaze on his. "I told you to stay hidden. To run. She could have killed you."

I press my lips, walking toward the shore with him, Diego leading the way. "I didn't want to run away."

He delivers a ragged sigh, bringing me closer. "Fuck," he murmurs.

"What?"

"We got her."

I nod. "We did."

"It's still not over. I won't be killing her right away, like I had planned." He looks over at Guillermo and Sebastien, who are taking turns dragging Yessica across the wooden beams and then disappearing through the tall grass with her.

"Where do we go from here?"

He runs his tongue over his lips, exhaling. "To the one place I love." He sighs. "Lantía. Home."

Before we go, we hear a bell chime and look to our left, at the boat coming to dock. Ruben appears and steps off the boat, coming our way.

"Glad to see you alive, Jefe!" Ruben says boastfully, lightly clapping Draco on his good shoulder.

Draco chuckles. "Thank you, Ruben. For what you did. I will never be able to repay you."

"Hey, now. You can repay me by remaining my best buyer!"

Draco gives him a light smile, bringing a hand up and squeezing his shoulder. "You have my word."

Ruben nods and then looks down at me. "La Patrona," he sings with a full smile on his lips. "Quite the beauty. And one hell of a fighter. I saw the way you got to her boat." He looks up at Draco. "You've got yourself a keeper, Jefe. Don't lose this one."

"Trust me," Draco murmurs, his eyes shifting down to bolt with mine. "I won't. Not ever again."

My heart flutters deep in my chest, my cheeks blazing red.

"I will have my men take care of these bodies for you. Clean up the area. Safe travels, Jefe." He looks at me again. "Patrona." Ruben steps back, tipping his fedora and slightly bowing his head before putting the hat back on and jogging back to his boat.

We make it back to the hideout, battered and exhausted, taking the tunnel and going through the same building.

Most of us are injured, but no one is complaining—no one but Yessica. It gets to a point where she's so uncooperative that they have to knock her out with a hard blow to the face just to get her to be quiet.

When we reach the exit of the building, I spot the three BMWs. Beside one of them is a black plastic bag with what looks like a body inside it.

As if Draco sees it at the same time as me, he tenses up, but keeps walking, though his breathing is a little heavier now. My eyes fill with tears in an instant.

Emilio...

Damn it, Emilio.

Emilio risked his life for me and then gave it for him.

From what I was told, Emilio didn't have many people that knew him other than us. He had no friends. He has a grandpa in a nursing home with dementia. A part of me wonders if his grandpa will even remember him—or miss him.

It breaks my heart.

As we climb into the backseat of the car, I know one thing for sure.

I will remember him forever.

He respected me, and I respected him just the same. He took care of me when he didn't even have to.

He was good to me…a good man, gone way too soon.

In this business, there must be devotion and sacrifice. He delivered both for our sakes.

For him, for Thiago, for Mom and Daddy, I will live on.

I will conquer. I will rise.

I will be what I need to be in order for their legacy to live on.

For Draco's legacy to live on.

45

GIANNA

It's been more than forty-eight hours since we landed in Lantía.

I'm restless, and so is he. I've debated whether or not to go to the shed—whether I want to see her one last time and remember the look in her eyes, or just stay put here and forget all about her.

Draco shuts off the TV and goes to the bathroom, picking up a can of shaving cream and a razor. He looks through the corner of his eye at me when I step into the bathroom.

We are still on the run, though we're taking a minor pit stop for now. Turns out we spent too much time at the marina. The cameras were only supposed to shut off for fifteen minutes—it's what security agreed to. We took longer than that, so they know who shot up that marina.

The images the media have aren't very clear—they're terrible cameras—but besides Draco, they're now looking for a woman with red hair as well as a brunette. Yessica and me.

He has enemies everywhere. They don't just stop at Yessica. They'll continue to flood in, knock on the doors, demand things from him and threaten his life.

He is still wanted. Still a threat to society, even though I no longer see him that way.

"What is it, Gianna? You look bothered." His eyes land on mine.

I press my lips, shrugging. "I don't know," I murmur.

He sighs and dispenses a handful of cream in his hand, applying it to his face. "I know what you're thinking," he murmurs.

"What?"

"How you want your face to be one of the last faces she sees before she's gone."

I look him over.

Spot on.

"I just want to see her."

He looks sideways at me. "Then go. But this time, don't set anyone free."

I bite a smile, rubbing his back as he smirks. After putting on a pair of jeans and a loose white blouse, I tie my damp hair up and make my way down stairs.

When I get to the main level, there aren't many people around. We have two maids and one butler, and they're most likely in the other kitchen, beyond the dining area. None of the guards are in this area. They're probably keeping watch at the shed. Draco wanted most of their eyes on her.

I walk through the smaller kitchen and Diego is standing by the doors when I walk out, just like I told him to. I walk past the pool, down the stone steps that lead to the rickety bridge.

And then the shed appears.

That old, familiar place.

My heart beats a little faster, breath faltering.

This place still gives me nightmares.

I pull the door open and step inside, the stench of urine consuming me. I hear noises, chains rattling, and my brows pull together when I hear men cursing, followed by deep and heavy grunts.

I continue my walk down the thin hallway, stopping in front of the second cell.

And there she is, standing but bent over.

Shackles are around her ankles, her wrists tied tightly with rope, bloody from trying to resist. Her red hair is matted, some of it hanging in front of her face.

She isn't alone.

Two of the guards are here, Sebastien with his cock in her mouth and Diego with his cock in her asshole.

I swallow hard, watching the chains yank and tug, hearing her groaning and moaning, and I'm not sure if it's from pleasure or pain. Diego slaps her ass while Sebastien grips her hair.

I know Draco didn't order this. And I also know he wouldn't care that it is happening. He told them he didn't care what they did to her. To make her suffer.

And it seems she is.

I almost get the urge to open the gate and stop them—tell them that's enough—but her eyes drift over to mine as Sebastien shoves himself deeper down her throat. Though her eyes are glistening, I see the anger in them. The hatred.

Her nostrils flare as he grips her head and slams deeper, cramming his entire cock in until it disappears. She whimpers, and I step forward, gripping the handle, but when she brings her bound wrists up and points both of her middle fingers at me, I release the handle.

I back away, listening to the chains rattle even harder and her moans turn into cries. I can't watch anymore. And I also won't stop them. So instead of interrupting, I turn my back and walk away. For now.

46

DRACO

After getting dressed, I walk down the hallway to the spare bedrooms and knock on the last door at the end of the hallway.

My nurse and maid, Juanita, answers it, smiling at me. "Hola, Jefe," she murmurs, letting me in.

I give her a slight nod, stepping into the room and looking at the bed. Patanza spots me and tries sitting up against the headboard, but she groans instead, wincing as she adjusts her arm in the sling.

"Relax, Patanza," I tell her, and she sighs, slouching into a comfortable position again. I take the chair beside the bed as Juanita goes to the bathroom and runs some water. "How are you feeling?"

"Better. Sore as fuck, but better."

I huff a laugh.

"How about you?" she asks, looking at my bandaged arm.

I glance down at it. "It's fine. Healing."

She nods. "Where's Patrona?"

I smirk. "Oh, she's Patrona to you again?"

She sucks her teeth, dropping her gaze. "She always was. I was just pissed at her. Said some stupid things."

I sigh, dropping my elbows on top of my thighs. "So did I. She knows it's just how we are." I look around the room. "Has Clark come to see you today?"

"Not yet." I see her face flush when I ask the question, her chin dipping. "He stayed here all night, took care of me, got me what I needed when it was time for Juanita to go. I don't think he caught much sleep. He said I kept waking up…said I was crying in my sleep." She shakes her head. "Like I'm some *stupid, abandoned puppy*. His words exactly."

I chuckle. "He's a true smartass. He might have Thiago beat."

She looks up at me when I say Thiago's name. "Thiago had a dry and dark sense of humor. Clark's sense of humor is a little more…blunt."

"You like him." It's a statement, not a question.

"He saved my life," she says, like that will prove she doesn't.

"He likes you, too. Gia said he went running to save you when he saw you go down."

Her face reddens even more. I've never seen her like this, not even for my cousin.

"Where is La Patrona anyway?"

I point out the open window, where the shed is as I stand again. "Taking care of things with our prisoner, I'm assuming."

"Good," she huffs. "Bitch deserves whatever comes her way."

I walk toward her, kissing the top of her head. I know she's only a few years younger than me, but she's always felt like a sister to me. Like I helped raise her.

"I don't know what I would have done had I lost you, Patanza," I tell her in Spanish and she looks up, her eyes glistening now. "You are more than just a soldier and a body to me. You are family. Thank you for always having my back."

Her bottom lip almost trembles. Almost. "Gracias, Jefe."

I step back. "Get some rest."

She bobs her head, and I turn, leaving her.

She's alive. She's safe. We all are, for now, but none of us will be satisfied until Hernandez is gone.

"Jefe," Patanza calls, and I look back. "Has Gia told you?"

"Told me what?" I ask, turning halfway, peering over my shoulder at her.

She shakes her head rapidly and pulls her line of sight away as Juanita comes to her side, helping her out the bed. "Never mind," she murmurs.

47

GIANNA

When I return to the shed an hour later, after taking a brief visit to the library and talking to Draco for a bit, everything but Yessica's bra is gone.

Her panties are shredded.

Her knees are dirty now, her mouth red and swollen.

She sees me coming in and goes still, breathing quicker, mascara running down her cheeks.

"Wow," I breathe. "Were you crying?"

"Fuck you," she spits at me.

I fold my arms. "I bet you're hungry. Thirsty."

Her eyebrows fuse together, lips pressing tight. I look back, nodding at the two butlers. They walk into the shed and set up a folded table and two chairs. Guillermo steps into the room and unlocks her shackles, like I asked him to do, and then slices through the thick rope around her wrists.

I walk over to pick up her dirty pants, handing them to her. She snatches them away, tugging them over her legs with haste.

"*Siéntate*," I command. *Sit.*

She glares for a brief moment, but sits nonetheless. When she does, I nod my head at Guillermo who lifts his gun and aims it at the back of her head.

"You try to run, try to lunge for me, or try anything I don't like, and he'll shoot you. Maybe not in the head, like he should do, but somewhere where it'll hurt."

"Why are you doing this?" she says, voice dry. Coarse.

I sit back in my seat. "You treated me to a nice meal when your people took me, so I want to treat you to one, too. This will be the last meal you'll ever have. May as well enjoy it."

She doesn't say anything, just glares at me, eyes misty. Her tongue runs over her lips as the butler places her plate down in front of her.

The butler sets some silverware down, pours water into a plastic cup, and then takes off, dusting his gloved hands off.

Sebastien comes into the cell with a handgun and gives it to me. Before he takes off, he gives Yessica a small sneer, grabbing his crotch, and she cringes, snatching her eyes away.

I place my Daddy's gun on the middle of my lap, smiling softly at her. When I know she can't stand the aromas smacking her in the face and making her belly rumble, I tell her, "You can eat."

She digs in, eyeing me several times, scarfing down the French toast and eggs. She goes between the bread and the fruit, and then to her cup of water, guzzling it all down and then looking at my cup like she wants more.

I slide the cup toward her with the tip of my gun, and she glances at it briefly before picking it up and sipping it.

"I remember what it was like to starve. To be thirsty." I sigh, sitting back in my chair, watching her eat some more. "I would have killed for a meal like this. Actually—I almost did kill someone when I was first brought here, and I ended up getting many meals like this later on." I lean forward. "How does it feel?" I ask. "To be at the very bottom again? To feel *worthless*? All your men gone. Your money, gone. No one working with you anymore—all of them siding with The Jefe again. With a man that will *never* love you."

She doesn't answer, but her eyes scream it all.

She hates me. She hates me so much. She's envious—wishes she was in my place so badly. This is torture for her, way worse than any kind of rape or punch or kick.

Hearing this, and the other things I have to say, is what will ruin her.

"Can I tell you a secret," I whisper, leaning over the table a bit more. "It's something I haven't even told Jefe yet." I run my finger over the lion's mane on my gun. "I haven't been feeling too well the past few mornings. It's been maybe a week and a half now of this nauseous feeling, and the constant headaches that come in the mornings and late at night. It's no coincidence. I knew what was happening to me before I even tested. I had one of his men buy and bring me a pregnancy test in secrecy, right before we found you. His name was Emilio. I liked him a lot. He was a good person, and you killed him."

Her glistening eyes are wider now. She's no longer chewing. Her face is pale. Eyes desperate and empty at the same time.

"I know you think it can't get any worse than me being his queen, his woman, but it does for you. Because his bloodline will continue, and it will continue through me. A Molina-Nicotera baby. The Jefe's baby." I sit back. "Even now, I'm not feeling the best, but I've been pushing through the nausea. Luckily, it's not too severe. No vomiting —*yet*." I twist my lips, my eyes lowering to her plate. "I don't know. I thought I would be...devastated or scared. I mean, I was scared of the idea of a baby at first—when we hadn't caught you. But we have you now, and now that we do, well...I feel a little better. I don't feel so bad about being pregnant with his baby. In fact, I'm kind of excited about it. Like I said, he doesn't know yet. I want to tell him when all of this is over. When you are officially gone, and his head is a little clearer."

She slams her empty fist on the table, dropping the plastic spork on the ground. Guillermo takes a big step forward, pressing the gun to the back of her head, but I hold my hand up, letting him know it's fine. He doesn't ease up.

"You think you're getting anywhere by doing this? *Telling* me this? I've been through worse—heard so much that is way worse than this, *sweetie*. What you say doesn't deter me. No one gives a damn about you or your baby. I hope that baby dies in your womb, and you bleed to death," she growls through her teeth. "Now if you're going to kill me, just kill me already and get it over with." Her voice is thick. She's so close to breaking down. She still wants to be strong.

I almost envy how strong she's trying to be right now. I remember doing something similar—trying to push through the pain and the torture. Trying to see the lighter side of things.

"Oh, you think I'm going to kill you?" I laugh, folding my hands in my lap. Her eyebrows dip with my outburst.

A door slams closed and footsteps march down the hallway, measured, heavy. She glances over her shoulder, eyelashes damp.

When *he* appears at the door, brows knitted, wearing all black with his fists clenched, I look at her and grin.

"I was just warming you up for the real deal, *sweetie*," I murmur. "Him."

48

DRACO

I have been waiting for this moment for some time now.

Gianna is long gone. I sent her to her room to shower and get some rest. I know she won't sleep. She'll wait up until I return.

She told me to take my time, so I will.

I have my guards drag Hernandez up to the mansion, down the corridor, the marble steps, and to one of the bedrooms near my galería.

There is nothing in this room but a full-sized bed with white sheets, maroon walls, and palm trees in front of the window.

One of my guard's shoves her forward and she falls on her knees, yelping.

She struggles to get up, so I yank her up by the hair, dragging her to the bathroom only a few steps away.

"Let go of me!" she screams.

I force her down in the chair placed in the middle of the bathroom and she breathes raggedly, looking up at me.

"I hate you!" she roars and then spits at my feet. "You think you're something? Let me tell you right now, Draco, you are *nothing*. You never have been anything! You're not important! I'm not afraid of you!"

I lift my chin. "Is that so?"

She swallows hard, her eyes focused on me, trying to catch my eyes.

I walk around the chair, stepping behind her, looking at her reflection in the mirror. She doesn't take her eyes off me.

"I've thought of all the possible ways to kill you," I murmur. "I couldn't decide on what I wanted more. To torture you, drag it out, and waste my time. Or to make it quick and simple, the same way you did my cousin." I slip a pair of gloves on both hands. "After letting Gianna toy with you a bit, I finally figured out the perfect solution."

I pull a pocketknife with a black handle out of my back pocket, studying the handle with my father's initials on it.

I then lower my arm and yank her up, wrapping my arm around her midsection, holding her body close to mine, and inhaling the filthy scent of despair, terror, and greed.

"You were always trash to me, Yessica. You know that? I never cared about you. You were just an easy fuck, fun to punish, and nothing more." I grip her tight, squeezing her body with one arm, the cold, hard pocketknife in my right hand.

"That's a lie. You love me. I know you do," she pants. She's working harder to breathe.

"You think so?"

"Yes. You always fucked me like you loved me," she answers, confident. Too fucking bold.

"Do you feel breathless?" I ask.

She frowns at the reflection.

"Do you like my body on yours?"

When I ask that, she bobs her head.

"Speak," I demand.

She tries too, but she's unable. Words try to spill out, but they're stuck. All I hear are moans and whimpers.

Her eyes get bigger and soon, her body goes limp in my arms. Her head falls back, but her eyes are still on my reflection.

"Do you know what's happening to you right now?" I run my fingers down her arms, caressing her flushed skin. She watches my hand, like she loves it, like it's all she's ever wanted. My touch. Me. "You are paralyzed, but you can feel every single thing I do to you. Your nerves are just fine, and your eyes see all, but everything else inside you has completely shut down." Her chin wobbles.

"There are these flowers that I am so fascinated with called Death by Indigo. At first I hated them and what they could have done to me, but they intrigued me later on because they made a point—had a purpose. Because they are just as dangerous as I am. That meal you ate," I whisper in her ear, grinning, "had the ground powder of that poisonous flower all over it. You were so hungry you couldn't even taste it, could you?"

She tries to speak—to move. She's frozen.

"You know something?" I clutch the handle of my knife again. "You were wrong about what you said before." I bring the knife up to her throat, looking at her reflection through the mirror, deep into her eyes. "When I fucked you, I fucked you like I *hated* you, because I will always fucking hate you. As soon as I end you, it will be like you never even existed, and I'll be living my life the same as before. The Jefe. The deadliest, most powerful motherfucker in the world."

After my final words are laid out, I slide the thin blade of the knife across the middle of her throat, slicing deep. My teeth grit as I spin her around, forcing her to look me in the eyes.

Her arms fidget like she's trying to reach up and grab for her throat, but I push her up against the counter, dropping the knife and wrapping my hands around her neck.

My thumbs press into the slit, squeezing, forcing the blood to spill faster. It cascades, spilling on her chest and on my shirt.

"I never loved you," I murmur in her ear, "but I will *always* love her. She is *mi reina*—my future—and you can rot and sulk in hell knowing that."

Blood gushes out of her mouth, and she chokes on the thick, dark red flood leaving her body, trying to move, begging for mercy with her eyes alone.

But there is no mercy.

This is for Thiago.

This is for Emilio.

This is for Gianna.

This is my chance to finally be fucking free.

When her eyelids flutter and her gags and sputters around the blood soften, I let her go and step away. She lands on her knees and falls forward, her face slamming into the hard marble floor. I stare down at her, watching the blood pour from her nose and mouth.

It pools on my floor, blending in with her flaming red hair.

I don't stop staring—don't make a fucking move—until I see the last breath bubble its way out of her motherfucking body.

When I know she's dead, I go to the counter and grab the wooden box on top of it. My winner's box, as my father would call it, delivered right to this room, like I ordered.

Every time I know I've won, I open it and take a prize.

I pull out a joint and my favorite gold zippo lighter, staining both with her blood. Pressing my back into the edge of the counter, her blood a puddle at my feet, I strike a spark from the lighter and take a pull from the joint, inhaling deep, letting the buzz cleanse my soul— letting it renew and restore me. I smoke the whole thing, not giving a damn about the mess on my floor.

As I take the final pull, I push off the counter, looking at the dead *puta* one last time and then smirking as I walk away.

I told that bitch I would kill her.

She should have fucking listened.

49

GIANNA

The door to his bedroom swings open, and he walks in, soiled in blood.

I don't ask questions, even though that was much quicker than I thought it would be. Instead, I climb off the bed and walk to the shower to start it.

He comes into the bathroom and starts to unbutton his pants. When the water is warm enough, I walk over to help him, lightly pushing his hands away and pulling his shirt over his head. I reach down, unbuckling his belt next and then unbuttoning his pants.

Tossing it all on the floor, he stands before me completely naked, his cock thick, hanging between his legs, and I slip out of my dress, taking his hand and leading the way to the shower.

No words are spoken as we step beneath the stream.

I look up at him as water pours over his head. His eyes squeeze tight as the blood rushes down the drain.

When it's all gone, he presses himself against me, cupping my ass in hand and bringing his head down. His lips press on my cheek and then my jawline.

I cup his face, my other hand wrapping around the back of his neck as I turn my head, getting our lips to connect.

With this act alone, he picks me up in his arms, and I link my legs around his waist. With his teeth clamping my bottom lip, he presses my back on the shower wall and delivers a hard, powerful thrust deep inside me.

It's tender and full, and my moan is louder than it probably should be, but I don't care. He sucks on my bottom lip and then drops his head to lick the water away from my skin before kissing me all over my neck.

God, it feels good.

He feels so good inside me.

"Fuck, I love you, Gianna," he rasps, warm water running over his full lips as he brings his head up and locks eyes with me. "So fucking much." His hips are still drilling upward, filling me up. He groans, hard and heavy as he drops his forehead on my shoulder. A wild growl fills the space of the shower, and he stills inside me, panting heavier, still cupping me in his large hands.

My fingers thread through the hair at the nape of his neck. We stay like this for a moment, breathing. Sighing. Relieved. I rest my cheek on his shoulder with a sigh.

We finish washing up, and when we're out, we put on robes and walk back to the bedroom. I linger by the bathroom door, twisting my fingers.

Before he can sit down on the bed I call his name.

He looks over his shoulder at me. "Si, Gianna?"

"I have something to tell you," I whisper, and suddenly my heart is pounding, but only because I don't know how he'll react.

He turns fully, eyes serious and focused. Either I've paled and now look like a ghost, or he's actually seeing one because he asks in an urgent tone, "What is it?"

"I… " My mouth clamps shut, my eyes burning now. "I found out a few days ago that I'm…*pregnant.*"

His eyebrows stitch together, and he stops moving all together. With a deep frown, he asks, "How do you know this?"

"I haven't been feeling well or like myself the past few days. When I came back to Mexico, I asked Emilio to buy me a test, and I took it the night you finally arrived in Puerto Vallarta—after we talked. It was positive. I still have the test—it's in my bag if you want to see it."

His throat bobs, his head dropping. He focuses on the floor for a brief moment, and then looks back up at me. "Pregnant…"

"Yes," I whisper. I bite back the tears. The rims of my eyes sting.

He sits down on the edge of the bed anyway, still watching me. He looks at my flat belly, watches as I run a hand over it, and then releases a heavy breath. "Come here," he exhales.

I go to him, stepping between his legs and wrapping my arms around the back of his neck.

"You want to carry my baby—even after all of this?" he whispers.

I nod without even thinking about it. How stupid of me. He doesn't want this. Why would he want this right now?

"Yes," I answer, and I can't fight it anymore. The tears fall on their own.

"No, Gianna. Don't cry. This…it's good news to me. Great, actually."

"It is?" I'm surprised to hear that.

"Yes." He shifts a little, holding my waist. "The only thing that concerns me about this is you. Are you happy with this? With *me*? And why the hell did you go after Yessica when you knew you were pregnant? You could have risked your life and lost the baby—"

"Draco, I did what I had to do so that our baby could have a living, breathing father. I refused to let her get away. We needed her gone so we can have a life together."

His mouth clamps shut, a hard sigh leaving him. I sit on his lap, squeezing him tight around the shoulders and then leaning back to look him in the eyes. "I don't think I'm too far along, anyway. Maybe a month or so. Juanita checked me. The baby is fine." I inhale deep and long, before letting it go. "Nicoteras love hard, just like Molinas do." I drop my hand, entwining our fingers. "And when I say I love you, I mean it. I don't want to be with anyone else but you, Draco. And I have no doubt, whether it's a boy or a girl, that he or she will be our little warrior."

"The risks—there is always someone after me, Gia. The baby will be in danger his or her entire life, and I won't—"

I cut him off before he can even finish, pressing a finger to his lips. "We will always, *always* be in danger. Even before all of this, my life was easily on the line. I was a mafia leader's daughter, for fuck's sake. I'm not going to let the threats of this world stop me from being happy and living my life. Yes, I'll be worried, and yes, I'll have to watch my back even more now. But what parent doesn't? I will do my best to protect this baby—our baby. I will be there for my child as much as I can. I will prepare our baby for the best of times and the worst."

He drops his head, like he's ashamed or something now. "I only want you safe."

"I will be fine."

He picks his head up, gripping my chin between his fingers. "If something happens to you—"

"Then you'll set the world on fire for me. I know. Trust me, I know." I laugh just as he does. After laying a soft kiss on his cheek, I rest my head on his shoulder. "It will be fine. I promise."

"Well, this news settles my internal debate. I'm stepping down," he declares. "Getting out of the heavy shit. I wont be this cartel's only leader anymore."

"What will you do?" I ask.

"I've spoken to Clark. He wants to take it on, with Patanza. They've agreed to do it together. Run the Molina-Nicotera Cartel."

I lift my head. "Yeah? Is that what you really want? To hand over everything you and your family have worked so hard for, just like that?"

"I'm doing what's best for us—for my future." He releases a long, weary breath. "It's time for me to retire—lay low for a while. Be a part of an actual family. Live life. My mother has wanted this for me for years. There is someone I trust handling it—Patanza won't tarnish the name of my cartel—so I'll do it. For you." He runs his palm over my belly. "For my baby."

He grabs my waist and twists me around, lightly placing my back on the bed. "We can get away, just you and me...until the baby arrives."

"Where?" I ask, smiling up at him.

"I'll have it figured out as soon as we get through tomorrow. First, we'll have to do a proper burial for Thiago and Emilio. My mother is flying here in the morning with Thiago's skull."

I frown. "His *skull?*"

"Yes. That bitch Yessica saved it, tried to make a statement with it during a set-up—almost killed me." I frown, sitting up a little but he presses a hand on my shoulder, relaxing me again. "There's a lot I need to fill you in on, huh?"

I laugh. "Yeah. A lot seemed to happen while I was away." I stroke his chin. "Good thing she's gone."

He drops his head, kissing the crook of my neck, making a swarm of butterflies tumble in the pit of my belly now. "Good thing indeed, Patrona."

The burial the next day is heartbreaking.

Everyone is dressed in all black for it, clean. No hats or guns are allowed, to pay our respects.

After Draco kisses the skull and then places it in the pit with Emilio's body, he steps back with a nod and Diego starts shoveling the dirt on top of them.

"*Te quiero, primo,*" Draco murmurs at my side. "Emilio."

We all stand until the dirt has become a pile and has covered them completely. Patanza steps forward with a small bouquet of chocolate cosmos in hand, laying it on top of the dirt pile. She kisses the tips of her fingers and then presses her hand on the flowers quickly before pulling away and standing again, turning and swiping her face with her good arm.

Clark rubs her on the back, and surprisingly, she doesn't dismiss or push him away.

My eyes are thick with tears, as well as Mrs. Molina's. Hers fall, but she's smiling. *Smiling.*

I don't even try to understand it.

And I don't know what it is about her smile, but it satisfies me.

It gives me so much hope for the future.

50

GIANNA

48 HOURS LATER

"I really don't know why I care about you so much."

As the words pass through my lips, a warm hand drifts over my belly, snaking around my hip, tugging me close. Rays of the sun beam down on the gold sheets. It's a warm day, the ocean breeze pushing through the curtains.

Now that I've had time to settle, I'm starting to love this home in Lantía a lot more.

Gusts of salty air spill through the crisp white curtains. I can taste it on my lips, smell the freshness of the water that comes along with it.

I shut my eyes as his hand presses into my belly, skating up to my breast. He cups it in hand, using the other to nudge me backwards until I'm flat on my back. His mouth wraps around my nipple, the other still cupping me in his large, demanding hand. A groan vibrates through his chest, and he sucks until it becomes a soft, pink pebble between his lips.

"Is that why?" he asks, letting up, his voice raspy and filled with sleep. I moan as he pulls his hand away and slides downward, his mouth pressing on my belly, moving to various places. "Or is this why?" His lips are soft, slightly demanding. I start to grip his hair, but he catches my wrist, forcing it down as he slides his face between my legs.

"Draco," I moan.

He ignores me, kissing the area just above my clit. I shudder when I feel his breath run through my already wet slit. So wet for him. So eager, just from his teasing lips alone.

I say his name again, and it falls so lightly off my lips.

"Stop your bickering." His breath is hot on my skin. Something hot and wet presses directly on my clit, swirling slow at first. His large hands grip my thighs and his fingers slide up, capping my knees and pushing them up to my chest.

He spreads me wide open for him, sucking, licking, and tasting *all of me*. His hands grip my thighs as I writhe, back bowing, sinful words leaving my body and surrounding us. He's always so hungry for me, always ready to devour.

It doesn't take long for my body to overheat, the bundle of nerves between my legs to scream and beg for release. I grip the sheets and allow every moan of pleasure to escape me, squeezing my eyes shut, relishing in every ounce of it he provides.

My body dies down, sated, euphoric.

Draco slides his large body up, resting his head on my chest, his hard cock pressing on my pussy. We're both naked.

We may have even celebrated a little too much last night, him over tequila shots and me with way too many tacos and too much sparkling juice. We celebrated the life of Thiago and Emilio, as well as our win over Yessica and getting all of his territory back.

I've never seen him so...*content*. Not even during all the days I'd spent with him before this happened. Even before I knew about Hernandez, he was always so hostile, so vicious.

Now, in his warm brown gaze, I see nothing but satisfaction. I see hope.

Like he's satisfied with life. Satisfied with himself.

Once, it was all about the venom. The poison and the power.

Now, well, it's just the passion. Some of the power. Some of the glory. But mostly just *love*.

He drops his head, the tip of his nose skimming over my jawline. "You know we can't stay here today, right?" he murmurs.

I catch his eyes as he lifts his head. "Why not?"

"Guillermo got word that the sicario is looking around Lantía for me, wanting to plan an ambush. They're getting close."

"Hmm."

He slides a hand beneath me, cupping the back of my neck, tilting my head so our lips meet. He presses his warm, supple lips to mine.

He kisses me once. Twice.

"This will never end, will it?" I ask, holding his gaze.

"What?"

"This. Going to different locations. Always on the go."

He chuckles. "As long as there is breath in my body, Patrona, it never will. Are you willing to go through that with me? With the baby too?"

I smirk. "Have you forgotten what I told you yesterday? I fucking love you. I want you. Para siempre." *Forever.*

He chuckles, low and deep and perfect. "Hearing that shouldn't turn me on so fucking much."

I grin. "*Jefe y Patrona*. The most wanted couple in the world."

"Mmm," he groans, gripping his cock, pressing it at my entrance. My lips part as he slides in inch by savory inch. When he's fully inside me, he says, "Mí reina. Eres tan perfecta." *My queen. You are so perfect.*

It doesn't take much for me to shatter again. My body still hasn't come down from the first powerful orgasm of this morning. I break into a million beautiful pieces, just as he grunts his release.

Just as he finishes, there is a bang on the door.

"Jefe!" Patanza shouts. "We have trouble!"

He pulls out of me and climbs off the bed. Picking up a pair of boxers and sliding into them quickly, he walks to the door and grips the door knob. She speaks before he can open the door.

"Someone talked—claimed they saw you coming to this area.

Guillermo just called, said he saw the colonel in the city. They're on their way here. We have to go. Now."

"Shit," he rasps.

I climb out of bed, rushing to the closet and yanking down the first dress I touch—a red maxi dress. I tug it over my head, no bra, slide into my sandals and open the drawer of the nightstand, pulling out Daddy's pistol.

Draco is already dressed in his jeans and white T-shirt from last night. He picks his gun up from the nightstand and tucks it behind his back.

"Boat is running?" he calls over his shoulder at Patanza.

"Sí. The maids and butlers are out of the apartments, and Mrs. Molina is already being taken down to the boat. They'll be here soon. We have to go."

"Everything else already set?" he questions, taking my hand and leading the way out the door.

"Sí," she answers over her shoulder, a pistol in one hand.

"Good."

Clark comes running out of one of the bedrooms with a gun in hand and his bag slung over his shoulder. "I'm not getting caught after all that shit. Let's get the fuck out of here," he says.

We rush down the hallway, down the many stairs and through the corridor. Past his infamous paintings and the dining room he loved to feast in.

When we get outside, behind the house and past the pool, Patanza and Clark rush to the right as Draco and I bustle down the stone steps.

I glance back as she and Clark crowd around something black on one of the walls. She presses buttons on it as he keeps watch and then they're making a mad dash our way

We're on the sand, the cold ocean water wrapping around my ankles as we splash through it and toward the speedboat that's already waiting.

Draco lets me up first and I climb the ladder, taking Sebastien's hand, letting him haul me up. Mrs. Molina is already waiting on board with a life jacket on, knitting away like she has no cares in the world.

Draco steps on board, Patanza and Clark coming on shortly after.

Patanza huffs, placing her gun down on the bench and then pulling a black device from her pocket. Clark and Draco keep watch of the mansion.

It doesn't take long for us to hear sirens wailing in the distance. To hear a loud thud as they barge into Draco's so-called castle. Men in black and some in green surround the house at all angles. I see one who's tall, sharp, sunglasses on. He looks toward the speedboat as we take off and shouts, pointing at us.

But it's too late.

Patanza presses a red button on the device, and the mansion explodes, bursting into flames, and burning with it, the sicario.

I hear Draco release a small breath, but I'm not sure if it's a sigh of relief or a sigh filled with sorrow. His arm wraps around my shoulders, heavy, tight.

We watch his favorite home burn down, the distance growing, putting us further away from the history of that place, good and bad.

I picture his paintings, how they hang on the walls, melting. The beautifully furnished rooms being licked by the flames. Everything in that home will soon be gone—everything, including the memories. All because of a single bomb.

A bomb that has set us free…for now, anyway.

"Where do we go now?" I ask.

"We take everyone to safe places," Draco answers, his gaze ahead, focused on the fiery flames. I bet he's thinking the same as I am—about all he is losing with that home. It was his favorite. He had everything there. It's where he spent most of his time growing up. "And afterward, I'll be taking you and Mamá to a place I hope you'll enjoy."

Patanza slides closer to Mrs. Molina, handing her a spool of thread she dropped. Mrs. Molina takes it, giving her a complacent smile, and Patanza nods once.

For the first time, their shared smile is not cold or filled with indifference and bitterness. It is real. Respectful.

I look at Clark, who has an unlit cigarette pinched between his lips. He smiles at me behind it and then winks. I smile back, mouthing the words "Thank you." He and I made a pretty good team.

My eyes shift over as mangled curls whip at my face from the growing winds. Draco's arm tightens around me, his throat clearing.

My eyes travel over until it lands on something that will always stand out to me.

The brown shed.

It still stands, tall and proud, with not a scratch on it. It's still the same—sturdy, rough, filled with the horrors of my past. Somehow, I know that shed will always be there. That memory will never fade—the memory of how we came to be.

The start of us, though tragic and frightening.

The story that went from hate, to war, and then to the one thing I never thought it would become: love.

El Jefe y La Patrona.

The fucked-up story of how we came to be.

Of how we became one.

Of how we fell in love.

EPILOGUE

DRACO

14 MONTHS LATER

After bombing the only house I ever loved, the home I became a man in, I sent Patanza and Clark to America to visit his family and fill them in on everything.

I had him deliver a message for me—that Gianna will be staying with me for as long as she sees fit.

I won't make her stay against her will. If she ever wants to leave, she can. If she thinks, in the future, that my child is better off without me, then I won't stop her.

It would break my heart—probably kill me—but I won't stop her, because if it comes to that point, she's probably right.

My three best guards—Guillermo, Sebastien, and Diego—are with me on this island, watching my back, keeping their eyes peeled and their ears open.

No one in the world knows where we are, besides Patanza and Clark. I bought this island a long time ago—a private island in the waters between Morocco and Portugal. It's used for tourists looking for a getaway spot, but we keep our distance from them. We're never bothered.

My mother lives in an upgraded hut on this island, not too far away from Gianna and me. Though I'm not fully out of the business, I am close to being so. I've handed most of my assets and territory to Clark and Patanza, who are working hard to keep the Molina-Nicotera cartel up and running.

Patanza always reports back with good news, despite the many hiccups that come along with the job.

Fourteen months have passed, and the world wonders where I am. They wonder how I've suddenly disappeared, speculate that perhaps I died in the explosion that took my home.

The best things that have happened to me have happened while away from the chaos. Gianna and I got married when she was six months along. The wedding was very small—probably nothing in comparison to her first one, but it was real. A marriage built on sacrifices and promises. A marriage that was destined to happen. She is mine now, just like she was meant to be.

I know we can't stay here forever.

In a few months, we'll have to relocate again. I hate constantly being on the run, but I have no choice. To keep her and my child safe, I must. I will do anything for them. My own life is nothing without them.

An arm wraps around my waist, and I look from the stretched ocean, down at Gianna. Curled up in her arm is a baby with tan skin, chubby cheeks, fingers, and thighs. On top of the baby's head is a curly bundle of shiny, ebony hair, and the baby's eyes are the greenest I've ever seen. Greener than her mother's.

My baby girl.

Mi hija.

Mi princesa.

"My girls." I kiss Gianna on top of the head and then step around to pick Leona up. Leona, named after her grandfather—Lion. "Como esta mi niña!" My princess giggles, a sweet, innocent giggle I love hearing every single day. I curl her up in my arms, rocking her gently, letting her listen to the roar of the ocean. It always soothes her.

I never knew I could love someone so unconditionally—not until Leona was born. When she came into this world and looked at me with those big green eyes, I knew—I just knew that I would do anything for her. I knew I had to get out of this business. For her safety. For her future.

She doesn't take my last name. No. It's too dangerous, but with the middle name Molly, I guess it's good enough. Close enough to Molina. Leona Molly Nicotera.

My world.

My everything.

Both of them.

Gianna stands on her toes, pressing a full, damp kiss on my lips. "I love you," she murmurs. "Para siempre."

A faint smile sweeps over my lips. "Para siempre, mi amor."

When I look at Gianna, my beautiful wife, I have hope. When I see her for the first time every morning, I know I can't fucking live without her. I can't live without either of them.

Same goes for my mother, who is walking the beach and collecting shells. She comes up to me when she feels us watching and coos to Leona on her way, extending her arms when she's close and reaching for her. Leona gives a playful grin, and Mamá laughs, rubbing the tip of her nose on hers. She's so in love with her granddaughter. This is what she's always wanted: To escape the madness, to breathe and live freely, to have a family.

These are people who love me, despite my ugly, shattered soul—despite the darkness that tries to consumes me. These people here, right in front of me, mean the fucking world to me, and apparently I mean just as much to them too.

I know we are not good people.

I know for damn sure I am not a good person.

Apart, we are savages—dangerous, lethal, and fucked up.

But together—*fuck*—we're perfect.

Especially Gianna and I.

We're real and passionate and…in love.

So fucking in love.

She pisses me off like no other. She lifts me up like no other woman can. She has held me down and has also pushed me to the brink of madness. She does so fucking much to me—so much that I can never understand…but it's why I love her.

She is the light that guides me through the darkness. She continues to test me—push me. Even after letting it all go, she still keeps me on my toes.

I don't know what this woman has done to me. I don't know how I sank this fast, like being trapped in quicksand, unable to pull out. Putting up a fight only makes me sink faster.

We started out as hate and war. Passion and venom. Venom to ecstasy.

But now, we hold the same poisonous bite, and have achieved all the glory.

People will always be out for us, wanting to kill us, wanting to hurt her and my daughter, if they ever find out about her. I dare them to fucking try it.

Coming for her or for my daughter is coming for me, and, trust me, we won't be going down without a fucking fight.

Rey and reina. King and queen. And soon enough, a *princesa* will rise and conquer the fucking world, too.

It's El Jefe and La Patrona against the world.

Always together, until death does us part.

Fuck Bonnie and Clyde. They don't have shit on us.

We may not be in plain sight, tucked away on this private island and away from the real world for now, but we will always rule.

I will always be The Jefe.

And the world better fucking remember that.

THE END

NOTE FROM THE AUTHOR

As I write this, I want you all to know how invested I was in these characters. I really wish you could see the many notes and deleted scenes I have on my laptop and in my notebooks, filled with Draco and Gianna and their crazy, wild antics.

These two were ... something. They tested my boundaries, pushed me to my limit. They gave me a creative spark that I never even knew existed. Though dark and dangerous, they are a powerful couple and I have no choice but to admire them. They fought hard. Loved harder. They gave me so much joy, even through all of the madness.

In my eyes they are flawed, damaged, broken, but to put it simply, they are perfection to me.

I lived life through them, chapter by chapter.

I felt their pain and their joy.

I felt it all, and to know this is the end is killing me. I never wanted it to end, but every story must conclude somewhere.

It seems like it's over, but their story will always continue and live on in my heart. I hope they can live on in yours too.

If you've made it this far, I hope you enjoyed the story. I hope it made you feel something. I hope that it entertained you while reading

NOTE FROM THE AUTHOR

just as much as it entertained me while writing it. I hope that it gave an escape from the madness.

Thank you for believing in this wild, damaged couple and seeing it through until the end.

Thank you for all of your love and support for this trilogy.

Truly, it means the world to me.

So much love,
Shanora

Feel free to follow me on any of these social media sites. I am always active and always happy to talk to my readers!

Facebook: facebook.com/ShanoraWilliamsAuthor
Instagram: www.instagram.com/reallyshanora
Twitter: www.twitter.com/shanorawilliams

Visit www.shanorawilliams.com to join my newsletter.

If you need a place to talk about Venom & Glory or even the first and second book, there is a support group you can join on Facebook. Just search for *Venom Trilogy Support Group* and request to join.
Please be cautious about joining before reading the books - there will be spoilers about the books in there.

DON'T FORGET THAT POSTING A REVIEW, WHETHER BIG OR SMALL, IS ALWAYS A BIG HELP!

ALSO BY SHANORA WILLIAMS

SERIES

FIRENINE SERIES
THE BEWARE DUET
VENOM TRILOGY
SWEET PROMISE SERIES

STANDALONES

DIRTY LITTLE SECRET
100 PROOF
DOOMSDAY LOVE
TAINTED BLACK
UNTAINTED
INFINITY

VISIT WWW.SHANORAWILLIAMS.COM TO CHECK OUT THESE BESTSELLING TITLES AND FOR MORE INFORMATION.